GARDEN

VARIETY

By Christy Wilhelmi

Fiction
Garden Variety

Nonfiction
Grow Your Own Mini Fruit Garden
Gardening for Geeks
400+ Tips for Organic Gardening Success

GARDEN VARIETY

VARIETY

A NOVEL

CHRISTY WILHELMI

wm

WILLIAM MORROW
An Imprint of HarperCollins*Publishers*

P.S.™ is a trademark of HarperCollins Publishers.

GARDEN VARIETY. Copyright © 2022 by Christy Wilhelmi. All rights reserved. Printed in the United States of America. No part of this book may be used or reproduced in any manner whatsoever without written permission except in the case of brief quotations embodied in critical articles and reviews. For information, address HarperCollins Publishers, 195 Broadway, New York, NY 10007.

HarperCollins books may be purchased for educational, business, or sales promotional use. For information, please email the Special Markets Department at SPsales@harpercollins.com.

FIRST EDITION

Designed by Diahann Sturge
Title page and chapter opener illustration © lacuarela / Shutterstock, Inc.
Garden map illustrations © Blue Ring Media; Grimgram; Vladislav Lytov; baby sofja; Abscent; Alexzel; Julia Shamayaeva; Shpadaruk Aleksei; Hennadii H; joom seeda / Shutterstock, Inc.

Library of Congress Cataloging-in-Publication Data has been applied for.

ISBN 978-0-06-311348-0

22 23 24 25 26 LSC 10 9 8 7 6 5 4 3 2 1

To Ed Mosman, the real Garden Master,
who shall forever be preserved in my memory
as the guy who magically appears whenever he is needed

If you have a garden and a library,
you have everything you need.

—Marcus Tullius Cicero

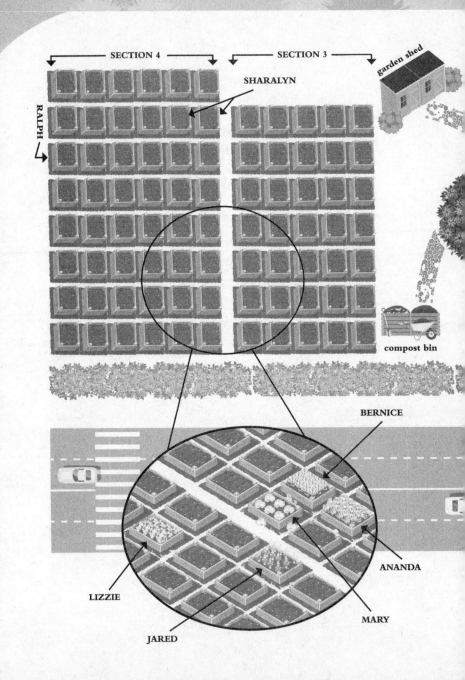

SECTION 4

SECTION 3

garden shed

SHARALYN

RALPH

compost bin

BERNICE

LIZZIE

ANANDA

JARED

MARY

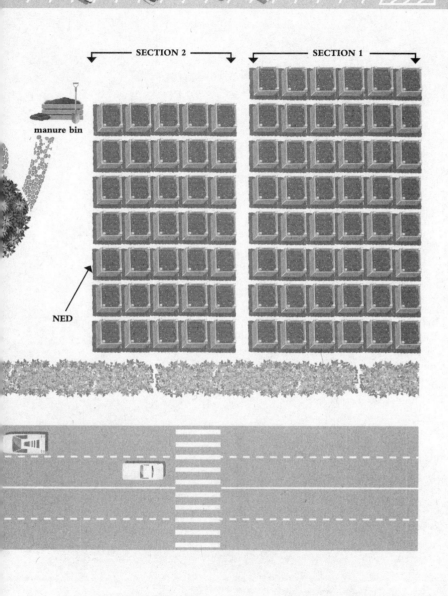

A map of Vista Mar Community Garden

GARDEN VARIETY

CHAPTER 1
The New Guy

October

Lizzie pulled the square of coarse sandpaper out of her back pocket. She stood poised over the retaining wall of her neighbor's garden plot, staring at the letters etched into the wood, "L+D" surrounded by a starburst. It might as well have been carved into her chest. Nobody else noticed it, this constant reminder of failure. *But it's gotta go.*

Lizzie wrapped the sandpaper around a small piece of brick and scrubbed away at the wall. She stopped and tilted back her sun hat. Her efforts hadn't made a dent; the carving went too deep. This job required a chisel.

She looked at her cell phone and saw she had a few

minutes before her next appointment. She rolled up the sandpaper and put it back in her pocket. Before she headed up to the toolshed, she pressed her hiking boot against the wall, covered the etching with her toe, and tried to picture what a mistake-free life would look like.

"'Scuse me!" A man's voice drifted over from the driveway. "I have an appointment with Lizzie?"

"Meet me up at the gate. I'll let you in."

She grabbed some paperwork she'd set down earlier in her plot on the way. At the top of the hill, Lizzie unhooked the padlock and swung back the tall chain-link gate. A man about her age stood with his hands on his hips, in tan shorts and a snug navy-blue T-shirt, squinting in the morning sun.

"Jared?"

"Aloha."

"Aloha!?"

"Grew up in Hawaii, where my mom's from. The greeting stuck."

"But your last name is Raju. That's Indian, right?"

"There are a few of us in Hawaii."

"Fair enough. Follow me."

The warm October morning air was tinged with smoke from a distant wildfire. Lizzie walked back down the hill past her own garden toward the vacant plot below. She noticed her companion had trouble keeping up with her.

"You okay?" she said. *Should have told him to wear better shoes.* She watched him slide in his flip-flops on the mulched pathway.

His sandals exposed damp earth, releasing a comforting, musty smell of soil.

As if he'd read her mind, he smiled and said, "Right. Garden lesson number one: shoes with traction."

"Good, you're a quick learner. We like those here."

When they came to a flat path halfway down the hill, Lizzie turned to him, but was a bit distracted as she was still thinking about how to erase the ill-fated "L+D" from the wall. She looked down at the application in her hand to double-check his name before beginning the speech she'd given countless times over the past eleven years as a section rep. She took off her sunglasses, brushed a wisp of her dark brown hair away from her face, adjusted her sun hat, and tried not to speak too quickly.

"This is Section Four, Jared. It's the youngest part of the garden. It's divided into east and west subsections. I oversee Section Four West, which is from that middle row of plots down to the street. Sharalyn, who you'll meet at some point, runs everything from the midpoint up to the top of the hill, that's Section Four East. Each plot is twelve by seventeen feet. You have one month to clear it and start planting. Everything I'm going to tell you is in the *Rules and Regulations*." She paused, pointed to the rolled-up booklet in his russet-brown hands. "You're not required to remember it all right now, but you will be expected to observe the rules, okay?"

"Got it."

Lizzie spotted a glint of excitement in his eyes. She'd seen it all before. People started out with a newfound passion for gardening, but when the shininess wore off in three months' time, she was left with an abandoned plot full of weeds and lost ambition. She wondered whether Jared would be one of those gardeners. *Too early to tell, so don't get invested. Make him feel welcome at least.*

She put her sunglasses back on and looked up. This time she had a good look at him. His tousled, shiny black hair curled just enough to be interesting.

Shit. He's gorgeous.

His profile reminded her of a Hindu god. If Marvel were casting for *Chakra the Invincible*, he'd be perfect. He couldn't possibly be single.

Don't even think about it. Bad idea. Remember the last time? And please stop thinking in movies.

"Do you watch films?" She couldn't help herself.

"'Scuse me?"

"Never mind."

She turned back to the pathway and led him toward an overgrown patch of weeds that sat across the path from two well-manicured gardens. In one of those tidy plots she saw Mary, on her knees, bent over a strawberry patch. She was older and, probably due to her love of blueberry pie, combined with formidable baking skills, carried her weight around the middle. Mary tried to blow a strand of silver hair away from her eyes, but it stuck to her mouth. She used one of her gloved hands to tuck the strand behind her ear, leaving a thin streak of soil across her olive complexion, then she tightened the strap on her oversized straw hat. The tails of her denim shirt were dusty with soil, and brown smudges smeared the cuffs.

Lizzie and Jared approached her plot. Mary, her back to them, was pulling snails from the strawberry patch and dropping them into a coffee can. She sat back on her heels and looked up from her work. With a brief but cautious glance to either side, she leaned forward and hurled the contents of the coffee can into the plot next to hers. Then she went back to hunting for snails.

"Hi, Mary!" Lizzie called out.

Mary started, caught her breath. "Ack! You scared the bejesus out of me." She peeled her muddy glove off her chest. Her gaze shifted from her glove to Jared, who stood in the pathway a few feet away. She took in his tall, lean, and muscular frame.

"Is this my new neighbor?" Mary lifted her chin in the direction of the abandoned plot across the path.

Lizzie turned to him. "Jared, please meet Mary, our president."

"Nice to meet you," he said with a nod and a chuckle. "No pressure, right?"

Mary grinned and shrugged. "I don't know, try me."

Lizzie watched Jared turn to look at the weedy plot adjacent to Mary's. He took in a deep breath and sighed—no doubt because of the waist-high grasses replete with sunbaked seed clusters at the tips. The soil looked parched and compacted, as if no one had cultivated it in years. Strewn among the weeds were two broken plastic chairs, one upside down with weeds growing through holes in the seat. The wooden retaining walls surrounding the plot had rotted in the corners, allowing soil to slip through from the pathway above. Rusted pipe held the rotten wood in place, a tenuous construction at best. The wall appeared as though it would fall apart with the slightest touch.

"This is it?" he said.

Mary smiled. "One month to clear and start planting."

"So I've heard." Jared stepped off the pathway, down into the sea of weeds.

Lizzie said goodbye to Mary. "I'll give him the rest of the tour before he realizes how much work he has ahead of him."

"Buh'bye," Mary said. Jared reemerged and walked back toward the main pathway.

"I saw that, by the way." Lizzie grinned. With her finger, she traced the trajectory of the snails' flight from the coffee can to the tidy plot next door.

"What?" Mary shrugged, a feeble attempt at innocence.

"Don't make me write you a citation."

"Why?" she asked, making doe eyes.

Lizzie gave her a sideways glance. "Catch ya later, Mary."

Jared followed Lizzie back up the hill, his eye drawn to the sandpaper peeking out the back pocket of her jeans. "Sandpaper? What's that for?"

"Nothing."

Okay, not very forthcoming.

At the summit, Jared stopped to survey the property. For the first time, he took in the big picture. *Whoa!* It was completely hidden from the street below by a wall of trees that also blocked most of the traffic noise, but the place was crazy big—hundreds of rectangular plots popped with green plants he couldn't begin to identify. Some plots reminded him of home—wild jungles of tropical fruits or multicolored flowers—and others were chock-full of orderly vegetables. Each plot shouted, *I have a green thumb!* He spotted metal, wood, vinyl, and bamboo trellises anchored into the ground, with overgrown vines threatening to break at least a few. Jared devised a quick fix for one overburdened trellis on the spot: a rebar stake and 22-gauge wire would do the trick.

"What's with all the mailboxes?" he asked Lizzie, pointing to one nearby adorned in decoupage.

"They're pre-internet. Every plot has one," she told him. Lizzie thumped on the metal curve of the mailbox. "It was the best way for people to communicate back in the day. Now they're mostly used for storage. And plot number. You'll need to paint your plot number and name on your mailbox right away. It's pretty faded."

"Copy that." He had already begun designing a cool mailbox in his head.

Plots terraced the hillside, bordered on one side by the steep driveway and topped by a parking lot. In the distance were two sheds made of wood and corrugated metal. They looked industrial and out of place against the plants, but he guessed they must be for tools and equipment.

Jared noticed a window in one of the sheds—no, scratch

that. It was a mirror set in a frame with an attached window-box planter. It reminded him of the honor farm stands on the island when he was a kid, the kiosks in the neighborhood piled high with mangoes and guavas next to a tiny money box. On weekends he used to chase the neighbor's rooster around the kiosk it guarded.

Fifty bucks a year for all this. Awesome.

He couldn't remember how long ago he'd filled out the application for a garden plot—maybe a year?—but it was long enough that he'd forgotten he had. When the voice on the phone said his name had reached the top of the waiting list, all the forgotten excitement about growing his own food had flooded back. He could picture ripe tomatoes in every color imaginable. Was it tomato season? Now he just had to figure out how to grow them . . .

As he and Lizzie walked past rows of gardens, Jared tried to sound as if he knew what he was doing. "What's in season these days?"

"Weather's finally cooling down, so it'll be time to plant fall crops soon."

What does that mean? Maybe he could ask his new neighbor, Mary. A good way maybe to get to know her. "Hey, that lady we met . . . Mary . . . does she have grandkids?"

Lizzie paused. "I have no idea. Never thought to ask."

He laughed. "And you've been here how long?"

Without missing a beat, Lizzie asked, "What made you decide to get a garden plot?"

He had to think about her question for a minute to recollect what started it all. "My mother used to grow all our veg in Hawaii," he said, "but when we moved to Seattle, it was a different ball game. I guess she wasn't used to having seasons. Now that I'm living in Southern California with perfect weather, worth a try, right? Plus, I love creative projects."

"You're an artist?" She looked back at him and picked up her pace.

"Well . . ." He caught up with her. "You've heard of that jack-of-all-trades thing?"

"Master of none?"

"Yeah, that. You name it, I've tried it—professional surfing, accounting, carpentry . . . Well, I still do that, but I've never done any one thing that I felt connected to, long term." He ran a hand through his hair. "Things come and go for me, so when my name came up on your list, the timing seemed right to give gardening a try."

Lizzie turned to face him but continued walking backward along the path. "Fair warning: gardening is not for the commitment-phobic." She whipped back around as if to punctuate her statement.

He cleared his throat. "Yeah, my dad says that a lot."

"About gardening?"

"About life."

There it is again, Jared thought. *Why does everyone think life requires commitment? Life is a ride. A convertible, not a contract.*

They passed a pomegranate tree with branches draped over a chain-link fence. A sign wedged against its branches said, WELCOME TO VISTA MAR GARDENS LOS ANGELES. Jared eyed the fence line and discovered that it enclosed the entire garden. He hadn't noticed this when he drove through the entry gate at the bottom of the hill; the sea of green plants had distracted him from everything else. He identified smaller gates along the perimeter of the fence, where gardeners came and went on foot, similar to the gate Lizzie had unlocked for him at the top of the hill.

Lizzie pointed out two hummingbirds speeding through the air, chasing each other above the pomegranate tree. The pair hovered over a set of dangling pomegranates, which were split open and ravaged: what remained after other birds ate their fill.

"Watch, it's a mating ritual." She motioned to one of the tiny birds. The hummingbird floated low over a nearby shrub, frozen in space except for the blur of its wings. It shot straight up into the air, like a rocket, then plummeted toward the shrub in an arc. When it reached the top of the shrub, millimeters away from the leaves, it let out a penetrating chirp, then curved around to start all over. Hover, climb, dive, chirp.

"Where'd his date go?" Jared wondered aloud. He glanced at Lizzie. She stared at him in—what was it?—disbelief. She let out a single laugh and moved on.

South of the sheds, in between the compost bins and the mulch pile, Lizzie pointed out crows, kestrels, and hawks patrolling the sky.

"When they aren't circling the grounds, searching for rodents, they're pestering each other for territory on one of these hawk perches," she said, gesturing to a thin pole that rose twenty feet high, topped by a metal spike that jutted out ninety degrees.

Two crows tried to scare a hawk off the perch, swooping close but never colliding with it.

They passed one plot filled with lavender—he recognized that one! Bees hummed by, checking flowers for pollen. Jared watched Lizzie brush her hand across the flower spikes and bring it to her nose. She inhaled, slowing her pace for a second. Across the path, in a different plot, butterflies fluttered on a bush with tall, purple, cone-shaped flowers.

"Wow. This place is amazing," Jared said.

"Yeah, we're pretty spoiled. But the best part . . ." She stopped to extend a hand toward the horizon, where the clear blue sky gave way to the ocean. "They don't call it 'Vista Mar Gardens' for nothing. The sunsets are incredible."

"I can't wait to see that."

"This is a good time to tell you that the garden closes at sunset."

"Closes?"

"It's in your *Rules and Regs*."

"So how do you know?" Jared smiled.

"Know what?" Lizzie replied.

"That the sunsets are incredible."

That triggered an exasperated sigh. Not the response he was going for. *For someone so connected to nature, she sure seems uptight.*

Jared turned toward the far-off edge of the garden and spotted an industrial warehouse that must have marked the end of the property. Turning the other way, he saw another warehouse, hidden behind fruit trees and pergolas. Behind him sat a flat, open field ending in a chain-link fence a few hundred yards away. Three hundred sixty degrees of open space was hard to come by in Los Angeles.

On the other side of the fence, across the street, were houses.

"And nobody's tried to build on this? This must be what, five, six acres?"

"Seven," Lizzie said. "From what I understand, the land was given to us a few decades ago. As I said, we're spoiled."

"Wow. Lucky. I could get used to this."

"I don't know what I'd do without it." Lizzie's tone softened.

Jared glanced at her. She was lean and tall, with suntan lines left over from summer across her forearms, her hair fluttered away from her shoulders in the breeze. The brim of her straw hat almost hid her dark glasses. He wondered what she looked like under all that.

The sound of chain and padlock clinking against the gate brought Jared back. They turned as a tall, lumbering man with wiry hair unlocked the gate and entered the garden.

"Oh shit," Lizzie said under her breath.

"Oh shit?"

Lizzie held up a hand. "Hang on a sec." She set off toward the wiry-haired man, who carried a duffel bag slung over his back.

"May I help you?" Lizzie's voice turned formal, authoritarian. The man didn't respond at first, but when he tried to pass her, she stepped in front of him.

"Where are you going, Mark?"

The man stuttered, "I'm . . . j-just getting a few things."

"You're not a member anymore. Your termination letter went out months ago."

"Yeah, but I was on vacation." He adjusted the strap of his duffel bag.

Lizzie took off her sunglasses, squinting into the morning sun to meet his eyes. "Your stuff belongs to the new plot owner." Jared couldn't help noticing her chilly matter-of-fact tone.

The man grew irritated. His eyes darted up to the sky. He grunted and clenched the handles of his bag with sizable fists.

"This is bullshit!" His voice rose. "I've been in this garden for ten years."

"Then you should have known better." Lizzie's voice rose to match his. "You stole produce from other gardens. You know the rules." She put her glasses back on and crossed her arms.

The man sighed and shook his head. He scanned the garden, looking lost.

Lizzie spoke softly. "There's nothing left here for you. It's time to turn in your key."

Without a word, the man spun around and took a step back toward the gate.

"Give me your key, Mark." She stepped after him. "Don't make me have to call the police."

The man lifted the catch on the gate, and Jared's pulse quickened. He started to lean forward to intervene, but right then, the man tossed his key over his shoulder. It landed in the mulch at Lizzie's feet.

Lizzie exhaled as she bent down to extract the key from the mulch. Jared strode up next to her.

She looked at him. "One of the unfortunate duties of being section rep."

"Remind me not to get on your bad side," he said. It looked like Lizzie smiled, but he couldn't tell for sure.

"Sorry about my language earlier." Lizzie tucked the key into her pocket. "Very unprofessional of me."

"What, the swearing?" Jared said. "I don't mind. They say cursing is a sign of high intelligence."

"That's good news. My internal dialogue reads like a Quentin Tarantino script, but it doesn't usually leak out."

"Don't worry. I don't judge."

She turned down the path and picked up the tour where they had left off. They heard a car door slam in the parking lot. Jared glanced to see if it was Mark getting into his car but instead saw a woman with dark skin, dressed in a black tracksuit, unlatch the tailgate of her truck. She dropped her car keys and a hose nozzle into a basket slung over her forearm. She smiled and pushed her fingers though the chain link to give a cheerful, fluttery wave.

"Another beautiful day in paradise," the woman said with a lilting southern tone as she came through the gate. When she got closer, Jared noticed a small pale scar on her cheek that folded into the dimple of her smile. And what a smile, so full of charm and warmth.

Lizzie introduced her as Sharalyn, the rep for Section Four East. "I'm giving him the plot right over from Mary," Lizzie told her.

"Oh, good luck with that, sweetie," Sharalyn said with a chuckle. Her soothing voice made her sound wise beyond her years.

"Yeah, fingers crossed," Jared said. "I figured if I rebuild the retaining walls, that will get me off to a good start with my neighbors."

"Yes, it will," Lizzie said as Sharalyn nodded. Lizzie's gaze drifted back to Jared. "And as soon as Ned finds out you're handy with tools, he'll put you to work."

"Mmm, lucky for us." Sharalyn waved goodbye and walked away. After a few steps she stopped, eyes focused in the direction of her plot.

"*Hey!*" Sharalyn yelled across the distance. "Get outta there!"

Jared followed her eyeline and spotted a willowy older man wearing a golf cap standing beside a plot filled with roses. He appeared to be picking the flowers. The man, startled at Sharalyn's scream, darted toward the field, pilfered bouquet in hand.

"Who is that?" Lizzie asked Sharalyn.

"I wish I knew! Some swamp rat who keeps picking my roses when my back is turned. He doesn't use shears, just rips 'em off—leaves frayed edges everywhere. I can't imagine how he gets in here. He's not a member."

"He's headed out the back gate," Lizzie said. "We should catch him."

Jared debated for a second whether he should run after the guy, but realized he'd never catch him in flip-flops. He didn't want to face-plant halfway across the field, either.

"That's okay, sugar. I figure he needs them. Someday I'll catch him and set him straight, though." Sharalyn sighed and fished her pruning shears out of her basket. "Guess I've got my work cut out for me today." She set off down the path.

Lizzie glanced at Jared and said, "Never a dull moment here."

"No kidding." Jared tried to remember where he and Lizzie had left off before the crazy rose-stealing-guy incident. *Oh, yeah . . .*

"Who's Ned?"

"He's our garden master. You'll meet him—he's always here." Lizzie smiled. "Let's go fill out your paperwork and get you a key." She pointed toward the shed.

They walked single file along the narrow pathway at the top of the hill. Jared inhaled the warm October air and imagined his hands in the soil, another new adventure to dive into. It reminded him of running around barefoot in his mother's garden, tracking clay into the house, his father scolding him, his mother's laughter. He wondered where this gardening thing would lead him next.

"Any questions so far?" Lizzie asked from farther along the path.

"Yeah. Do you have any advice about growing cannabis?"

Lizzie gave a weak laugh as she picked up her pace.

"I'm kidding. You get that one a lot, don't you?"

"Yep."

Lizzie took a quick look at her cell phone to gauge if she was on time. She had given these tours so many times over the years, but it had been a while since she had assigned a plot.

She lifted a wayward blackberry cane blocking the pathway,

holding it up for Jared to pass. They were near the entrance of Section One: the original expanse of land that had been developed more than thirty years earlier. Unlike Section Four farther down the path, Section One was tethered to the past by its aging wooden pergolas and climbing roses.

Lizzie pointed out a sign attached to the gate: PLEASE LOCK THE GATE BEHIND YOU.

"There's another sign outside the gate that says No Trespassing. Make sure you lock the gate when you come and go—we do put out the occasional restraining order."

"In a garden?"

"You saw what happened earlier. People also sometimes break in to steal the fruit from the orchard, but mostly they're inside jobs. Members will take bagsful from the orchard, instead of the four pieces of fruit per day they're allowed, and they steal from each other's plots." She watched Jared shake his head. "Yeah, theft happens more often than we'd care to admit."

They walked past rows of young broccoli and cabbage plants. Overgrown rosemary arched out into the pathway, attracting bees to its purple flowers. A well-established grapevine had taken over a pergola above one plot's small seating area, all but burying the chairs and mosaic-tiled footstool underneath. The faint sound of an engine intruded on the quiet.

Lizzie pointed out the miniature picket fence lining a plot nearby. "Fences are illegal, but these have been around so long, they're grandfathered in."

She turned to Jared. "Walk each section. Observe what other gardeners are growing. Each area of this property has its own microclimate. What grows well here might fail in our section. You'll also get ideas for how to organize your plot. There's a lot of history here."

Jared looked overwhelmed. Or maybe distracted.

"Tulsi?" He pointed toward a basil plant nearby. He stepped off the pathway into the plot. "It is tulsi. I recognize this one." He pulled a green leaf from the plant, brought it to his mouth.

Great, he's already breaking the rules.

Lizzie paused for a moment. She tried not to shame her gardeners before she had instructed them about what they were and were not supposed to do.

"We ask people not to step into anyone else's plot unless the gardener is present, or you have permission."

"Seriously?"

Lizzie's aggravation grew slightly. "And you're definitely not supposed to eat anyone's crops."

"Oh. I figured, you know, it's only one." Jared smiled, jumped back up to the path, and shook mulch out of his sandals. "Plenty for everyone, right?"

Another snarky scofflaw. Just what I need.

She tried to stay calm, but his casualness fueled her inner schoolmarm. "Maybe this garden isn't a good match for you."

"What? No, I just— There sure are a lot of rules."

"They're here for a reason." Her voice rose. "The place runs smoothly because of the rules and regs." Things didn't look good for the new guy. "Besides, all of us board members, we're volunteers. We don't get paid to put up with behavior like that.

I have plenty of other people waiting for a plot if that's a problem for you."

Jared put up his hands. "Relax, it's not a problem."

In the awkward silence that followed, the engine sound grew louder. Lizzie realized it was shredding day. She waved for Jared to follow her. "Come on."

The closer they came to the whirring equipment, the more uneven and soft the ground became. Years of shredded straw and composted manure lay underfoot. The rumbling engine cloaked the garden with the thick din of oily machinery. Two structures made from sawed-off telephone poles stood like roofless, three-sided log cabins. Piled high with horse manure, the shredding bins each rose nine feet tall. Three men worked atop one of the piles on a platform with an industrial shredder.

Lizzie spotted Ned, who wore a battered straw hat with a few good-sized holes, checking to make sure the manure passed through the shredder into the pile below. She also recognized Ralph, heavyset and baby-faced, standing next to Ned. He flushed when their eyes met. Next to Ralph stood Leo, a slim, older Japanese man who wore goggles against the dust billowing from the shredder as each batch passed through.

Ned hollered something down to Lizzie, but the noise drowned out his voice. She shook her head, lifted a hand to her ear. Leo reached behind the shredder, flipped the switch, and waited for the beast to come to a halt.

"Is that a new gardener?" Ned said in his heavy Boston accent. He took his hat off to wipe his brow. His silver hair had long ago disappeared from the top of his eighty-year-old head, but Ned employed the classic comb-over technique to create a still-youthful hairline. Long silver wisps fluttered in the breeze. He ran the sleeve of his Vista Mar Gardens sweatshirt across his ruddy face. The shirt was almost as tattered as his hat; the frayed collar had separated into two layers years ago, and the logo was barely visible from years of laundering.

Lizzie introduced Jared, and then added to Ned, "You'll be happy to learn that Jared is handy with tools. He's ideal for retaining-wall duty."

"Geez, you make me sound like a workhorse," Jared joked.

She squinted. "I did, didn't I?"

Ned's eyes lit up. "That's great! We've got plenty of retaining walls falling to pieces over in Section Two. You can get your community hours by fixing them up."

"That's a good deal." Jared glanced at the other two men.

Leo nodded and touched the brim of his baseball cap. "You come to composting on Saturdays, and I teach you how to make very good compost." He was in his late sixties, his skin weathered from many years outdoors, but his small frame was still wiry, and he carried himself as though he were twenty-five.

Ned chimed in, "Leo's our master composter."

"Nice to meet you, Leo." Jared then lifted his chin toward Ralph. "Hey. What do you do here?"

"Me?" Ralph flushed again. "Oh, you know, not much."

"He's being modest," Ned said. "Ralph's the glue of the garden."

"No, that's you, Ned." Ralph zipped the collar of his puffy vest higher, like a turtle disappearing into its shell.

Ned shook his head. "You built us a website overnight—he's a hacker, you know, a genius with code, or whatever it is—and it even tracks community hours. We used to have to do that by hand."

"Programmer, Ned, not hacker," Ralph said through his down shell. "I sit in the dark and write code all day."

Lizzie watched Ralph's embarrassment rise. Somehow, his shyness boosted his boyish cuteness factor. He looked at his shoes as Ned regaled him, pulling his gloves out of his back pocket and thwacking Ralph on the arm with them. Ralph's eyes shot to Lizzie's, but darted away.

"A computer geek. Cool." Jared nodded at Ralph. "Hey, do you own Spock ears, too?"

Silence fell over the group. Everyone stared at Jared.

"Sorry, too personal?" Jared said.

Ralph rolled his eyes at Jared, clearly insulted by the *Star Trek* inference. "Um . . . lightsaber."

Lizzie stepped in, unsure of whom she wanted to spare more, Ralph or Jared. "Maybe we should go." She saw Ralph's forehead bead with sweat when she spoke.

Ned jumped into action, giving Ralph a quick pat on the back. "You're talking over my head, genius. Come on, let's get back to work."

Meanwhile, Jared's wide-eyed consternation remained unchanged as Lizzie hooked his elbow to lead him away. She said, "Happy shredding, guys."

The composters said their goodbyes—at least Ned and Leo did. Ralph stared at his shoes. Someone flipped the switch, revving the shredder back to life, as Lizzie and Jared turned to walk the path toward the main shed.

They stepped up into the corrugated metal building, where Lizzie pointed out the emergency landline phone, the map of the property, and the schematic of the plumbing for the entire garden. "If anything goes wrong, this is where you come. You'll find shutoff valves for all the water mains pinpointed on that map. There's a list of phone numbers for our volunteer plumbers, the police, ambulance, whatever. Except pizza—you can't use the phone for personal calls, okay?"

"Yes, ma'am," Jared said.

Lizzie gave him a sideways glance. "It's 'miss.'"

"Ah, I see."

"Take a seat. I'll get your forms." She pulled a set of keys from her pocket and unlocked the padlock on the office door. Propping the door open with her foot, she pulled several pages from paper trays along the office shelves. "I'm giving you a few back issues of our newsletter to give you an idea of what goes on here each season. If you care to write an article, you'll get credit toward your community hours if the editor includes it in the newsletter."

"That's okay. I'll be too busy building retaining walls," he said with a grin.

Lizzie sat down and reached across the table for Jared's copy of the *Rules and Regulations*. She smoothed the rolled-up pages flat, or tried to, and began going over each of the major points with him. Then she saw it. That glazed-over look in his eyes she knew all too well: too much information all at once. "Read it over when you get home and call me if you have any questions—I'm always happy to clarify the rules."

"Okay." Jared yawned. "Sorry. Late night."

"Do I want to hear this?" She preferred not to learn too much about people too quickly.

Jared laughed. "It was nothing scandalous. Good wine, cheese, and a chocolate chip cake I'm still thinking about."

"Sounds like a good time." It was exactly her kind of evening, but she wasn't about to express that with any notable enthusiasm.

"Well, you should come next time."

Lizzie's chest tightened.

Jared continued. "New faces are always welcome at my parties."

"Let's see how you do in the garden first. You're on probation for two months."

"Probation? What does that mean in a garden?"

"It means that if you don't get busy in your plot, I can kick you out without going through our fair and lengthy citation process." Lizzie tapped the pages in front of her. "It's all in the *Rules and Regs*." She passed it back across the table after writing down her number. "Call me with questions."

After Lizzie padlocked the office door, they walked to the parking lot above the garden. When they came through the gate, a cream-colored Ford Falcon station wagon lumbered past. It had more rust than paint and looked as though it were held together with grime and corrosion. It teetered over the speed bumps, creaking with age as it crawled across the asphalt. Ned stuck his hand out the window as he passed them. He waved and pointed at Jared, calling out, "Welcome to the garden!" Then he disappeared around the corner and the sound of his Falcon faded.

Lizzie dropped a key into Jared's hand. "Good luck with your plot."

"Thanks. Before I go, I think I'll rustle up some salad greens for dinner tonight," he said as he surveyed the garden through the fence.

"Please tell me you're joking."

Jared smiled, winked, and walked toward his car.

CHAPTER 2
The Neighbor

Late October

K urt Arnold stood at the top of his staircase, peer-
ing out the dusty second-story window toward the
blight-of-the-neighborhood that blocked his view of
the ocean. He could swear they planted another tree
yesterday. Someone should do something about it.
Someone should fine them.

"Damn it."

He slid open the window, inhaled in search of rank
odors of decay from the upwind compost pile. He
couldn't detect it today—must not have been warm
enough yet. But he determined it was only a matter
of time.

The hazy film on the window helped his case. Dust

from those foul compost piles drifting across the field reminded him every day of something that never should have been there in the first place. He picked up his spray bottle of blue glass cleaner. It infuriated him, how many paper towels were required to remove the grimy film. He didn't bother with screens anymore, he left them off to make the task easier. Stretching as far as his arm would allow, he still couldn't reach that outside lower corner from inside the house. It taunted him, as did the gardens across the field. They ruined his view and soiled his otherwise peaceful existence.

His ocean view had been beautiful before that wretched community project went in thirty years ago, a decade after he built the house. He had worked hard to make it the home they would live in for the rest of their lives. The garden ruined everything, but for most of that time, he had been too busy working to care.

Retirement offered Kurt a daily opportunity to fume. He'd sold his publishing business fifteen years ago, earning him enough money to live comfortably for the rest of his life, which promised to be lengthy, given his excellent health. After spending a fair amount on home renovations (to make his retirement—and wife—more pleasant), he'd settled back in his Eames lounge chair and decided that this, indeed, was the life.

Kurt's children had long ago left home for other interests, other lives. Ken, the eldest, married his college sweetheart and started a family in New Haven, staying close to his alma mater. They never came to visit. Too busy to get away, Ken always said over the phone. At least he called. Lisa, the youngest, was rarely heard from. Were it not for the phone calls Kurt's wife made, he wouldn't even know Lisa was alive. The girl had more important things to do in her day than appreciate those who gave her life.

"What can you do?" his wife's voice echoed in his head. At some point you have to let them go. But he certainly didn't expect they'd run for the hills when released.

Kurt looked out across the field and identified the tips of what must have been cornstalks cutting into the horizon. What else grew beyond the crest of the hill? He speculated that the people growing that corn were foreigners, or worse, illegal immigrants. He'd seen enough during his treks across the field to lodge complaints to know that those people brought their sizable families to work in the garden with them. The garden administrators should have to produce proof of citizenship for all its members. He could arrange that, couldn't he, as a member of the neighborhood council? He'd have to look into that.

The original deed to his house, signed all those years ago, stated that "no part of said premises shall ever be used or occupied by any person not of the white or Caucasian race." Though the notion was outdated, he observed that the neighborhood's residents weren't the issue. Hoodlums turned up too often for his comfort. He nearly put bars on the windows last year, after Phyllis and Dick's house was burglarized twice. He couldn't confirm it, but his gut told him crime had gone up since that garden appeared. He assumed someone from the garden was responsible for the recent break-ins. They have the perfect view—all these houses, lined up and waiting for some degenerate to come by and break in.

If people can't afford to buy groceries from a clean, well-regulated market, they should go back where they came from. This nonsense about growing your own food, getting back to the land, whatever, was ridiculous in this day and age. What's wrong with grocery stores, anyway?

As usual, the more Kurt fixated on the garden, the more irate he became. And there it was: the billowing cloud of stench rising from their filth piles, wafting toward his now clean windows (except for that damned corner). He slammed the window closed, stormed down the stairs, and grabbed his golf cap on the way out the door. He set a brisk pace across the field, pausing only to unlock the gate with the key that he, as former neighborhood council president, had acquired years ago. They had never asked for it back when he stepped down. Their loss.

Step by step, he formulated his rage into words, stumbled on a gopher hole, and almost slipped out of his loafers. He approached the crest and—there!—the smell of fuel that assaulted his senses, along with the deafening sound of the shredder. Perfect timing. *I'll catch them in the act of air and noise pollution. I'll report them and demand a fine.* He opened the inner gate at the entrance to the garden, which for some reason sat unlocked, and continued on his mission.

Ned and Mary shuffled past each other in the cramped office quarters. The tiny room in the main shed was packed with file cabinets, a couple of old coffee machines, and stacks of outdated newsletters. Ned pulled open a file cabinet drawer halfway—all that the space allowed—and riffled through an open money box for a new watering key. He tucked it into his pocket, closed the drawer, then turned to sidle past Mary, who was reading through the day's mail.

"So long, Mary. Give those grandkids of yours a squeeze for me next time you see 'em." They nodded to each other, then Ned stepped out into the fresh October air. The smell in the air meant one thing: fall was really here. Fall crops would soon be ready, and he'd pick his fill of kale. He didn't miss Boston on days like this. He smiled. *The Northeast may be blessed with fall color, but we get year-round harvests.* Ned reached for the crinkled notepad in his pocket and scrawled "drop off a key in D-62's mailbox."

He turned down the path and was nearly knocked over as someone barreled past him down the hill.

"Hey there, what's your hurry?" he called after the man.

The thin man spun around and locked eyes on Ned. There was no mistaking that face. Kurt Arnold had gotten in somehow. Kurt stormed up to Ned—a little too close for Ned's comfort—and launched into a tirade, gesticulating up the hill.

Ned sighed. The curmudgeon was back. He had almost forgotten about Kurt, but the complaints spewing from his lips were as familiar (and unswerving) as the march of changing seasons. Ned put a hand up and shook his head.

"Now hold on a minute there, Kurt. We already moved the compost operation for you once. That took a ton a work."

"I still smell it all the way over at my house. I'm downwind, you know." Kurt pointed toward the street. "You've got to move it somewhere else."

Ned pushed back in his gentle way. "Look, we resituated the compost already. We also moved the mulch pile out of sight, and we cut down those eucalyptus trees that you said blocked your view. We even made those gardeners along the top of the hill stop growing corn when you asked—which was a real pain by the way. It took us months to rearrange everything and reassign different plots. Rewrote the *Rules and Regs* and everything."

Kurt stood fuming. A moment later, Mary rounded the corner. Ned saw Mary. Kurt saw Mary. Mary locked eyes with Kurt. They were two wildcats about to pounce on each other. This wouldn't be good.

Ned always dealt with Kurt, ever since Mary had threatened to set his house on fire one day when he had come to complain about the noise from the shredders. Ned had realized a few years ago that these demands would never stop, that Kurt would never be happy. Once Mary realized it, too, she stopped playing nice and started threatening him instead. She also brandished weapons—pruning shears, on one memorable occasion—though Ned never knew whether it was just for show. Either way it scared the living hell out of Kurt.

"Get that *alter kocker* off my property!" Mary pointed her hand trowel at Kurt.

"Go to hell, you old hag," Kurt said, sinking to a new low.

"Dragging you with me, you useless dirtbag." Mary started down the hill toward them.

Ned stepped between them. "I've got this, Mary. You can go."

"Give me two minutes with him, Ned." She tried to push past him. "Then we can compost him and be done with it."

"Mary." Ned bent to look her in the eye. "I've got this."

Mary clenched her jaw, then turned away. "Yeah, good luck with that." She trod off.

Ned couldn't blame her. Sometimes he wanted to put a banana in the guy's tailpipe, too. But he had his own way of handling Kurt.

"You know, we might build a double-decker shed with a nice rooftop deck to watch the sunsets. We'd gain a real nice ocean view. Sounds great, right?" He enjoyed watching Kurt turn red as a furnace about to blow.

Kurt, whose sense of humor could best be described as nonexistent, said, "Over my dead body."

"Careful. Mary would be happy to arrange that."

After winding him up, Ned spent a few minutes soothing the old goat. Ned assured Kurt they would try their best to keep the manure dry so it wouldn't smell, which appeared to be enough to pacify him for the moment. After Kurt left for home, Ned strolled through the orchard until his heart rate returned to normal. He picked an early apple (or two) for later, polished them on his flannel shirt, and put the incident behind him. Who would have guessed there'd be this much contention around a garden?

Mary wanted only one thing: to water her plot. That, or to power wash that bastard Kurt into the middle of next week.

She hiked to her plot, uncoiled the nearby hose, and screwed on her favorite nozzle, trying not to blast her freshly planted seedlings into the earth.

Calm down, breathe deep. Ned's got it.

Within a few minutes, calm creeped in. Her seedlings looked happier, adding to her sense of accomplishment. She was even breathing slower. *Good.*

She turned off the hose, unscrewed the nozzle, and tucked it into her mailbox for storage. After coiling the hose, Mary brushed her hands across her jeans to dry them. As she climbed back up the hill, she passed several mailboxes with white pieces of paper poking out. That was odd; she hadn't approved any flyers for distribution lately. She scanned other mailboxes and discovered the same flyer in each one. Mary pulled open the closest one and wrestled the flyer out from under a rusty hand trowel.

"Are You Tired of Being Ignored?" it said across the top in a bold font. "If you're annoyed with frivolous spending, theft, lazy gardeners, or disorganized operations, tell us!"

"What the hell is this?" Mary turned the page over. No revealing handwriting, no names, nothing.

She read further. "Leave us a note at plot A-17"—*Of course. Bernice. Why am I not surprised?*—"and we'll take your concerns to heart. Be prepared to vote for a fresh start come April."

It wasn't the first time her neighbor had threatened to usurp the throne. If Mary had a nickel for every time a section rep warned her that Bernice was conspiring . . . *Ha, let her try.*

Her threats were idle at best. Bernice couldn't possibly gather enough support to actually consider going through with it.

Mary crumpled the flyer and walked back down the hill to toss it into Bernice's plot before leaving.

"Maybe it's time to move," Kurt's wife said when she caught him glaring out the window later that evening. "Maybe if we were somewhere else you'd focus on something else."

She was probably right. If he had used half the time he'd spent seething about that eyesore across the street on other, more lucrative endeavors, he would've tripled their investments by now. Not that he needed to.

He picked up the hammer he had set on the windowsill and tapped a nail into the wall to the right of the window. This extra picture frame he'd found in the closet was perfect for the photo he'd printed out from his computer. Thirty years ago, he had taken the picture from this very window, before that blight appeared. The photo showed the view the way it should be. The way it would be again.

He owed it to himself to put things right.

CHAPTER 3

Weeding

The Next Morning

Lizzie struggled to pull her garden gloves off in time to answer her phone. Third ring. *Stupid gloves don't work on a touch screen.* Fourth ring. *No time to check who it is.*

"Hello?" She tried to mask the irritation in her tone.

"It's good to hear your voice."

"Dylan?" Lizzie glanced at the screen to make sure. Her heart sank to her stomach.

"Please, don't hang up," he said.

She wanted to, more than anything. But part of her ached to know why he had called.

"I thought I'd check in, see if you're okay."

"Why? What have you heard?" she said.

"Nothing. I had a feeling we should talk."

"Four months and you finally had a feeling?" *How nice for you*, she wanted to add.

After a long pause, Dylan said, "Look, I hope you understand that things just . . . happened. They just *happened*, okay? I don't regret it, and I hope you're okay with that. It's not your fault."

Lizzie's hands shook as he spoke; his voice still disarmed her, lulled her into silence. Inside, her anger rattled around but she couldn't put her feelings into words.

"Anything else?" was all she got out.

"I want us to be okay."

"I've got to go." She hung up, still shaking. Lizzie sat back on her heels, looked up at the sky, and, because she knew she was alone, bellowed into the open air. A nearby tree shuddered as crows took flight in response. She sighed.

Should've left the phone in the car. She glanced over at her neighbor's retaining wall, at their etched initials, still there. *Where's that chisel?*

The morning was crisp; the air carried a trace of wildfires still raging in the distance. Lizzie loved dawn, loved being in the garden before everyone else. It was the perfect place to think without anyone interrupting or demanding anything from her. But the voice from the past had disrupted that peace. Dylan knew she'd be up early on a Sunday, even if the sun wasn't yet. She bent down to touch the leaves on a row of broccoli. When she brushed them, dew that had beaded up on the leaves overnight rolled toward the center of the plant. Lizzie rationalized herself down from her emotional tree.

Distractions are good. Forget about the phone call. About Dylan. At least try.

She knelt to begin her careful ritual, unfolding the leaves at the center of each plant in search of caterpillars and aphids. They gathered on delicate new growth and, if left unchecked, could ruin a head of broccoli or cauliflower. In the early morning light, all the evening's revelers stood out, easy to spot for removal or relocation. Removal first: she tossed green caterpillars on the ground and squished them under her hiking boot. In the case of aphids, she brushed the tiny gray-green insects off the plant with her thumb. Most people wore gloves for this task, but this morning Lizzie didn't care. She tackled the job bare-handed.

But not when she got to the snails. She put on one glove to pick them off; they were too slimy any other way. She grabbed half a plastic water bottle from the pile of empty halved bottles in the corner, inspected it for holes, and collected the snails and slugs for transport. She found them under the nasturtiums, behind the potting table, attached to the underside of her watering can. When the bottle was full, she walked to the top of the garden to hurl the snail and slug collection into the open field.

"If you can find your way back to my plot, Slick, you can eat all you want."

She gazed toward the ocean for a moment to take a break from pest control. The sun rose, revealing a cloudless sky. The ocean stretched out, deep blue and peaceful.

We're so spoiled.

Lizzie wished she could garden on weekday mornings, but

work demanded her time. As an alternative, her boss allowed her to clock in early so she could get to the garden well before sunset. She kept a set of coveralls in her trunk to throw over her work clothes at the end of the day. But it never gave her the satisfaction that came from spending hours at a time gardening on the weekend.

Lizzie turned back to the garden. Next, weeds.

She put on her other glove; it felt gritty on the inside. If she would remember to take them out of her garden bag every once in a while and wash them, they might do their job. Her hands were chilled, which made putting on the glove more difficult, but once she shimmied it over her damp fingers, its warmth began to thaw her hand. The shaking had subsided, too.

She stood in the center of her plot to observe each raised bed, each pathway, and each corner of her garden. That damned devil's grass was back. It found its way into the corners from the neighbors' plots. The only way to get rid of it was to dig it out by the roots. Or terminate the neighbors' memberships and take over their plots. Not going to happen, but still, the idea made her grin. She added to her mental list of to-dos: write a few citations after weeding.

Lizzie reached into her garden bag to pull out two soil-caked knee pads. After struggling to fasten them, she knelt on the damp pathway of pine-needle mulch to begin weeding.

She spotted some chickweed, grabbed it near the base, and pulled. The satisfying sound of roots being unearthed, snapping and releasing from the soil, was followed by the visual confirmation that the entire root had come out. Clover, mallow, and mystery grasses all came free with a gratifying yank. This made up for the morning's disruption. Sort of.

True, weeding was therapeutic, but it only went so far. Lizzie's mind wandered while her hands worked. She circled back to the phone call, to the memories that had plagued her for the past four months, to the man who broke her heart into a million pieces.

Dylan, the beautiful artist who didn't talk much, whose silence only made him more alluring. A year ago, she assigned her neighboring plot to him. She found his quiet charm intoxicating. She dove in headfirst. He wouldn't let her in, and she couldn't keep him out.

Eight months later—long after he had carved those letters, after he had abandoned his plot for other adventures—the damage still festered. Lizzie's stomach churned. How blind she'd been, thinking they had a romance worthy of *The Notebook*, that he was the Noah to her Allie.

"I CAN'T SEE you tonight. I'm not feeling so hot," he'd said over the phone. "Not accepting visitors."

"Okay," Lizzie said. But she was disappointed. All day at work she looked forward to seeing him. No, she didn't look forward to it; she obsessed. She couldn't do anything but think of being with him. Everything had happened so fast with them, so passionate, so unrestrained. So many promises made. He called her his girlfriend. So fast. She still had everything to learn about him. But that didn't stop them from settling into a comfortable relationship. With relationships comes security. He needed her.

So she made cookies. She took them over to his house as a feel-better-soon gift. When she got there, another car was parked in her spot on the driveway.

"Not accepting visitors, huh?" She sat there for a few minutes, not sure what to do.

Maybe it was a friend. *No, he doesn't have friends; we have that in common.* The more she tried to picture what was happening inside, the more nausea built in her stomach.

What possessed her to park, get out of the car, and walk to the door carrying a warm bag of cookies? Why didn't she light it on fire and hurl it at the porch? It would've been a perfectly appropriate thing for a jilted girlfriend to do. The humiliation was too much. She should have left, but instead she smiled as Dylan answered the door. She anticipated the look on his face, his guilt as he accepted the fragrant cookies.

But instead, his slow surprise was followed by a sheepish look. He turned toward the bedroom, to the figure leaning against the wall on his bed. Lizzie caught a glimpse before he blocked her view.

"Thanks . . . for being cool about this."

He took the cookies and shut the door, leaving an embarrassed and speechless Lizzie to wonder how he and his new girlfriend would enjoy them.

LIZZIE CAME BACK to the present moment to discover that she'd pulled out all her radishes. She wiped tears from her eyes. *When will you get over it?*

Dylan never returned to Vista Mar. His plot had decayed

along with their relationship. She had waited to reassign it, waited for him to show up and claim his things so she could tear him a new one. After one too many reminders from Ned about the abandoned plot, she ripped everything out with her bare hands one hot July afternoon in a fitful attempt to purge her anger. Lizzie rehashed the words she never got to say—words she couldn't force out of her mouth on the phone—that he was a lying, cheating coward who didn't have the balls to tell her he had moved on to something new. She was old news, discarded, disposed of, not good enough anymore. Dylan called to unburden himself, not to apologize. But her yearning for an apology wouldn't subside. She knew she'd take the pain to her grave if she couldn't let it go, and she wanted to let it go—but she wanted that apology more.

Dating seemed pointless after Dylan. Not that it had been exactly fruitful before him. In fact, Dylan had been the last straw after a run of dating disasters. She had tried hookups, one-night stands, blind dates, and other attempts at relating to the opposite sex as a single adult female. They had all ended the same way, with Lizzie obsessing and overanalyzing it to death. The string of negative experiences left her with an eroded sense of good judgment, and an unshakable distrust of others. Her spectacular crash and burn with Dylan simply reinforced the fact that she wasn't equipped to have relationships, not even the frivolous kind. Luckily, there were no prospects on the horizon.

She enjoyed living alone, liked doing whatever she desired, whenever she liked. Daily writing prompts from her screenwriting guru's newsletter kept her occupied, plumbing the depths of her imagination, crystallizing sparks of creativity into numerous unfinished screenplays. Occasionally Lizzie would send query letters or treatments to agencies in an ongoing quest for representation. The search yielded few results, but each day she'd inch toward finishing at least one manuscript.

The rest of the time she occupied herself by living inside other people's movies instead of real life. She looked forward to her annual movie binge over the holidays. How many films could she watch during her two-week vacation? Last year she counted twenty-eight, mostly romantic comedies and Oscar noms, but a few classics, including *Some Like It Hot* and *The Philadelphia Story*. Lizzie was proud of her all-time record: forty-five flicks in fourteen days. If she ever found someone who enjoyed holing up in a dark room for weeks to watch movies, they'd be a perfect match—if she didn't ruin it—but for now she was content to indulge in cinematic oblivion alone.

Lizzie had a knack for choosing the right movie with the right life lesson at the perfect moment. She'd scroll through the options and pick a film that offered a relevant solution to whatever problem the world had presented her that day. Whether it was "it's time to move on" or "don't get on that plane," Lizzie found poignant messages in her chosen films. Most of the time, anyway. At the very least, watching movies took her mind off work and the lack of fulfillment it gave her. Work was, after all, just another J.O.B.

I wonder if that new guy Jared will be a good gardener.

She couldn't yet determine into which category Jared fell:

garden flake or true enthusiast. He appeared active enough, emailing her with garden-related questions throughout the week, but it was still too early to tell.

She reminisced about her own beginning at Vista Mar Gardens, twelve years earlier. From the moment she drove a shovel into the soil, she was addicted.

Her phone pinged. Should she look at it? What if it was Dylan unapologizing again?

Aloha. Is redwood OK for raised beds? It was Jared.

Kiln-dried, yes. Solvent-dried, no. Toxic, she texted back. **Cedar is better.**

Dang, thanks. U saved me from certain death.

We wouldn't want that. She hit send before she could edit herself. She covered with **Best to email instead of text, OK?**

Old school . . . I can dig it.

Whatever, Shaft. She set the phone down, her heart unexpectedly aflutter.

Was he gardening for the same reasons she was? She had added her name to the waiting list after she read Rachel Carson's *Silent Spring*. Apartment living in Los Angeles didn't afford the space to grow food on-site, so a plot in a community garden was the obvious choice. Years later, she binge-watched a series of documentaries about conventional agriculture and the woeful state of the American food system. The films all blurred together at this point, but the topics still burned in her brain: pesticides that kill beneficial insects, weed killers that wipe out Monarch butterfly habitats, synthetic fertilizers that destroy soil microbiology, and GMO crops that cross-contaminate the seed supply. It was crazy. Scared stiff to find out that genetically engineered corn generates its own pesticide—and that it's in almost everything people eat—she had ramped up her plan to gain more control over her food sources.

When she got the call, she was so excited she couldn't sleep. She spent late-night hours planning out the most efficient use of the twelve-by-seventeen-foot space and designed the perfect garden. After taking ownership of her plot, she tackled the weeds, the sandy soil, and the rotten retaining walls with gusto, eager to put her stamp on a plot of land. Her first year in the garden was the most successful. Everything grew. Maybe because no one had worked the soil in a while, or maybe it was beginner's luck. Okay, maybe it was because she coddled those plants like a new puppy.

She had covered the seedlings in each raised bed with a clear plastic tarp draped over stakes in the corners. The plants had loved the makeshift greenhouses and her seedlings thrived. Green shoots climbed their trellises and made the first-time gardener look like a pro.

The past few years, though, had not been as fruitful. Lizzie observed more changes in the garden than usual. More diseases, more pests, but mostly the warmer weather. For years, the November board meeting had taken place in the pouring rain, everyone huddled close to a sad excuse for a space heater that struggled to cut through the chill. But for the past five years, those meetings had been held on warm, clear days with no rain in sight. Blue skies were always welcome, but Vista Mar members searched for clouds with worried eyes, knowing the land was drying out. Flower bulbs came up earlier, tricked into thinking spring began sooner each year.

Don't tell me there's no such thing as climate change, Lizzie fumed. Any gardener could attest to the changes. Big changes: Fewer days of rain. Rain in July instead of November. Humidity? Where the heck did that come from? Mexico's weather was moving north. Even the USDA hardiness zone map had shifted. Los Angeles used to sit in zone 9b, then 10a, now 10b. She used to plant fall crops in September, but for the last few years Lizzie and her fellow gardeners had to wait until late October or early November to avoid the heat. She looked up from the soil and took a breath. She scanned nearby plots and observed many empty patches of land still awaiting cooler weather for safe planting.

Drought was the new normal, and the board had been forced to impose watering restrictions. No irrigating between 9:00 A.M. and 4:00 P.M. Boy, did that cause a ruckus.

The beauty of Vista Mar Gardens was in its members' diversity. Young, old, straight, gay, new, and veteran gardeners who came from all over the world: India, Russia, Poland, Japan, Uganda, and every corner of the Americas. Despite disagreements between members, this second home was a wonderful place to be. But when the board had announced irrigation restrictions, it was as if someone imposed martial law on the community.

"How am I supposed to get here to water before nine? I have a life, you know."

"I can only come during my lunch break. My garden's going to die!"

"Why can't we put the whole garden on a drip irrigation timer?"

Suggestions and defiance resounded, but the board didn't see any solution except to follow the new rules. Over time, everyone got used to the shortened hours and, along with the rest of Los Angeles, reduced water consumption by 17 percent that first summer. That had made Lizzie smile. She loved the idea that their actions made a difference.

Weeding gave her hands something to do while her brain worked out problems. By the time she finished weeding, she'd figured out how to fix a broken drawer in the kitchen (use those mystery screws from the closet to hold the slides in place), decided on a five-minute recipe for dinner that night (wilted greens over leftover brown rice with marinated tempeh), then made a list of steps to take to solve world hunger (start with establishing a worldwide victory garden program). She'd also outlined the beginnings of a screenplay—about gardening, of course. It was a much better use of her mind to problem-solve than to wallow in old heartbreak.

Her reverie was interrupted by the sound of footsteps down the path. She glanced up and watched Jared carry two planks of cedar lumber down to his plot. He caught her eye.

"Hey, thanks for the pro tip."

"No problem." She stood up, dusted off her knees, and found herself walking toward Jared's plot for no reason. "Going for a matching pair?" she said, nodding to his recently installed retaining walls.

"Say again?"

"Nothing. Matching raised beds to go with your retaining walls"—she fumbled her words—"is what I meant."

He chuckled. "Yeah, I guess so. Do you approve?"

Lizzie was taken aback for a second. Was he trying to impress her?

"We're supposed to get materials approved before we build, right?" Jared asked.

"Oh." Lizzie looked down. "Yes, that's right. I guess nobody remembers that part." Of course he wasn't trying to impress her.

In that awkward moment, standing there, she noticed she was thirsty—and hungry. Really hungry. Her stomach croaked loud enough for Jared to hear.

"Was that you?" he asked.

"I left without breakfast this morning."

"Who does that? Breakfast is the most impor—"

"Yeah, yeah, I know." She shot a glance up the hill. "Self-care is not my strong suit."

When it came to meals, Lizzie exhibited bachelor tendencies, eating straight out of a pan over the sink in her tiny apartment kitchen. Overscheduled, no time to sit down. She could hear her mom's voice the whole time: *Don't you have any chairs?*

Jared brushed past her, probably to go retrieve more wood from his car, but she only noticed the soft cotton of his shirt as his sleeve grazed her shoulder. He smelled of fresh laundry and cinnamon. He smelled like dessert.

"Be right back," he said.

She wished Jared good luck with his raised beds and walked back to her plot in search of a snack. She kept emergency rations in her gardening bag for occasions such as these. How old was this one? The mangled protein bar looked as if it had been closed in a car door. She tore open the metallic wrapper and bit off a sticky segment. She chewed, watching Jared return to his plot with additional timbers. He set them down and knelt to work in the far corner. After she crinkled the wrapper and tucked it back into the depths of her bag, she peeled her eyes off Jared's back and continued to weed.

In the middle of a big city, it was easy to get lost in the sound of traffic and road noise. Vista Mar was walking distance from her apartment, and both the garden and her apartment were equidistant from a small, local airport. Living near an airport meant jet engines were the perpetual soundtrack of her daily life. After a while in the garden, though, Lizzie was able to tune out the urban disruptions in favor of the Foley effects supplied by nature. The garden provided an oasis. Hummingbirds called out to their mates, bees hovered above leftover flowering basil, and an occasional crow put on a show for anyone watching. You could probably hear a snail chomping on the cabbage leaves here. She loved the quiet.

"Hi, Lizzie."

The voice shot through her. She looked up from her pile of weeds to find Ralph standing on the path with his hands in the pockets of his puffy vest, thumbs jutting out. She swallowed her heart down out of her throat and said hello, trying not to let on that he had scared her half to death. He already looked as though he was going to burst from nervous tension.

Ralph stared at the ground and ran the toe of his work boot through the mulch beneath his feet. "It's going pretty good," he said, his voice more nasal than usual.

That's odd. I didn't ask him. Lizzie picked up her hand trowel.

"What are you growing this season?" she asked. *Why is he here?*

"Um"—he squinted up at the sky—"I'm growing some kale, and chard, and . . . well, my roses, of course . . . Oh, here." Ralph's chubby hand reached into his back pocket and reappeared grasping two violet radishes by their green stems. "Pink Beauty."

He tossed them toward Lizzie, and they landed atop her garden bag. He ran his fingers through the tight curls of his black hair and stuffed his hand back in his vest pocket. He didn't look at Lizzie. "I'm probably going to try some rhubarb this year, but I'm not sure yet."

"Oh, that'll be nice. There used to be a rhubarb patch in the plot down there," Lizzie pointed her hand trowel a few rows downhill, "but when they left, the new owner ripped it out."

"That's a shame. I plan to try a variety called Paragon because it's rare. It's going extinct, so they're trying to get more people to grow it."

"That's wonderful," Lizzie said. "I love when people take an interest in that stuff."

"You do?" A smile overtook his face.

"Of course. Any time we preserve a species, it's better for everyone."

"I concur." Ralph's face lit up even more. "If you have time, I'll show you a bunch of heirloom catalogs I get. They're full of rare varieties. It's really cool. There's this one rhubarb, it's Himalayan, and it's used as a laxative in Chinese medicine. Of course, you're not supposed to take laxatives on the Sabbath . . ."

Lizzie was surprised Ralph took an interest in Chinese medicine. Did she want to know about the laxative part? After a moment of following that thread further than she ought, she realized no one was talking. She looked up at Ralph and his awkward grin, feeling a sudden urge to leave. Trapped in her own plot with Ralph at the entrance, she did her best to finish the discussion.

"I'd love to get the names of those catalogs. I can check them out online. Will you email them to me?" She looked past him toward Jared working in his plot. Jared shifted two pieces of lumber and walked toward his car for more.

"Oh." Ralph turned to follow Lizzie's gaze. "Sure."

Lizzie watched Ralph fall into silence as he paced along the pathway in front of her plot. She assumed that at some point he would finish ruminating and say something. She pulled another weed or two before checking on Ralph. He stopped pacing, but still gazed at his feet.

"So I'll look for that email, okay?" Lizzie tried to nudge him out of his reverie.

"It's just that . . ." Ralph's head popped up. "I bookmarked pages, you know, and made notes, cross-referenced between catalogs. You have to experience it . . . in person."

Ralph blushed a shade darker.

"Oh," Lizzie said.

"Heads up," Jared called from the pathway. Lizzie looked over in time to spot a banana flying toward her. Ralph looked startled as Lizzie caught the flying fruit. He squinted into the morning sun to see who had lobbed it at her.

"Breakfast." Jared smiled. He gave Ralph a chin lift hello.

"Oh." Lizzie laughed. "Thanks. I found a mangy snack bar in my garden bag, but this is better. Sure you don't need it?"

"Naw, I ate breakfast." He turned back toward his plot.

Ralph cleared his throat. Lizzie had forgotten he was there. She held the banana and tried to figure out what to do.

"So about those seed catalogs . . ."

Ralph jumped in. "When's a good time to meet?"

"Ralph, I'm so busy with work and everything. October is always crazy."

"Forget about it. It's not that interesting." He stared at the now limp radishes on Lizzie's garden bag.

"I'm sorry, but—"

"No explanation necessary." He started down the path.

Lizzie called after him, "Tell you what. Maybe in December when the new catalogs show up, we can share a few of our favorites at the potluck. Yeah?"

He didn't stop, but shouted over his shoulder, "If it comes up."

CHAPTER 4
Opposing Forces

November

"All right, everyone, let's get this underway," Mary spoke into the mic. "We have a lot to cover."

Board meetings at Vista Mar Gardens were held every other month on the third Sunday morning. The members of the board—including east and west section reps—would gather under the canopy of the giant magnolia tree in the center of the garden to approve minutes from the last meeting and discuss new business on the agenda. *More like* bored *meetings*, Lizzie thought.

They assembled around a grouping of tables resembling oversized spools of thread. Green deck chairs circled the tables and weeds poked through the mulch underfoot. Each plastic chair possessed an unfortunate design flaw; it cradled a hidden cache of water, deposited by the ocean air the night before. Board members—those paying attention, anyway—tipped the chairs forward and wiped the seat dry before sitting down. An unsuspecting few discovered the soggy seat the hard way. Lizzie used her grubby jacket to wipe down the chair, but others used paper towels from the roll Ned had brought down from the office along with a pot of coffee. Ned's coffee was as reliable as his uncanny ability to turn up at the right moment. No meeting took place without a fresh pot. Ned also provided an assortment of baked goods, usually a classic pink pastry box filled with sweet rolls, scones, and muffins.

Lizzie had arrived early and stood by the refreshments table, watching the board members gather. They exchanged small talk about the weather and their gardeners. Lizzie didn't often encounter other section reps outside of meetings, so this gave her a chance to catch up.

"Anything scandalous happening in your section?" she asked Ananda, the rep for Section Two West. Lizzie limited her conversations to garden matters. Never about life outside the gates.

"Bernice and Mary are at it again," Ananda whispered. "Something about snails, I think."

"What is it with those two?" Lizzie asked.

"Girl, I have no idea. From what I heard, they used to be friends, but something happened when Mary became president. That was before I got here though." Ananda waved her hands over her head to clear the negative energy. "Mary used to scare me."

"Yeah. She comes off as angry sometimes, but she just cares a lot. Also, she's at the age where she's not required to take BS from anyone anymore."

"Wait, we have to be old for that?"

Lizzie giggled and turned to locate a seat at an empty table.

Board members were volunteers. Mary governed as president, overseeing the board. Ned, the garden master, ensured the garden itself was taken care of. The rest of the board members—eight section reps, treasurer, and secretary—answered to Mary and Ned. Section reps policed the members and helped keep the garden running smoothly. While the board members were happy to get together to solve any problems, most of them continued on because no one else campaigned for the job. How many times had Lizzie's biennial reelection gone uncontested? She'd lost count. Every once in a while, a new gardener complained about how long it took to get anything done, but once they discovered the section reps weren't paid, the complaining stopped.

Sharalyn arrived, dressed in her trusty black tracksuit, found a seat next to Lizzie, and asked after her half of Section Four. Ned found himself in a talk-hold with a regular garden member who'd shown up to join the meeting. He tried to get away, but the woman kept grabbing his sleeve to add "one more thing." Then there was Bernice.

Bernice was a thin, silver-haired woman who'd been on the board for as long as anyone could remember. She always wore a crisp white oxford shirt, sleeves rolled up, and new denim jeans tucked into her Wellington boots. Though it rarely rained in

Los Angeles, Bernice carried wellies in the car for all garden-related matters. She came to each board meeting with strong opinions about every item on the agenda but some days stronger than others. This day, Lizzie had appraised Bernice's determination the moment she'd arrived—she looked stern and ready for a fight. Bernice found an empty seat beside Lizzie, set her three-ring binder on the table with a smack, took a copy of the agenda as it circulated, and glanced over the page. She sighed and shook her head.

"Shouldn't we start?" Bernice asked in her tight British accent. "We're two minutes overdue."

"I called the meeting to order two minutes ago, Bernice." Mary gathered her papers. "Before you decided to join us."

Lizzie tensed, reminded of Ananda's gossip. Were these two going to hash it out here, in front of everyone, à la Joan Crawford and Bette Davis? Why did Bernice have to sit right next to her? Lizzie had absentmindedly chosen a chair in the center of the meeting area, which left no path to escape unnoticed. She observed the other board members; most of them chatted with each other, unaware of what was to come. Lizzie took a deep breath as Mary quieted the group.

Mary took the reins of the meeting with grace, ushering them through the first agenda item.

"May I have a move and second to approve the minutes from the September board meeting?"

Hands shot up. Several people said, "Move."

Bernice raised her finger in the air. "Just a moment."

A collective sigh was uttered. The meeting was indeed underway.

"I call for a correction to the minutes; there appears to be a mistake."

Mary exhaled. "Yes, Bernice?"

"The minutes state that we agreed unanimously to increase funds dedicated to composting. That's incorrect. There was indeed one opposed—the record should reflect such."

Mary nodded. "Didi, you got that?"

Didi, the board secretary, nodded back. "Got it."

"Anything else before we move on?" Mary scanned the group. "Okay, then, a second, please."

Lizzie's hand popped up. "Second."

"All in favor?"

Mary took in the show of hands, thanked them, and continued. "Item 1 A: Update on the orchard. We're low on volunteers for monthly weeding, and the pruning committee could use an extra hand or two. So if any of your members need community hours, send them my way."

Lizzie heard Bernice grumbling. She shifted her glance in time to witness Bernice saying to her neighbor, "Her precious orchard. If only she gave as much attention to all the problems in this garden."

Bernice raised a hand. "You don't plan to increase the orchard budget again, do you? I believe we can all agree that forty percent was a more than ample increase for your pet project."

Mary focused her steely gaze on Bernice. "Let the record

show that the increase in budget allowed us to transform a weedy patch of neglected fruit trees into a productive grove. I procured thirty new fruit trees with a bit of sweet talk— donations that didn't use any budget funds—and as a result our garden members reap the benefits, harvesting more fruit than ever before, year-round."

Bernice harrumphed, flipped open her binder, and pretended to read something important to herself.

"If we're done with that, let's get back to the agenda," Mary said. "Item 1 B: We've been hit by thieves again." Ned shook his head while several other board members cursed under their breath. "Not only did someone strip all the fruit from the lemon tree at the bottom of the hill, but we found about fifteen mail-boxes smashed in—we assume with a baseball bat—in Section One East."

"What?" Lizzie stood up to survey the garden. She spied a damaged mailbox at the edge of a corner plot, dented in the middle, rendered useless. A few others close by all showed similar damage. Red flags snapped off, doors hinged open on impact. Lizzie thought about the scene in *Stand by Me* where the guys drove around playing mailbox baseball. The damage here wasn't as bad, but still infuriating. How had she not no-ticed that on the way in?

The garden's mailboxes were more than a way for members to communicate among themselves. They also showcased each member's artistic expression. Some gardeners decorated their mailboxes with bright colors or mosaic tiles. Others painted theirs with flowers or gnomes. The mailboxes brought color and cheer to the garden. Their destruction, the broken tiles strewn on the ground, violated the community spirit among members.

The section reps mumbled to one another. Jason, Section Two East's rep, said, "How about surveillance equipment? I know a guy. He'll hook us up."

Jason had probably been a Montezuma cypress tree in a past life. Just shy of seven feet tall, he had an ominous presence at first glance. His hands were as big as the business end of a shovel, and he could turn a compost pile in under a minute. Despite his brown baby face and bleached curly hair, his physical appearance reminded Lizzie of a character straight out of *Stand and Deliver*. Even though they knew he was as dangerous as a labradoodle, she and the other section reps called him "the Bouncer."

"We *need* twenty-four-hour security," Ananda said. She had pulled her purple-streaked dreadlocks back into a neat ponytail. She smoothed her batik skirt over her knees and tucked her hands under her thighs. "Our community isn't safe." The freckled, light-brown skin between her violet eyes crinkled with concern.

"I know, I know." Mary put up her hands to calm the group. "We don't have the budget for a full-time security guard, and we wouldn't be able to afford replacements for any stolen camera equipment either." The section reps fell silent.

"I've been picking this apart all night, believe me. My idea is to install floodlights in strategic places throughout the garden to see if that scares off unwelcome visitors. I know it doesn't sound like much, but I've talked it over with Ned, and he agrees it's a good first step."

Sharalyn and Lizzie exchanged glances. Outside of posting guard dogs, or volunteering Jason for night patrol, what else could they do?

Sharalyn whispered, "Maybe that'll scare off that swamp rat who's stealing my roses."

They both shrugged and shifted focus back to Mary. Bernice sat with arms folded. Her face had twisted into a ball of tension at the mention of hiring security, but she relaxed as Mary mentioned floodlights.

"That's a good idea, Ned," Bernice said.

Mary rolled her eyes, but continued. "If we place motion-sensor lights near the compost bins, the orchard area, and all the entrance gates, hopefully that will keep undesirables from coming in. Ned priced out several options and estimates that it will cost less than three hundred dollars for fifteen floodlights with batteries."

"We'll only use twelve of them," Ned chimed in, "but we'll get a few extras in case some get destroyed. And that includes one security camera. If we install it on the west hawk perch, it'll be too high up to be stolen."

Didi raised her pen into the air. "I believe this requires a vote."

Mary nodded. "Motion, please?"

Jason raised his hand. "I move to approve spending three hundred dollars for floodlights, a camera, and batteries . . . and to electrify the fence." He smiled. A round of chuckles went up from the board.

Didi grinned. "I'll leave that last part out of the minutes."

"All in favor?" Mary asked. All hands went up.

"All opposed?" No hands raised.

"Motion passed. Okay, moving on. The next item of business: the cats."

Groans floated across the group.

"Two garden members are here to make a statement about the cats. Let's try to keep this to five minutes, folks." Mary gestured for the guests to step forward.

Meanwhile, across the garden, Ralph thundered down the hill to deliver a message to the new guy from Lizzie's section. He found him—the tall, GQ-looking athletic guy with equally GQ-looking wavy hair—hammering away at some framing boards for a new shed. Right where Ned said he would be.

"Jared?" Ralph bent forward to ease the sudden stitch in his side.

Jared paused his hammering and looked up. "Yeah. It's Ralph, right?"

"Yeah." Ralph was surprised the guy remembered. "Ned asked me to bring you this." He reached into his puffy vest and produced a folded piece of lined paper. "Specs for the addition."

"Great. Thanks." He took the note and tucked it into his back pocket. "How's it going?"

Ralph shrugged. "Okay. Are you getting settled in here?"

Jared motioned to the project surrounding him. "I guess you could say that. Ned seems to believe I'm settled in."

"Mm-hmm." Ralph looked down at his feet. He felt sloppy next to this guy, though he wasn't the one sweating. He struggled for something else to say, to find out more about him.

"What do you think of Lizzie?" is what popped out of his mouth.

Jared gave him a sideways glance.

"I mean, uh, as a section rep," Ralph said. "How's she treating you?"

"She's great. A little, you know, strict, but she helped me get started. Seems like she's got a good heart once you get past the rules." Suddenly the sound of music filled the air. "Sorry, hang on a sec." Jared pulled the sonorous device from his back pocket. "Yeah?"

Ralph recognized the ring tone: Rolling Stones' "You Can't Always Get What You Want." He turned away, pretended not to eavesdrop on the conversation, but it was pretty useless.

"Hey, Sean . . . Can I call you back? I'm in the middle of something . . . No, not a 'chick.' God, are you still in high school, man?" He laughed and nodded. "Yes, I'm at the garden . . . Someday I'll bring you, then you'll get it. Look, I'll call you later . . . Don't be a jackass. Bye." Jared slid the phone back into his pocket. "Sorry about that," he said to Ralph.

"Do you call all your friends 'jackass'?" Again, the words came out, unbidden.

"Only the ones who are." Jared chuckled. "I'm sure you have friends like that, from a different time in your life? We get new friends, and the old ones don't quite fit anymore, but they know you from forever ago, right?"

"Yeah, sure," Ralph said, but he couldn't think of a single person from high school or college who still talked to him. High school sucked. This guy was probably prom king.

"Anyway, you were saying?" Jared brought the conversation back around.

"Uh, nothing. Just delivering the note."

"And Lizzie?"

Ralph felt heat rush to his cheeks. Suddenly he was sweating beneath his down vest. He turned to walk back up the hill. "Oh, yeah, whatever. It's nothing."

"Okay, cool." Jared went back to hammering.

Ralph unzipped his puffy vest and billowed his shirt front to cool off while trudging toward the gate. He'd failed in his mission: find out Jared's intentions with Lizzie. Had he not been caught off guard, flustered, he might have extracted more information. *He's probably a jerk*, Ralph concluded. *He probably doesn't even see her—he's too busy being Mr. I'm-So-Sexy.*

Bob and Caroline Sawyer trundled to the microphone with a roll of papers in their hands. Bob was the kind of man who believed that plaid flannel was perfect for any occasion. He took off his baseball cap, smoothed his salt-and-pepper hair, cleared his throat. Caroline, in a button-down shirt with chickens appliquéd on the collar points and denim pants to match, distributed flyers to each board member as Bob launched into his speech. This wasn't the first time Bob and Caroline had spoken at a board meeting. In fact, this marked their third visit in a row. And while garden members were more than welcome to attend board meetings, and were encouraged to bring items to the agenda, most gardeners found the meetings less than scintillating and avoided them at all costs. Bob and Caroline, however, had a bone to pick. And pick they did—for twenty minutes each time.

Over the years, Vista Mar Gardens had become home to many feral cats. Garden members assigned as cat volunteers oversaw the births of unexpected litters, arranged trips to the vet for spaying, neutering, and vaccinations, and mourned the occasional death. In return, the cats, who found a steady supply of rodents and other enticements on the property, helped control the vermin population. The cat care volunteers were a spirited bunch. But some gardeners maintained that the cats were a nuisance. They resented that the board spent budget funds on cat food, arguing that feeding the cats made them lazy and, therefore, lousy mousers. Bob and Caroline were entrenched in the latter faction.

Lizzie scanned the flyer Caroline had handed her. It depicted several species of birds.

Oh God, we're going to be here all day.

Lizzie peeked over at Sharalyn, who looked up from her page to Lizzie, and concurred with her unspoken thought by lowering her eyelids to half-mast. They tuned in to Bob's homily at the front of the group.

". . . So, we've proven that cats endanger the birds in our garden. We surveyed gardeners in our section and found that while the cats prowl, most gardeners say there's still a rat problem. I find the tips of my lettuces chewed through every week. It's the rats! We believe—"

"Does anyone else smell smoke?" Mary interrupted.

Lizzie rose from her chair to follow her nose. Midway down the hill, toward Section Four, she spotted a plume of black smoke rising.

"What the—?" She pushed her chair back and bolted for the gate. Jason, Sharalyn, and Ananda followed close behind.

When Lizzie reached a vantage point along the fence, she yelled back to the others, "Call 911! The palm tree in Section Four's on fire!"

She ran toward the smoke with Jason at her heels. By the time she reached the north edge of the property, the base of a forty-foot palm tree was engulfed in flames. Lizzie felt heat and embers blow toward her. Flames charred the tree's coarse bark as the fire climbed fifteen, maybe twenty feet, encircling the tree.

Lizzie's mind ran wild. How did this happen? Wayward cigarette? Spontaneous combustion? Or something more deliberate? *Stop questioning and do something!*

Jason landed next to her, breathing hard. "*¡Ándale pues!*" He nudged her arm and held up a hose.

"Right." She ran to the hose bib and cranked it on. Jason leaned into the smoke, the jet spray disappearing into blackness. The tree sizzled and creaked as the wind picked up. Flames reached toward a nearby avocado tree and a neighboring plot full of dry weeds and old wooden trellises. Lizzie held her breath, more in fear that the fire would spread than to avoid breathing the smoke.

The rest of the board reached the site. Ned called to Lizzie that the fire department was on its way. Sharalyn and Ananda pulled hoses from nearby plots to help Jason.

Mary stepped up between Ned and Lizzie, out of breath. She stared into the fire. "That son of a bitch."

"What?" Ned looked at Mary. She smoldered like the flickering flames. "Wait. What are you getting at?"

"You know who did this, Ned."

"You're saying this was deliberate?" Ned asked, aghast.

"Hell, yes." She pointed to the top of the tree. "Look at this palm, it's probably blocking his view."

Ned said, "Yeah, but arson? That's not really his style, don't you think?"

Mary scanned for evidence through the black smoke. "Oh, he'd never get his hands dirty, but he's behind this." She trudged up the hill as fast as her lungs would allow, stopping at eye level to the crest of the hill. Lizzie followed behind to see what Mary was, indeed, getting at. She watched Mary study the palm tree. Her gaze shifted toward Kurt Arnold's house across the field, then back to the palm tree. The tree pierced the sky above the crest another twenty feet, enough to block the view for the old curmudgeon.

Sirens blared around the corner and, lights blazing, the fire truck pulled up the driveway. It didn't have far to go to find the fire. Firefighters jumped from the vehicle, pulling hoses from the truck in every direction. A deep voice boomed over the clamor, "Step back. Clear the area."

Jason and his hose gave way, and seconds later a blast from the far-stronger fire hose worked to extinguish the blaze. Firefighters moved in on the avocado tree and doused the nearby plot that had started to catch fire. The tree continued to smoke and sizzle as Jason coiled and rehung the garden hose. The smell of burned wood blanketed the garden.

Mary turned to face Kurt's house in the distance. She extended her middle fingers high and stabbed the air, hoping Kurt was watching from his window. She turned to Lizzie and said, "You bet your ass I'm going to find out if he had anything to do with this."

"This calls for a tasty snack," Jason bellowed through lingering smoke. He turned and jogged back toward the refreshments table at the meeting area. The group dissolved into laughter and followed his lead.

Mary yelled after them, "We still have a meeting to finish." A few of the board members groaned.

"I'll finish up here, Mary," Ned said, gesturing to the fire chief. "You go ahead."

"Thanks, Ned," Mary said as she turned to head back. "Be sure to tell him about my theory, will you?"

"You got it."

As Mary passed them, Lizzie and Sharalyn took one last lingering look at the smoldering tree, then looked at each other. Close call, with minimal damage—just the palm tree and a branch or two of the avocado tree nearby—but still, it could've spread to the whole garden if it had been noticed any later. Sharalyn reached out to squeeze Lizzie's arm. Lizzie inhaled and felt a sudden rush of tears at the touch of Sharalyn's hand.

"You okay, sugar?" Sharalyn leaned in.

Lizzie, perplexed by her own reaction, replied, "Yeah, I don't know why I'm crying."

"Maybe you need squeezes more often."

"No, I'm fine." She waved her off. "I think it's just adrenaline."

"Mm-hmm."

"No, really. I'm fine." She saw Sharalyn's probing eyes. "I'm not lonely, Shar."

"I'm not saying you're lonely, but everybody needs a squeeze now and again."

Lizzie squinted back at Sharalyn. "Maybe."

When they arrived back at the meeting area, they found Bob and Caroline still standing at the microphone. They began talking again before everyone found their seats.

Once Bob and Caroline finished their sermon and stepped away from the microphone, the board sped through the rest of the agenda. Aside from one additional interruption where Bernice argued the difference between a tree and a shrub, quoting the *American Horticultural Society Encyclopedia of Garden Plants*, the meeting went well.

Mary's call for a vote to adjourn was followed by a shot of hands in the air.

"Move," the group said in unison.

"Second!" the section reps sang out. Jason started stacking chairs.

Lizzie folded up her meeting agenda, tucked it into her back pocket. As she made her way to leave, she overheard Bernice engaged in heated conversation with Ananda. Part of her—the curious part—wanted to witness what was going on, but the other part remained content to play ignorant.

"This is not an issue of cleanliness," Bernice said.

Ananda stood with her arms down, hands clenching and releasing the fabric of her skirt. Her words came slow and calm, as if they were a mantra during meditation, but her expression showed that the meditation wasn't working. "Bernice, I hear you and I respect your words, but I don't understand why—"

"This is an issue of breaking the rules and regulations." Bernice's voice ascended in volume and pitch.

"Why do you have such a problem with people storing tools in their plots, Bernice?"

"I don't care about everyone else's plot. I care about your plot because it's directly across from mine and I have to look at your pile of junk every day." Bernice pushed on. "The *Rules and Regulations* clearly state that no tools or equipment may be stored in a member's plot unless elevated and vertical. You have a mountain of broken tools and your collection of old patio furniture is unsightly—"

"It's not old—"

"Furthermore, it makes an ideal location for vermin to populate. You must remove it, Ananda."

Bernice clenched her jaw. Her thin hands shook. Lizzie

pictured her fuse sizzling toward its inevitable end. Bernice took a deep breath, let out a sharp exhale.

"We've ruminated on this enough. Here"—Bernice slapped a yellow piece of paper down on the table—"is your citation."

You can do that? Writing another section rep a citation was unheard of. In fact, most reps rented plots in the section they oversaw. No one wrote themselves a citation. As it turns out, Ananda was the only section rep with a plot in a different area of the garden—the section under Bernice's jurisdiction.

"A citation?"

"Yes, and if you don't fix it in two weeks, I'll write you another." Bernice was in her element.

"That's not fair."

"It doesn't matter if it's fair, it's our policy. You're well aware of that."

A citation: the dreaded yellow slip of paper, tucked into the member's mailbox for any number of infractions in the garden. Unattended plots filled with weeds, trellises shading a neighbor's garden, plants growing too close to the boundaries—all were grounds for a citation. Lizzie wrote plenty herself, for too few community hours, or uncivil acts, such as the fistfight she had broken up the previous month between one neat freak and his lackadaisical neighbor. Section reps were supposed to keep the citations flowing, but some were far too lenient and left abandoned plots for months before issuing citations. Bernice, however, stayed on top of her duties.

After two unresolved citations, the member would be terminated—kicked out of the garden. Once that happened, the gardener had ten days to clear the plot and turn in their gate key.

"Bernice"—Ananda was shocked, and her voice began to climb—"I have plans for those things. They came from my mama's house when she passed. I haven't figured out where to use them yet." She paused. "I'm waiting for a sign." Ananda traced figure eights on her skirt to calm herself.

"Well, dear, let this be a sign." Bernice fluttered the citation in front of Ananda. There was a touch of sympathy in her words, but she continued on. "I'm sorry about your mother, but the garden is not the place to store family heirlooms. Please find another location for them, or I will be forced to write a second citation." She dropped her arms to her sides. "I'm not unreasonable, you know. We have one job as section representatives, and if we don't set a good example, what's the use of our being here? We can't show favoritism—that would damage our credibility. You have authority in this garden, Ananda. You can't be an exception to the rules."

Out of the corner of her eye, Lizzie spied Mary, who had lingered, listening to the conversation between Bernice and Ananda. Mary shot Bernice a scowl. She picked up a stack of papers and sauntered past the two women.

"Oh, Bernie, pull that stick out of your ass," Mary said as she passed. "The girl's lost her mother. Give her a break."

Bernice turned toward Mary and yelled after her, "It's Bernice, thank you very much, and don't tell me how to do my job. If you knew how to do your own . . ." She trailed off as Mary walked out of earshot. A rush of blood darkened Bernice's pale face and she blurted, "And stop throwing snails into my plot, Mary Burcham!"

Bernice looked ruffled by Mary's assault, but she attempted to smooth her feathers. She turned back to Ananda.

"This doesn't change anything, Ananda." She tried to regain her previous intensity. "The citation stands."

Ananda stood distraught. "I'll take care of it." Angry, dejected, and nearly in tears, she looked like a schoolgirl in detention. She gathered her Guatemalan backpack and coffee mug, picked the citation up off the table, and left.

Bernice let out a sigh. She looked over at Lizzie standing a few tables away. Indignation took over her countenance.

"These people drive me batty," she said to no one in particular, but really to Lizzie, while collecting her things. "Granting themselves exemption to the rules." She walked toward Lizzie, who searched for an escape route. Should she feign obliviousness or engage Bernice and get it over with?

"Exactly like my husband." Bernice shook her head. "He's always looking for ways to defy the law of the land." She came a little too close and drummed her fingers on her three-ring binder.

Lizzie didn't care to learn much more about Bernice, but the silence dragged on. "Yeah," she said.

"My Norman fancies himself a bit of a schemer. He derives great pleasure from bending the rules. I marvel at how we've stayed married all these years."

Lizzie acquiesced. *All right, I'll bite.*

"How long have you been married?"

Bernice lit up. "Forty-five years, and not a day goes by that he doesn't try to coax me into breaking some rule or other. I'm sure if I did, I'd be the one to end up in prison while he'd go gallivanting off fancy-free." She chuckled, amused by the idea.

Who'd have guessed we had anything in common? "That's me, too. I grew up Catholic. Fear of getting in trouble guided all my decisions." Lizzie paused. "Still does, sadly. I'm too afraid to do anything wrong because, with my luck, I'll be the one to get caught."

"Well, then you understand." Bernice fluttered her fingers in the air. "Why, the other day I caught him—nearly turned him in myself—for down . . . loading, or whatever you call it"—she stirred the air with her free hand—"one of those pirated music programs. Stealing classical music. Can you imagine! 'Everyone's doing it,' he said." Her face darkened. "Well, I won't. I'm constantly keeping him in check." Bernice's demeanor shifted when she spoke of Norman. Sternness gave way to a combination of frustration and love: a refreshing change.

"You have your hands full, don't you?"

"Like it or not, yes," Bernice said.

Lizzie capitalized on the lighthearted moment as an opportunity to depart. "Luckily for me, I've only got my garden to keep in check. I'm going to see if my cauliflower plants are still alive. Talk to you later, Bernice."

"I actually have a question for you, dear," Bernice said.

Lizzie turned halfway around, taken aback by the affectionate *dear*. Bernice leaned in, pressing her binder to her chest.

"As you're aware, I'm Mary's section representative, but I try my best to avoid working in my plot when she's here. I'm sure you understand." She leaned in still farther; Lizzie noted Earl Grey tea on her breath. She lowered her voice to a whisper.

"You're close by. Have you witnessed her . . . you know . . . throwing things? That shouldn't be thrown?"

Lizzie's stomach tightened. She squinted and bit her lower lip. How was she going to get out of this one? Neutrality was the key component of her strategy as a board member. At least, maintaining an appearance of neutrality. The truth was, she cared more for Mary than Bernice. When she looked into Bernice's eyes, Lizzie suddenly understood her intentions clear as day: catch Mary in the act, cite her to the point of termination, run for president, rule the garden.

"Hmm, well, I'll keep my eyes peeled, now that you ask, but I don't run into Mary that much." It was the best she could do.

"I would appreciate that," Bernice gave a tight-lipped smile. "Oh, and one more thing, dear. Would you mind distributing these to your section? It's just a teensy flyer." She extended a stack of flyers toward Lizzie.

Lizzie took them, nodded, and turned away, feeling dirty in a rare moment when her hands were actually clean.

CHAPTER 5
Broccoli

December

Christmas cards flooded Kurt Arnold's mailbox. Polite messages from former business colleagues, portraits of them with spouses and children he'd long forgotten, all in their Sunday best with the ubiquitous family pet bedecked in Rudolph antlers or a Santa hat. Or worse yet, family vacation photos intended to fuel jealousy. "Happy Holidays from the Bernsteins in Bali," one card read in silver ink across a picture of five happy, sun-kissed travelers poised in front of their private helicopter. Not that he hadn't sent multitudes of comparable photos in his younger days, but coming from others it felt pretentious and annoying.

None of the holiday cards scattered across the table,

however, came from either of his two children. Maybe Ken's and Lisa's cards had come in an earlier delivery and he'd missed them. He scanned the room, up to the garlands draped across the cabinet shelves with photos and cards pinned to them. No such luck. Maybe they would surprise him with a visit instead. It had been years since either of them had come home for Christmas. Far too long.

He picked up the phone to dial Ken. When it clicked over to voicemail, he contemplated hanging up. What did he have to say anyway? The beep forced his hand. He mustered a smile, knowing Ken would hear it in his voice.

"Hey, Ken, it's your father here. Wondering where's my Christmas card? You usually send a picture that shows how your little rug rats are doing.

"So, uh . . . is Kyle still clinging to his mother for dear life or has he finally manned up? What am I saying? You turned out all right, I guess. Anyway, if you find time for a visit, we have room. Give me a call."

The sound of keys in the front door interrupted his debate on whether or not to call Lisa. A job best done by his wife, he determined. She'll have something to say, at least. He never cared for those awkward silences his daughter employed. That sort of behavior would never have been tolerated by his own father.

"More cards, my dear," his wife said. She tossed a thin stack of envelopes on the table.

"Any from our spawn?" He leafed through each one. When

his wife didn't answer, he added, "I invited Ken to come for the holidays."

"Oh? And what did he say?"

"It went to voicemail, as usual."

"He has a full life, Kurt. A trip is a lot to arrange," she said over her shoulder as she tucked groceries into the cupboard.

"Of course, but you'd think they'd encourage their kids to spend time with their grandparents."

"I talk to them on FaceTime all the time. You can always join in."

FaceTime. Hangouts. Skype. Since when did an honest phone conversation become insufficient? Apple and Google need not record the intimate details of his private life, thank you. If a person's kids and grandkids wanted to talk, they could call.

Kurt rose from the table and climbed the stairs to his usual lookout. Darkness fell a minute earlier each day, so there was nothing to observe out the window, but he imagined that damn palm tree still standing. Defiantly. Very much alive. He listened to the sounds of his wife preparing dinner below, the clank of pots and pans, the smell of broccoli steaming on the stove. It threw him back to a time when everything was perfect.

"DADDY, DADDY!" LISA's tiny feet hurried up the stairs.

"There's my little girl." Kurt hoisted her up to the window to look out toward the ocean.

"I made you a present." She handed him a paper heart, zig-zagged with waxy colors in every direction.

"Aw, thank you, my lovely. Whose heart is this?"

"Mine," she said.

He noticed a stick figure drawn in the middle of the heart. "And who is this?"

"That's you!" Lisa pointed to the golf cap on the stick figure.

"You captured my likeness perfectly." Kurt pressed it against the window; light passed through the paper, illuminating streaks of color. "You're going to be—"

"See? You are in my heart, Daddy. Look." She pointed to the stick figure, then traced the edge of the heart.

Kurt couldn't help but choke up. He might be in charge, but she held the reins to his heart. He kissed Lisa's shiny hair and looked out to the distant ocean. "I see. I'm the luckiest daddy in the world."

THE SMELL OF overcooked broccoli wafted upstairs. Kurt's wife rediscovered cooking when he fired their housekeeper six months ago. She catered to his palate and preferences, but she lacked the skills to provide anything too elaborate, so he wasn't about to dampen her spirits with unreasonable requests. He had grown accustomed to her simple meals with plain fresh food. At least she *tried* not to overcook everything. Sometimes she succeeded. He could easily dine out for lunch and eat her over-done vegetables in the evenings, as long as it made her happy. As long as she was content to stay put.

"Dinner's ready," she called from downstairs.

Kurt returned to the kitchen to find a plate of rubbery

chicken and limp, army-green broccoli on the table. He poured a generous glass of wine to make up for it.

"I found another listing today," his wife said in her singsong voice. She slid a magazine above his dinner plate. "It's only five million. What do you say?"

"We should buy two," Kurt said between sips of wine.

"I'm not kidding." She reached around his elbow and shifted the ad closer to his plate, right where his wineglass would go, to make sure he saw it. She pointed to the Tudor-style mansion listed under Beverly Hills. "It's a better neighborhood. More suited to our . . . comforts."

"You mean your comforts."

"My dear"—she swatted Kurt with her dish towel, then rotated a vase filled with the hand-picked roses Kurt occasionally brought her—"I love this old house as much as you do, but we've outgrown it. We—"

"What's to outgrow? The children left. We have more room than we need."

"You know what I mean. We're not the same people we used to be. We're . . ."

"Richer?"

She sighed, but coated her usual exasperation with a sweetness that always seemed to work on him. "Well, that, yes, but you said it yourself. The kids are gone. Why not move into our dream home, have fun?"

Kurt stared at his wine. "This *was* our dream home," he said. "I made it our dream home."

"Okay, dear. Remind me of that the next time you complain about the manure across the street, would you?"

He tossed the magazine aside to set his wineglass down in its proper place.

End of conversation.

Kurt stacked up the holiday cards and stood to carry his plate to the sink. The double-wide stainless-steel sink he'd installed as a surprise for his wife's birthday a few years ago. She had found it so charming, watching the CEO of a successful company caulk a brand-new sink, putting the finishing touches on another project with the pride of an old handyman. Her high-powered handyman. Kurt knew she never understood why he could sell a business he'd built from the ground up with sweat equity, but he couldn't sell this house he'd built with sweat and love. She didn't know every corner of the kitchen, every molding on the staircase like he did. He picked up the magazine from the table and tipped it into the custom recycling bin he'd built for her ten years ago, precisely the way she had envisioned it.

Kurt escaped to his usual place at the top of the staircase, looked out into the darkness toward the garden. *Move*, he thought. *Why should I move? They should move. All those trees should move. The whole garden should move.*

He glanced down the stairs to make sure his wife didn't see him fuming. It only reinforced her argument that moving was a splendid idea. She didn't know he'd been plotting away at the window, his plan to make everything better—the view, the ambiance, everything. But mostly the view.

Forty years ago that view lay untarnished, pristine. Ten years on, the city came along and broke ground on the community garden. At first it didn't bother him, but over the years, as he gradually ascertained what went on over there, what type of people worked over there, it became a reminder of everything wrong with the world. Some neighbors disagreed with him. When they asked if his view was actually blocked by any of the garden plots, he ignored them, pointed instead to the trees. Those trees were growing, had grown, to the point that they blocked the lower quadrant of his view. And they would only get taller. Something had to be done.

He had tried on several occasions to rid the neighborhood of the garden entirely. Complaints to the city had yet to accomplish anything to his satisfaction. But he wasn't finished. Kurt's house was there first. Therefore, it would remain. No room for both this house and that garden. He knew people, people above those people to whom he had lodged complaints before. He took his phone out of his pocket to dial.

"Mr. Mayor. Kurt Arnold here. How's that bottle of Glenfiddich 40? Empty? Well, I'll bring you another . . ."

One cool Saturday morning in mid-December, Lizzie drove through the gates of the garden with her harvest basket in tow. She had looked forward to this day for weeks. December gardening is impossible in many parts of the country, but in Southern California the garden's activities didn't stop. Lizzie always felt giddy about harvesting her early broccoli in December, and today she would do exactly that.

Dinner would be spectacular. The simplest recipe, showcasing the vegetable's freshness: steamed for no more than five minutes, with chopped garlic, a dash of chili pepper flakes, a drizzle of olive oil, and salt; served as a side with two eggs over easy. She'd dip the broccoli in the savory yolks.

Maybe I'll have it for lunch instead. Why wait?

There is nothing more satisfying than taking homegrown ingredients into the kitchen to make a meal. *This is the stuff of life*, she thought. In perfect alignment with the simple lifestyle she'd dreamt of in college: to make bread and lie in a hammock all day. Harvesting made her want to cook food, to rectify her bachelor tendencies and sit for a long, drawn-out meal. It made her want to abandon her full-time job to immerse herself in gardening every day, instead of a few hours a week after work or on weekends. Everything felt vibrant and alive while harvesting fresh produce.

She walked down the hill toward her plot. On the way, she unsheathed her Felco pruning shears from her garden bag to inspect them for dirt or rust. She wiped both sides of the blades on her jeans, secured the safety lock with her thumb, then slid the shears into her back pocket. They shifted right into place; the blades nestled into the hole at the bottom of her pocket. Lizzie had been meaning to sew that hole closed, but why bother? Some people invested in a leather holster with a belt clip, but the hole in her jeans served the same purpose and didn't cost a thing.

She rounded the corner of her row and looked out over the

Pacific. The crisp air lent itself to the scene—blue skies and a calm ocean.

"We're so spoiled." She traced the blue-green horizon with her eyes. *Mid-December and we're growing food outdoors.*

She stepped over the retaining wall into her plot. When her foot touched down, her eyes focused on the broccoli.

Something was very wrong.

"No!"

Lizzie dropped her garden bag and lunged toward the raised bed in the back corner. She fell to her knees and grasped the edge of worn wood. Then she saw the destruction.

Two broccoli plants were tilted sideways. Others looked somehow shorter than the day before. Yesterday they had stood tall. Long stems and vibrant leaves had reached out to touch their neighbors. Today green leaves had turned ashen, the stems sunk into the ground. She finally comprehended what she was looking at: a hole where the broccoli once grew. Most of the plant disappeared underground, tips of the leaves peeking out of the soil. She reached in to pull the leaves out of the hole. The plant was severed at the roots, chewed halfway up the stem. Only the wilted leaves remained—even the head that she was to harvest that day was eaten away.

Gophers.

"You fargin' iceholes." She'd been using the phrase as a fill-in for cursing for a long time, ever since she'd seen *Johnny Dangerously* years ago. But the expression fell short in the moment, so she threw the wilted leaves on the ground and blurted out the real deal.

All her hard work—months of care—nurturing crops only to have them stolen or destroyed overnight. Violated. There would be no steamed broccoli with eggs, no risotto with tender broccoli greens. She had laughed aloud in the grocery store when she walked past the vegetable aisle. She'd boasted to friends that one day she would feed herself solely from this garden. But the truth embarrassed her: with survival skills like this she'd starve. The gophers, meanwhile, ate well at her expense. Disappointment buried her pride, bruised any remnant of accomplishment. All she had left was a piercing sense of loss.

Calm down. It's just broccoli.

No, it was *not* just broccoli. Lizzie's frustration built to a peak, laser focused on everything resembling failure in her life: Dylan, her attempts at self-reliance, the lack of acknowledgment at work. Nothing went according to plan.

Tears welled up in her eyes. Free-flowing, pity-party tears. The gophers that had vandalized her broccoli unknowingly unearthed every letdown of the past year.

She found herself pacing through her plot. She stepped on a soft spot in the corner, where her foot sank six inches. Of course—along retaining walls was the bastards' favorite place to burrow. This wasn't the first time. In fact, it happened most years. But tricked by oh-so-typical gardener's amnesia, she and her neighbors ventured to plant season after season, forgetting the tragedies of the past. And still it crushed her every time. She stomped at the soft patch until her foot fell all the way through. She stood there, eyes wet and shin-deep in failure.

Lizzie batted at the nasturtium patch, which was much closer to eye level with one foot in the hole. An oversized grasshopper sprang toward her and she leaned back to dodge it.

"Holy crap, you're huge." Lizzie pulled her foot out of the hole, grabbed the garden hose, and twisted the dial on the nozzle to "jet," or as she called it, "kill." She blasted the grasshopper into the soil and looked the other way. Most of the time they escaped, but it was important to at least try to take them out. Gophers, on the other hand, required the Mafia.

Vista Mar Gardens had a crack team of volunteer gopher hunters. When trouble arose, one need only leave a note in a mailbox and the matter would be handled. Leave a stick marking the affected area, and when you returned, you would find a trap set in the very spot. A few days later, the trap would be gone, and so would your troubles. One trapper, who called himself the Cleaner (an obvious homage to *Pulp Fiction*), tried to *sell* his services to the garden members. $15 PER GOPHER, his posted sign read. 10 FOR $150. Lizzie had laughed at his idea of a deal. When the board found out he took money for his volunteer services, they put a stop to it and searched for a new gopher hunter. Luckily, there were plenty of vigilantes among the membership. Each section of the garden gained its very own trapper. The hope of growing food without interference returned.

All's fair in love and war. Lizzie drove her hand trowel into the corner of her plot, revealing a tunnel that led under one of her raised beds. She felt guilty, making someone else do the dirty work. But in this battle of woman versus nature, after the enemy pillaged her land of its precious children, she easily justified extreme measures.

She stood up to look for a stick to mark the hole when she heard shuffling behind her.

"Hey, Lizzie."

She recognized Jared's voice and looked over to find him standing on the pathway in front of her mailbox, shovel in hand. He wore khaki shorts with a light blue T-shirt that said, BE THE CHANGE . . . —GANDHI. Lizzie didn't know shorts and a T-shirt could look that good on anybody. The sweat above his temples caught the sunlight.

He's sweating in December?

She swallowed her frustration about the gophers and said hello, stepped over a mound toward the front of her plot. "You've been digging trenches?"

"Ned asked me to level the foundation for a new shed. You know about the new tractor? It's going to live in this shed I'm building." He gripped the D-handled shovel with both hands and leaned his weight forward against it.

Lizzie couldn't help but notice Jared's triceps. "Is he flexing?"

"Say again?"

Oh my God. Did I say that out loud?

Lizzie scrambled to recover. "Um, Ned . . . Is Ned, you know, flexing his authority over there? Making you guys work too hard?"

Jared shifted the shovel to one side and rested his other hand on his hip. Morning sunlight bounced off his bicep, at the curve where the sleeve met the arm. Despite her attempt to stay focused, Lizzie imagined her fingers tracing that bicep. This was not fair; no one should be that distracting. He was way too attractive.

Something about this guy is kryptonite. Is he like Dylan? No, he's fit, he's nice, he's . . .

Jared interrupted her thoughts. "Oh. No, he's just excited to have an able-bodied guy with construction skills on hand. I enjoy doing this. It keeps me busy on weekends."

Her heart slowed back to normal. *Skilled. He's also skilled.*

Jared explained Ned's plan for the new tractor shed, its location, how they'd use the tractor. Lizzie knew all this from the last board meeting, but Jared shared the details with bubbling enthusiasm, so she didn't let on.

Jared asked, "How are things going?" He lifted his chin toward her raised beds.

She pointed to the mounds and the cavernous spaces where her brassicas once stood. "Well, I got pillaged by gophers this morning." She flipped a hand toward the leaves scattered on the ground. "That's what's left of my broccoli. I guess I'll leave a note for the trapper."

"I'll do it for you."

"Oh, that's okay, I'm heading over to the main shed soon, so I'll leave him a note when I go."

Jared smiled. "No, I mean I can set a trap for you."

Lizzie took a second to understand. "You're in the gopher Mafia? When did this happen?"

"I've been catching them in my own plot for a few weeks.

Figured I ought to earn some community hours by decreasing the population *around* my plot, too." He put on a thick New York accent: "It's a service to Section Four, not only myself."

"Spoken like a true mafioso."

"So if you want, I'll go get my trap, and we'll hope for the best."

"Absolutely."

Jared hoisted his shovel over his shoulder and strode down the hill toward his plot. Lizzie's eyes followed him as he walked away. His shorts fit like a dream.

"Keeps you busy on weekends, huh?" Lizzie blurted out.

Jared turned around. "What?"

"You're joking, right? A guy like you with no one to do on the weekends."

His eyes grew wide. Jared laughed. "'No one' to do?"

Lizzie blanched, mortified.

"'Nothing'! I said 'nothing to do.'" *Oh God.*

"Sure you did." He saluted with a smile, then turned and left Lizzie cringing in the pathway.

CHAPTER 6

The Membership

Late December

December in the garden elicited a flurry of activity, including the final workday of the year at Vista Mar. Members, obligated to fulfill the last of their community hours, arrived early and ready to toil. They lined up and waited for Ned to dole out tasks: weed the north path, turn the third compost pile, move mulch piles from here to there, and any other tasks requiring many hands.

With the end of the year approaching, Ned's mailbox had filled with notes on scrap paper or tattered seed packets.

Dear Ned,

I need to get a few more hours this month. Do you have any work in Section 3 for me?

Thanks,
[Name of desperate gardener]

[Every possible way to contact them imaginable]

Ned always kept a laundry list of tasks for gardeners, so this job was easy.

After a long morning of hard labor, members gathered under the giant magnolia tree in the meeting area for the regular meeting. This quarterly event gave members a chance to learn about recent board decisions, get updates on unfinished business, and hear announcements for upcoming events. Flyers circulated, announcing early spring workshops. But before the meeting, a feast.

Each family brought a dish to share, placing it on the long wooden counter custom-built for these potlucks. People always brought an assortment of harvest treats to choose from: baked butternut squash, crisp arugula salads, and marinated beets. Sweet dishes rounded out the meal: pumpkin pies and home-raised honey in glass jars with toast points on the side. One gardener made sugar-free cookies with stevia she grew.

Lizzie scanned the crowd for gardeners from her section and spotted Jared chatting with Ned over a cup of coffee. Ned seemed as enamored with him as any woman would have been. *Must be Jared's skill set that charmed him.*

Lizzie strode up to the two men. "Is this your new best friend, Ned?"

Ned laughed and squeezed Lizzie's arm. "You bet. With this guy around, before too long, we'll get everything on my list done."

"He took care of my gopher problem, too." She turned to Jared. "My veggies thank you."

"Just your veggies?" Jared smiled.

"I . . . Well, I mean . . ." Her stomach did a flip-flop.

Ned smiled, squeezed her arm again. "Ah, now you owe him."

"I'll figure out how to extract payment later," Jared said.

Lizzie struggled not to react. *He's flirting, isn't he?* She needed a quick comeback. "That's not creepy at all, Jared."

Ned laughed at them both. "Be careful of this one, Lizzie. He's got his eye on you."

So embarrassing. She felt herself start to sweat and couldn't escape fast enough. Usually, split-second decisions would trigger a flood of film scenes in her brain. At least one of them would give her the actionable solution she needed for the situation at hand. This time, nothing. A blank screen. Ned had turned to leave, so she latched onto his arm, pretending to ask him a question as they walked away from Jared. She led Ned toward the buffet, where they each grabbed a plate.

Next to a spool-table, Ralph was stretched out on a plastic chair with a paper plate at his elbow. The bleached white paperboard showed greasy puddles beneath a crumpled, fluttering napkin, the last traces of what had been a pile of buffet offerings. He read from a thin, colorful book while resting his hands on his belly.

Lizzie paused in front of him with her plate. "Comic book?" she asked.

Without looking up, he replied, "It's a graphic novel, thank you."

"Right. Sorry. What's it about?"

His eyes darted up to her face. Color saturated his cheeks, and he rolled up the book, tucked it into his back pocket. "Oh, it's not very interesting."

She stood looking at the top of Ralph's head for a second, realizing that he wasn't going to say anything else. It made her even more curious about the graphic novel. Maybe it had an embarrassing plotline he didn't want to share? Or was he still upset about the seed catalogs? One of her new gardeners in a Vista Mar Gardens sweatshirt waved her over at that precise moment, saving her from a more awkward departure. She slipped into a conversation as she stepped away from Ralph.

The woman patted the bench and scooted over to make room. "You grew up in Los Angeles, right, Lizzie?"

"Born and raised." She squeezed into the space that was offered to her.

"So you're used to this gardening in winter business."

Lizzie grinned. "It's wonderful, isn't it?"

The woman's wife leaned forward and adjusted her baseball cap. "I'm still figuring it out. Our old garden in Michigan must be under four feet of snow right now."

"Why? What's going on over in your plot?" Lizzie asked.

The wife said, "Well, for one thing, all the bulbs I planted in November are already up. What did I do wrong?"

Another member on a nearby bench had been listening to the three of them talk. "Nothin'," he chimed in as he twisted around. "It's confusing, right? I'm from New York, so I feel your pain." He shifted on the bench to face them, stretching out his barrel chest. "It took a couple years to get used to it. My plot's full of flowers over the holidays. I get paperwhite narcissus in October, hyacinth in November. By January, my dahlias are going bananas."

"Right," Lizzie said, "and when those start to wither, the gladioli pop up. By the time the rest of the country gets close to last frost, the irises are blooming here—plus lilies in time for Easter."

"That's nuts!" The woman from Michigan shook her head. "Back East, we were lucky if we had crocus popping through the snow by then."

Lizzie laughed. "You won't find this in any gardening book. We Angelenos learn by trial and error."

The wife looked perplexed. "No kidding. None of this makes sense."

The New Yorker leaned in and asked, "Is this your first year here?"

The couple spoke in unison between bites of food. "We got our plot in June."

"And you have all your brassicas in now, right?" Lizzie asked.

"Well, just kale and chard," the wife said. "But we weren't

sure about the timing for anything else. It sounds like we should've planted all the cool-season crops already."

"Exactly. Then in March and April, the summer crops go in the ground."

"That's so backward." The woman in the sweatshirt laughed. "Thanks, we'll give that a try in spring."

"You're very welcome."

Lizzie excused herself and went back to the buffet for seconds, chatting with other Vista Marians in the meeting area over their bountifully portioned plates. She overheard nearby members already talking about tomatoes, and which varieties they would soon start from seed. True enthusiasts wait all year for the first sign of warmth to plant tomatoes, and that hope will lead the gardener by the nose through all the hard work that comes before it.

She found herself scanning the tables for Jared. When she located him, he caught her glance and smiled her way. She pretended to wave to someone behind him to his left when she couldn't hold his gaze.

"Hey, Terry, how's it going?" she yelled from across the tables. Jared turned to look behind him; she hoped he wouldn't notice that no one had waved back.

Lizzie watched Mary as she rounded up stragglers and gathered steam to start the meeting. Most of the time, regular meetings remained uneventful, but occasionally they were as charged with controversy as board meetings. The last meeting of the year, however, offered pure enjoyment. Everyone exchanged hopeful sentiments of new seasons to come. One gardener's tale of a pathetic squash harvest was seconded by another's story of cucumbers that never set fruit. They both resolved to hand-pollinate and be more diligent about treating powdery mildew next year. Members traded recipes for this season's harvest of kale and next year's bumper crop of zucchini. Some gardeners brought seeds saved from their plots as gifts for neighbors.

As Lizzie spotted several people swapping seed packets, Ananda pranced up and handed her a tiny manila envelope, labeled "Early Girl Tomato" in colored marker. *How sweet.*

"Thank you, Ananda, that's really thoughtful." But then she realized the problem. "Did you save these yourself?"

"Yeah, it's my first time," she said. She looked so proud. Ananda had been elected to the board after only a year at the garden. What she lacked in knowledge, she made up for in enthusiasm.

Lizzie debated whether to seize a teachable moment about the seeds or not. *Carpe diem*, she decided.

"Can I give you a little advice about these?" she asked Ananda.

"Sure. What's up?"

"This Early Girl is a hybrid tomato. Are you familiar with hybrids?"

"I guess . . ."

"Okay, quick before the meeting starts." She spotted Mary and Ned in conversation, so she had a few minutes. She and Ananda sat at a table, and Lizzie continued.

"If a plant is an heirloom—seed that's handed down from generation to generation—or an open-pollinated variety—one that's bred and pollinated via the wind, birds, bees, et cetera—the seed from fruits of that plant will grow up to be the same as its parent: true to type." She paused and Ananda nodded.

"Unfortunately, hybrid seeds don't work that way. They're bred by crossing two parents that are genetically different but are of the same species—for example, crossing a pumpkin and a zucchini, which are both *Cucurbita pepo*, to get an oblong pumpkin. It's called an F1 hybrid. Saving seeds from the oblong pumpkin doesn't mean you'll get another oblong pumpkin. It will revert to the traits of one of its parents, or produce something in between. It's a wild card, unreliable. We're not supposed to save seeds from them."

"Aw, man!" Ananda was dejected.

"And—please don't hate me for saying this; I'm just the messenger—these days, more and more hybrid seeds are patented, so it might even be illegal to save seeds from that Early Girl."

"Seriously?"

"Seriously."

"Are we ready, folks?" Mary stepped up to the mic. "Our last meeting of the year."

Lizzie whispered to Ananda, "We can talk about this more later if you want."

Ananda nodded and shifted her gaze to the podium.

The jovial holiday spirit continued throughout the meeting. Mary upheld her tradition of giving loaves of pumpkin bread decorated with festive ribbon to each board member as a thank-you for a year of volunteer service. She presented each section rep with a tasty mini-loaf and asked for a round of applause at the end. She always gave Ned his last, an oversized loaf, which never failed to elicit peals of laughter from the crowd. Everyone knew Ned was the linchpin holding the garden together; he deserved every bit of recognition that came with that giant loaf.

"Aw, you shouldn't have." Ned waved a dismissive hand but had torn open the plastic wrap before he even got back to his seat.

Mary's final announcement of the year always focused on renewal notices.

"Please update your contact information with your section rep and pay your membership fees on time. The waiting list is long, so if you don't send in your dues, we'll reassign your plot." Despite her affectionate gesture of pumpkin bread, when Mary dispensed stern warnings, everyone took her at her word. "You know what I mean: 'We're not just lucky to have a plot here . . .'"

Everyone joined in unison: "We're spoiled."

"Meeting adjourned," Mary said.

Bernice's hand flew up. "You forgot to ask for public comment."

The crowd stopped halfway out of their seats and turned to look at Bernice.

"I have an announcement," Bernice said. She stood up with a stack of flyers in hand and began passing them out to the membership. "I will be running for garden president in the new year. I imagine many of you agree that we're desperate for a new approach here at Vista Mar. I should be happy to have your vote in the coming election."

Lizzie shifted her gaze to Mary, who stood silent, wide-eyed. Should she have told Mary about the flyers earlier? She had the chance to warn her weeks ago, but didn't want to get involved at the time. Mary's reaction triggered a sense of guilt as Lizzie recalled her decision to stay aloof.

Mary gathered herself enough to ask, "Anything else, Bernice?"

"No, that should be sufficient."

"Meeting adjourned," Mary said, on autopilot.

Gardeners murmured among themselves as they collected chairs to stack in the back of the meeting area. Members claimed their empty dishes, and the crowd dispersed back to their plots. The year had come to a close with an uncertain future, but gardening carried on.

Lizzie retrieved her platter from the nearly empty potluck table and sat on a damp bench to polish off the crumbs from her coffee cake after the crowd thinned out. She pressed her finger into the plate, sweeping up the remnants of the crumble on top—the best part of the dessert—and closed her eyes to savor the taste of sugar, butter, and spice melting on her tongue.

Bernice as president? It rubbed her the wrong way. She should've warned Mary last month.

"It's a good day for that," a man's voice said. Lizzie jumped in her skin.

She looked up to see Jared. "God, you scared me."

"Sorry. Next time I'll whistle or jingle my keys when I approach, okay?"

"That would help," she said.

"You left in a hurry earlier."

Lizzie couldn't look him in the eye, so she casually observed his legs. "Oh, you know, private audience with the garden master. How's your garden?"

Jared always wore shorts, no matter how chilly the weather. Though this was a mild winter, the wind still whipped through, blustery and cold.

"It's going well. I've been eating salads from my lettuce patch since early November."

Lizzie nodded, noticing his calves. She hadn't realized how well-defined they were. She wondered whether he jogged or played soccer. Or maybe cricket? The hair on her neck stood up.

"I'm going to plant more to carry me through spring." He smiled, proud of himself.

"I'd say you're having a good first year," Lizzie said. "So this gardening thing is working out for you?"

"Yeah. I'm surprised, actually." He shifted his weight. "I didn't expect to get so into it. I figured I'd fail miserably, get bored, and leave, like my friends all said. But I'm really enjoying this."

Lizzie nodded. "It's addictive, isn't it?"

The word triggered something, and his eyes lit up. "Oh my God, it is."

He sat next to Lizzie and launched into his discovery of kohlrabi, his newfound passion for wild arugula, and his obsession with seed catalogs. The floodgates opened, and he unloaded everything in detail.

"And there's Baker Creek Heirloom Seed Company. I went nuts, bought all these crazy seeds—most I have no idea how to grow. I overbought, so if you want some . . ."

Her pulse quickened at the mention of Baker Creek. Lizzie easily matched his enthusiasm. They talked, garden-nerd style, for half an hour, sharing tricks about pest control, new seed exchanges, and tomato-growing techniques.

"How do you know all this stuff?" he asked. His golden eyes caught her attention.

"Failure, mostly." Lizzie laughed. "But, you know, you learn as you go."

Jared paused as though he had another question brewing.

"So what's the big deal about fava beans?" He shrugged. "I see them in so many plots."

Lizzie grinned. "Oh, that's a secret."

It took a second for Jared to realize she was joking, then he laughed and nudged her arm. "Aw, come on."

At his touch, Lizzie instantly felt warmth flood her body. She almost forgot what they were talking about, she was so distracted by his smile. There must have been an awkward silence, but for who knows how long.

"So are you . . . going to tell me?"

"Oh." She woke from her daze. "Nitrogen."

"Huh?"

She pointed to a nearby plot, every square inch of it a green sea of tall stalks topped with white flowers tinged with black.

"Some gardeners grow them as a cover crop," she explained. She told him cover crops were essential at Vista Mar Gardens since the soil was as sandy as the beach and lost nutrients as quickly as any gardener added them, even after amending with tons of compost.

"Fava bean leaves pull atmospheric nitrogen into the plant, which 'fixes' into the roots in the form of small pink nodules. After about a third of the flowers open on the plant, before it sets fruit, you cut the stalks—the biomass—down, chop them up, and either turn them under—plow into the soil—or put the green biomass in the compost bin." She went on to explain how, either way, the plants break down and add organic matter to improve soil texture, and the roots release their captured nitrogen for the next crop of plants to absorb.

"I grow favas that way, but other gardeners let theirs grow to maturity and harvest the beans. At that stage, the plant still produces biomass for the compost bin, but the nitrogen has been reabsorbed to produce a crop of beans. Either way, you get something out of it."

Jared was fascinated. "I figured I'd try growing a few crops from seed next spring instead of buying plants from the nursery. Am I crazy?"

"No, you're ready." She noticed he sat up taller when she said that. "Next month is the perfect time to start seeds. You can direct-seed another round of cool-weather crops in early February, or plant warm- and hot-season crops in March or April. Either way, you can start seeds in trays to transplant out six to eight weeks later. Count backward from when you plan to plant out."

"I'm up for the challenge, but I'll probably text you for emotional support if something goes wrong."

"Email," Lizzie reminded him.

"Right, email."

"Well, text if you're in a panic."

They laughed. Lizzie flashed back to his first day when she had assigned him a plot. He'd come a long way. Maybe he wasn't so commitment-phobic after all.

"It's funny," she said, smiling. "I've got two constants in my life: movies and gardening. They're both great addictions to have, but with gardening you get to eat the results."

"True." He paused. "Your friend Ralph, he's into movies, too, right?"

"Video games and comic b—sorry, graphic novels mostly, but yeah."

He leaned in toward Lizzie with a warm smile. "I think he's got a crush on you."

Lizzie gave Jared an incredulous look. "Naw, he's just looking for connection."

Jared shifted on the edge of the bench. A split second of silence followed when Lizzie wondered whether to change the subject. He took a slow, deep breath. "Hey, we should do something *garden-y* together some time."

Is he asking me out? She felt a rush of heat to her neck and hoped he didn't notice.

"Yeah. That sounds good." *Good*, she scolded herself. *All you can say is* good?

"There's this restaurant on Abbot Kinney that's more of a

garden or a nursery than a place to eat, but they serve local-grown produce, artisan breads, cheeses. It's nice, but casual. Dolly's. Have you ever eaten there?"

Lizzie's heart raced. *He asked you to a restaurant. Dinner—or lunch, don't get ahead of yourself—with a man. An attractive man. It's happening, right now.*

"I've driven by it, but I've never been there. I'm dying to go, actually."

"Great. Well, I'll give you a call and we'll find a time, okay?" Jared stood up and brushed off his backside.

"Sounds good." There's that *good* again. She tried not to appear desperate.

Jared touched her on the shoulder as he said goodbye and left her sitting on the bench wondering what had just happened. Lizzie felt the phantom warmth of Jared's hand ripple down her spine. She'd been certain she was alone in her attraction to him, but his invitation seemed proof of something mutual.

Wait a minute. Don't get carried away.

Some guys are embarrassed to talk about gardening with other guys, so he might need a girl friend, a friend who is a girl, to talk shop with. *Don't get excited until you have the facts. Stay distant until proven otherwise.*

Lizzie wrangled herself into that frame of mind, but her body still tingled with the prospect of going to a restaurant, date or not, with Jared. She picked up her empty platter, swept clean of coffee cake crumbs, and floated up the hill toward her car.

CHAPTER 7
Bed Prep and Roses

January

Hey, the line's back there." Ralph pushed his wheelbarrow into Jared's path toward the compost bin.

"Oh." Jared stopped short, looking past Ralph at the row of eager gardeners in line with wheelbarrows in tow. "Sorry, didn't realize compost drew a crowd in January."

"Compost always popular," Leo, the compost king, said as he maneuvered between the two men on his way down the hill.

"Some of us waited all morning. Early bird gets the compost," Ralph said. Leo laughed and gave Ralph a thumbs-up.

"Shoot, I'm meeting someone soon. I can't stay long. Mind if I jump in here with you?"

"You mean cut the line?" Ralph tilted his head back to meet Jared's eyes.

"That's okay. I'll come back later."

"It'll be gone by then," Ralph called after Jared. Either Jared didn't hear him, or he didn't care.

Ralph unzipped his jacket to air out his nerves. The morning had started out cold, but as the sun rose the weather began to resemble spring more than January. The sky was clear, the air crisp, the sun shone warm upon the soil. A prodigious day for bed prep.

Leo opened a bin of cured compost, and Ralph and other members descended upon it with the fervor of shoppers at a Black Friday sale. They eagerly transported each wheelbarrow of black gold to their plots. Leo had designed the garden's compost bins to take composting to new heights. The process was an art form.

"How did you learn all this, Leo?" Ralph asked as he set his wheelbarrow down next to Leo to catch his breath.

"After *taishoku*"—he snapped his fingers, looking for the right word—"retirement, I study agriculture for two years at UC Santa Cruz. Retirement make me dead inside, but compost is life. I learn best way to make perfect compost."

"You must be doing something right. My roses love this stuff." Ralph nodded toward the contents of his wheelbarrow.

"Not me. We." He pointed to Ralph, then back to himself.

"We shred the garden waste . . ." Leo pointed to the tall piles of last season's crops in the corner of the composting area.

"Smaller is better, you always say," Ralph added.

"Yes, small, and put brown and green in layers. *Tanso* and *chisso*—carbon and nitrogen. And you . . ." Leo grabbed Ralph across the middle and gave him a jiggle.

Ralph looked down at Leo's hands. "And I irrigate the pile, because shoveling is hard." If it had been anyone else, he would've been embarrassed, but Leo's tummy pats were affectionate and grandfatherly.

"Come with me." Leo gestured for Ralph to leave his wheelbarrow. Ralph followed and watched Leo check a "cooking" compost pile for moisture; moisture helped create the perfect environment for beneficial bacteria and other microorganisms to do their work.

He pointed to a few dry patches. "More water," he said.

Ralph took note and promised to hose them down later.

Leo smiled, reached out, and flicked a red flag jutting from the side of the compost pile. "Go ahead, I dare you reach inside."

"Hell no, I'm not sticking my hand in there. It's a hundred and sixty degrees!" Ralph laughed and folded his arms away safely. He'd witnessed Leo pull this trick before on at least one rookie composter. Leo grinned, plunged his hand into the steaming pile, and pulled out an egg. He cracked it on Ralph's shoulder, and peeled away the shell. It was soft-boiled.

"The power of compost." Leo held up the egg like a prize. "Breakfast." He turned to walk up the hill to the office.

"That's gross, you know," Ralph called after him. "It's manure. You're going to wash that, right?" He was pretty sure he heard Leo laughing in the distance.

Lizzie relished preparing her soil for the coming season. Well, most of the process, anyway. What came before soil prep wasn't her favorite thing to do. Early morning, she began cutting down the entire bed of cover crops by hand with pruning shears. If ever there were a time for profanity, this was it. The constant repetitive motion, manually cutting swaths of biomass, caused hand cramps and abrasions that spawned Lizzie's most flowery speech. She remembered what Jared had told her about swearing—a sign of intelligence.

I must be a genius. But then again, if I were—and if I weren't so irrationally afraid of slicing through my leg with a sickle—I would've bought one by now.

After several blisters and excessive cursing, she completed the task. She added the chopped greens to her compost bin (a secret stash apart from the main composting operation—most of the time, she was too exhausted to haul it over there) but left the roots to break down in each bed. She layered her beds with a decomposed mixture of horse manure and shredded straw. Next, Lizzie grabbed her hose nozzle from the mailbox, buried under several of Bernice's election campaign flyers. She watered the bed to stimulate further decomposition. When she finished, she assessed her work. Perfect, just perfect.

A gardener walking down the north path drew her eye away from her raised bed. No, wait, not a gardener. He looked familiar, or at least his golf cap did. Before she could nail it down, she spotted him plucking calendula flowers by the handful from a plot along the path.

"Excuse me?!" she shouted toward the man. He rotated away from view and quickened his pace up the hill. She saw him try to stuff a big wad of flowers into his raincoat pocket.

"Excuse me!" Lizzie set off after him. "Who's your section rep, sir?"

He tossed the evidence into a plot as he passed and kept moving away from Lizzie.

"Are you Kurt? Kurt Arnold? Sir!" She'd never seen Kurt but had heard him described as tall and thin, like this guy.

He ignored her and disappeared over the crest of the hill at a brisk pace, far more agile than she expected from someone his apparent age.

Lizzie tailed him and reached the crest in time to observe the mystery man's exit through the back gate. He stepped off to cross the street, but turned, noticed Lizzie approaching from across the field, and proceeded down the sidewalk along the fence instead.

"Sir, you're trespassing," she shouted through the fence, breathless from trying to catch up to him. He kept walking.

"*No hablo inglays*," he said, with no trace of a foreign accent.

"Nice try. You're trespassing and if I catch you here again, I'm calling the police."

He stopped walking and turned to face Lizzie through the

chain link. "First of all, it's not trespassing if you have a key. Second, you can't trespass on public land."

"This land is owned by Vista Mar Gardens, and unless you're a member, you're not allowed in here."

"Is that so?" He tilted his head to one side.

"Plus, I've witnessed you stealing," she added.

"Owned by the garden . . . How could this half-baked organization afford land in Los Angeles?" He looked past Lizzie, pensive, surveying the property from ground level.

"I don't know and I don't care, but it's ours. And you're officially banned from setting foot on this land."

He stood silent, immersed in thought.

"Interesting," he muttered, continued on his way. Whoever he was, and Lizzie had a good idea, he didn't appear at all bothered by her threat to call the police, or the fact that she had witnessed him stealing. He sauntered off like he'd been struck with a brilliant idea.

While walking back toward Section Four, Lizzie noticed Sharalyn's head pop up from her plot at the top of the hill, shears in hand. "What was that?"

"You didn't see him?" Lizzie stopped at Sharalyn's garden. Despite the cool air, Lizzie felt sweat roll down her forehead.

"See what?"

"I think it was Kurt Arnold." She took off her hat, wiped her sleeve across her brow, smoothed her hair back.

"Aw, *hell* no!" Sharalyn threw a handful of thorny rose canes into a pile of other garden debris. "Did you catch him?"

"I threatened him, but he didn't care."

"See? A real swamp rat."

Lizzie returned to her plot, sat down at the entrance, and rested her feet on the brick pavers of the step below. She lay back onto the thick layer of pine needles that she'd spread in the wide pathways between her raised beds the day before. Fragrant pillows of pine mulch cradled her head. *This is the life. It smells of Christmas all year long.* Warm sunlight peeked over the tops of the trees, which meant others would arrive at the garden soon. *Time to go.*

"'So much time and so little to do. Wait a minute. Strike that. Reverse it. Thank you,'" she said as she sat up, not bothering to check for anyone within earshot. Had she noticed the gardener walking past her plot when she spoke, she wouldn't have said it out loud.

The gardener turned around and smiled. "*Willy Wonka.* I loved that movie as a kid."

Her embarrassment did not dim the satisfaction she felt after mulching her plot, which gave her a much-needed sense of order. It countered all the chaos at home. Bills to pay, not enough money, and no raise with her recent promotion at work, though she had asked her boss well before budgeting deadlines.

She'd made it through the holidays, but then all the bills for the gifts on credit came knocking at her door: time to pay up. The lack of a Christmas bonus or even so much as a holiday card from her employer left her craving appreciation as another year came to a close. She had taken full advantage of her time off from work—not quite a record-breaking movie binge this year, but she had still watched some good flicks—and enjoyed a satisfying dose of holiday cheer visiting her parents at their condo on Christmas Day.

New Year's celebrations had lacked something, though she couldn't put her finger on it. Lizzie stared up at the clouds, searching for answers. The start of a new year came with high hopes and promises of greatness, but fell flat on January 2. Was it the age-old lack-of-a-boyfriend story? She shook her head. *No, that's not it.*

She had connected with Jared during the holidays; they had even talked a couple times.

"You in town for New Year's?" he had asked over the phone.

"Yeah, I don't have any plans, though," Lizzie replied. "Probably lying low, watching a movie." She debated whether to ask him to join her, but held off. There was an awkward pause on the other end of the call.

"Sounds mellow."

"I'm not much of a party girl, especially New Year's Eve."

"I get that," he said.

Lizzie listened for a spark of interest. Jared wasn't inviting himself over, nor was he inviting her out on their promised date.

"Hey, well, at some point, we need to schedule that garden-y dinner, okay?" he said.

While it wasn't an entirely lackluster response, it wasn't the definitive enthusiasm she'd hoped for. Maybe the excitement was wearing off. Maybe she'd read too much into the original invitation. If he couldn't follow through—well, she didn't need anybody, anyway.

Here, today, before the gardeners arrived, she felt free and limitless. Everything flowed with ease. If right now a gardener demanded something from her, she could help without feeling overburdened. An hour ago, that had not been the case. But with new mulch in the pathways, beds prepped, and her garden in order, all was right in the world. Stretching out her arms, Lizzie made an angel in the pine needle pathway. She rested her hat over her eyes and envisioned herself from overhead, admiring the shape of her mulch angel.

Now for the fun part.

She sat up to reach for a glass jar of seeds nestled in the rosemary bush at the edge of her plot. That morning, she'd stashed the jar in the shrub to keep the seeds out of the sun. She extracted it and smiled at its contents: forty or so seed packets crammed into a large, wide-mouth, lock-lid canning jar. Precious cargo.

Cool, dark, and dry, little ones. Stay cool, dark, and dry.

Light, heat, and moisture—the three factors that make a seed grow into glorious vegetation—are the same three that destroy seed viability during storage. Lizzie kept her seed jar in the refrigerator with desiccant packets in the bottom. When she brought it to the garden, she stored the jar in the shade, either wrapped in fabric or wedged into nearby shrubbery for dry cover. She took pride in her collection, and in the fact that her attention to proper storage kept her seeds alive for years.

Lizzie unlocked the lid to select tomato, pepper, spinach, and an assortment of lettuce seed packets to sow in trays. She set them on a makeshift potting table, rescued from an alley in

Venice a few years ago. Below the table were two black plastic seeding trays, which she dusted off and set next to the seed packets.

She filled the tray with seed-starting mix and tamped it down. Next, she dropped one spinach seed in the center of each cell, scooped a hand trowel full of planting mix out of the galvanized metal bucket at her feet, and layered soil over the seeds. Then she pressed each cell down gently to compress the soil. Compression is key, she had learned years ago, because the act of compressing the soil in a seed tray creates capillary action to draw water up from the reservoir below to the roots.

Lizzie grinned and laughed at herself. *I'm such a nerd that I know this.*

Before she got distracted to the point of forgetting what was planted where, she slid the plant marker into the soil and slipped her homemade greenhouse dome—half an old tomato cage wrapped with plastic sheeting—over the tray to capture the condensation that would form as the seeds germinated. Then she reached for the next tray and the second packet of seeds, repeating the process until she finished planting each tray with spring and summer varieties. Lizzie lined them up on her potting table and stood back to observe her work, delighted by the prospect of what was to come.

It's a thing of beauty.

She fished her phone out of her garden bag and snapped a picture of the scene. It signified the beginning of the next planting season, where dreams are big and expectations high. She visualized those lettuces, tomatoes, and spinach sprouting, growing tall in her garden. She could almost taste the first tomato off the vine.

Lizzie noticed other gardeners arriving and guessed they were indulging in the same dreams. She imagined their elaborate plans coming to life as they dug new beds or rearranged their gardens for better efficiency. Some gardeners put up new trellises and cleared away old plants. Most pushed grubby wheelbarrows of compost from one end of the property to the other, all in the hope of more productive soil for the coming season.

She spotted Jared in his plot. "Happy New Year," she shouted down the rows.

He turned toward her voice and waved. "*Hau'oli makahiki hou.*"

"What?" She laughed.

Jared lifted his hands toward her. "You too."

He jogged up the hill toward Lizzie, something she didn't expect. Glancing at her seed trays, he said, "Am I behind schedule? I wasn't planning to start seeds for another month."

She waved him off. "I'm early." Wasn't he going to say anything about their date?

He made small talk, but no mention of the promised dinner at Dolly's. Maybe he'd changed his mind. Maybe he'd moved on to something else. Someone else.

"Hey," he said, "I have to go up north for a couple weeks. Could you water my plot while I'm gone?"

Oh, so that's it. It figures.

"I can hook you up with your neighbors. You can arrange

with them. I've got my hands full with section rep duties." She tried not to look annoyed. Well, not too annoyed.

"That'll work," he said. "Hey, I've gotta go. I'll be in touch. Thanks for the contacts."

He trotted off, oblivious to her disappointment. He'd be in touch. What did that mean?

Lizzie turned back to her seed trays. They looked perfect, but even perfection couldn't pierce the haze of disenchantment settling over her. And that damned etching on her neighbor's retaining wall. Why was it still there?

"No better time." Lizzie tucked the seed packets into her garden bag and jogged to the toolshed. She found a mallet and chisel and dashed back to her plot. She stepped over her neighbor's herbs and walked along an undulating path toward the back wall of the plot. She noticed a few painted pebbles strewn along the path, left behind from Dylan. He had painted them to decorate his garden, symbols of their time together, now faded, paint chipped. She kicked mulch over them on her way to the etching.

It doesn't have to look good, just gone.

She stabbed at the carving with the chisel, tried to decide the best way to remove it. The wood was soft from years of age. *This shouldn't be too difficult.*

She angled the chisel and tapped the handle with the mallet. A few slivers of gray wood broke free. Lighter virgin wood revealed itself from beneath. A fresh start. Lizzie hammered away at the etched letters until nothing remained but an oval scar of pink wood.

With the force of a weed pushing through soil, breaking through her fantasy of spring garden prep and this fresh start, Lizzie's less-than-stellar life outside the garden blossomed into focus. It pulled at her, reminded her she had bills to pay and quick meals to eat over her sink. She slung her garden bag over her shoulder and picked up the mallet and chisel to return to the shed on her way out. She looked back at the scar. It was gone, but not really.

Damn you, Dylan.

"You carving a sculpture, sugar?" Sharalyn spied Lizzie through the forest of rosebushes as Lizzie crested the slope.

"Doing some retaining wall repair." She paused and set her garden bag down next to a wild Cécile Brunner climbing rose. The plant had woven itself across an arch at the entrance of Sharalyn's plot, offering petite pink blooms and a delicate scent. Sharalyn watched Lizzie breathe in the heady perfume of a Gold Medal yellow rose close by.

"Well, if you have a pair of pruning shears in that bag, you can help me cut these back."

"As much as I love your garden, I've got to get home." She straightened up. "Don't work too hard."

"This isn't work, sugar. This is love."

Lizzie bent to pick up her bag and, as she stood up, nestled her nose in an apricot-colored Gentle Persuasion blossom.

"Take it," Sharalyn offered.

Lizzie looked up. "Are you sure?"

"They're all coming down, you might as well."

Lizzie unsheathed her shears and snipped the flower.

Sharalyn added, "Looks to me like you could use a little pretty."

Lizzie swung the rose overhead as a wistful goodbye and walked off in the direction of the shed.

Sharalyn was proud of what she considered to be the most productive rose garden anyone ever laid eyes on, even in the off-season. Floribundas, hybrid tea roses, and climbing varieties wove together in a lush landscape of color and fragrance. Some considered the amount of time Sharalyn spent in her plot excessive, but she didn't care. She took the words *pride* and *joy* to new heights, showcasing her passion for roses as only she could.

It won't be pretty for long, though.

This time of year, Sharalyn cut all her roses down—and loved every minute of it. January—official pruning time for roses, like a Southern California winter haircut. Sharalyn's ritual: First, she stripped off all the leaves, which made the plant's structure more visible. Then, she removed all horizontal branches with sharp pruners. Next, she cut back each vertical cane to the right height: not lopped off like a sailor's crew cut, but staggered, varied, to mimic nature's way of doing things. Finally, because any rosarian worth her salt knows as much, she squeezed a dab of glue on the tip of each fresh cut to prevent pesky cane borers from finding a new place to forage. Her plot reminded her of the Louisiana shoreline after a storm, twigs and sticks strewn all about, leaves fluttering in the mulch amid decapitated canes. Aside from cleanup, it looked perfect. Come spring, it would be a showstopper.

Sharalyn pictured her old rose nursery back in New Orleans, more a blooming botanical garden than a shop. Her knowledge of heritage estate cultivars made her successful there, and popular here at Vista Mar. Sure, New Orleans was zone 9a and Los Angeles was zone 10b. They were different, much less rain here, but the problems were the same. In the early years at Vista Mar Gardens, same as back home, powdery mildew confounded her. Soon she learned that a good spraying of her homemade milk-and-water remedy took care of that. Among the roses, she planted garlic to help fend off pests. She also planted a row of green onions along the border of the rose bed for double duty.

She watched a hummingbird settle over her patch of collards, and her mind shifted to that stack of new cookbooks teetering on her tiny nightstand at home. What was on the menu tonight?

We finished the last of the homegrown black-eyed peas with ham from New Year's. Collard greens with andouille sausages, maybe? I could make that in my sleep.

She stepped into her second plot, which overflowed with greens: chard, kale, and collards formed a border hedge at the entrance. The bean tower she'd installed when she first got her plot was designed to stand up against October winds on the hillside. Made from half-inch galvanized metal pipe she'd ordered special from a welder friend of hers and anchored two feet underground, it resembled a small set of monkey bars in a children's playground. Every spring she raised a crop of good old-fashioned dry beans that easily climbed the beast. Heir-loom True Red Cranberry beans—perfect for red beans and rice.

As she picked thick stems of collard greens from the plant, she invented a new recipe. No better place to ponder good cooking than while harvesting greens; ideas for savory dishes flowed up through the plant stems into her hands. Every time she touched the waxy leaves of her Swiss chard plants an idea for a new casserole popped into her head.

Good Lord, that sounds tasty. Forget the andouille. That might be the cover recipe for my cookbook. Hmph, you'd better put pen to paper if you plan to write a cookbook, Missy Thing.

Southern Cooking for Tiny Spaces, she'd call it, or maybe *Creole Cooking on the Water*. She wasn't sure yet. Cookbooks abounded for every lifestyle but hers; plenty about southern food, and even more about Creole seafood, but not a single book about how to cook it all in the compact quarters of a galley kitchen on a planing hull–style houseboat. Or any boat, really.

Smaller than the family's shrimping boat back in Louisiana, her houseboat was. Seafaring had its hooks in her soul—she couldn't pull herself away from it. She and her husband had their choice of ports in any of the beautiful marinas along the coast, but they chose Los Angeles because Marina del Rey had provided the lowest rent (at the time), the most welcoming people, and the best view of the Hollywood sign. Okay, maybe she'd taken some license with that last part, but don't tell her brothers. Let them imagine she lived close to the stars.

You're going to have to figure something out soon, Missy Thing.

Rent's going up. You might as well buy a house for what they're asking. She loved the marina, but with increases, throwing money away on rent made less and less sense. Time to build some equity.

The sound of footsteps interrupted her reverie. She glanced up in time to view Jared's athletic backside heading past her down the hill. *Wasn't he just here?* He didn't see her, but he looked to be in a hurry. She'd seen him flirt with Lizzie a while ago. Watched Lizzie try not to flirt back. Why all the fuss? They seemed cute together. Besides, Lizzie could use some fun now and again.

Not that it's any of my business.

Sharalyn surveyed her plot. Spring planting was coming soon. She could spout volumes about roses, but when it came to vegetables, she was charting new territory. Always learning something new, good or bad. This was only her fourth year at Vista Mar Gardens, but she had learned as much from her failures as her many successes. She mapped out the space for zucchini in her head. *Only one plant this year. I know better.*

Lizzie had warned her when she joined the garden that one zucchini plant is more than enough, but Sharalyn romanticized about summer squash and all the zucchini bread she planned to make. If she'd known back then that she'd be tossing thick batons of squash onto her neighbors' boats to offload the surplus, she would have heeded Lizzie's advice. She wasn't about to repeat that mistake. Some things can only be learned from experience.

What other mistakes have I made?

The mental review of the last four years released an avalanche of lessons learned: that time she tried growing tomatoes without cages. What a mess that was! And the year she planted an entire raised bed with wild fennel, only to discover a few months later that, again, one is enough—oh, and by the way, you'll never get rid of it. *I dig out those roots every year, and they still come back.*

Would've planted it in a corner, had she known, not taken up precious space with that invasive weed. And the most recent lesson, when she forgot to stop watering her potato patch once the foliage died back. Ended up with a pile of putrid potatoes, the whole crop ruined.

Sharalyn took these lessons to heart and, at the very least, tried to help others avoid her mistakes. She didn't have children to pass her wisdom on to, so she shared with her friends. Or as some would say, she overshared, to the point that some thought her nosy. She'd been accused by more than one friend of caring too much about other people's gardens, and other people's lives. She couldn't help but tell them, "That's not such a bad thing, is it, having someone looking out for you?" Maybe not. Or maybe it would take a few more years of mistakes to learn that lesson.

She detected Jared's footsteps returning up the hill, then music—the Rolling Stones, maybe? It stopped when Jared answered his phone. Sharalyn couldn't help but overhear; he stood right down from her corner plot.

"Hey, bunny," he said into the phone.

Bunny? That piqued her curiosity. She leaned back to hide

behind a trellis. She saw him, part of him, anyway, between her neighbor's cauliflower and the edge of her mailbox.

"Sorry, I'm running late . . . No, I want to. I am coming to see you; it's been a while. You've been on my mind a lot . . . What's wrong?" He lifted his hand to his forehead; he was clutching a bouquet of handpicked flowers. From his plot, no doubt.

"Bunny, hey . . . Don't get upset. I'll be right there. I'm on my way. I miss you, too . . . I don't understand what you mean. Stay put, it'll be worth the wait, I promise."

He smiled as he put his phone away, lowered his head with a deep sigh, and rubbed his brow. Sharalyn watched him take another deep breath, straighten up, and leave for his car.

Her head swirled with curiosity. Her heart swelled for Lizzie. What was that all about? Who's "bunny"? No wonder Lizzie's kept him at a distance. *Should I tell her? No, I should mind my own business. They'll have to figure it out themselves. With no help from you, Missy Thing.*

She couldn't think much about anything else, and the collard recipe went right out of her head. After a few minutes waffling back and forth, she wrestled a promise out of herself. If she happened to spot Lizzie walking by, maybe she'd pass on the information. Otherwise, she wouldn't go out of her way. Sure, that would be the neighborly thing to do.

CHAPTER 8

Realtors and Suits

February

Ned loved his role as garden master in February. Well, all year long, but February was tops. The commotion of brand-new gardeners obsessed with growing their own food. Year-end "nonrenewed" plots reassigned to fresh blood in January meant new helpers on work crews. If he looked close enough, he'd find a few more carpenters for retaining wall repair, a few more experts for the Pruning Committee, and a few compost geniuses out there. It didn't matter that he'd witnessed this annual turnover for thirty years, it still excited him.

"You'd think I'd be jaded by now."

"What's that, Pop?" Charlie, Ned's son, looked up from where he knelt in Ned's weedy garden.

"Every time February rolls around, I'm tickled all over again." Ned lifted the handles of his wheelbarrow to dump a pile of compost into his plot. Charlie stopped chipping away at a thick mat of devil's grass and looked up in time to watch compost tumble into a raised bed, covering a patch of weeds in the process.

Ned grimaced. "Probably should've dug that out first, huh?"

Charlie sighed. "You asked me to come help you, and you do this? Lucky you run the place, or you'd get kicked out."

It was an anomaly, Ned's garden. He was the only member of the board who deserved a citation for infractions any day of the week. On rare days when he coaxed Charlie away from work, they'd pull weeds or shift Ned's growing collection of stuff—all of which he planned to use someday—from one side of his plot to the other: rolled up plastic picket fencing, twisted tomato cages, and that pile of broken bricks intended for a pathway.

"Let me pull those weeds, Pop." Charlie stood to stretch his legs but bumped against Ned's mailbox. It teetered on its rotten post before falling to the ground with a hollow metallic clank.

Charlie asked, "Should I put in a work order for a new post for you?"

Ned chuckled. "I'd have to give it to myself."

"You're the cobbler—you know, with holes in your shoes." Charlie laughed.

"Something like that. I'll tell you, though, sometimes I come here and it's all cleaned up. It's my secret garden angel. They pull weeds and throw out some of this stuff. If your mother were still alive, I'd say it was her. You remember how she used to toss my shirts?"

"Didn't you pull them out of the trash when she wasn't looking?"

"Yeah." Ned put his hands on his hips. "I can't keep anything around here."

Ned reached into his pocket for his stack of to-do lists and smoothed them out. He brushed lint off the dog-eared corners. Hose leak in Section Two, broken mailbox post in Section Four, plumbing request from someone in Section Three. What about the work requests? Not as many as in December. Everyone understood only the garden master held the authority to assign work for credit outside of communal workdays. Section reps couldn't do it; Mary, as president, couldn't do it. Only Ned could.

A booming voice broke through his reverie.

"It's a friggin' miracle," shouted Jason the Bouncer, approaching in his usual white muscle tee and black shorts. He carried a bundle of fruit tree branches on his shoulder. "Now maybe your neighbors will shut up. They been naggin' me to cite you for months."

Ned waved. "Happy to comply, boss. What's new over in the orchard?"

"Getting a head start on the stone fruit trees before the rest of the pruning crew gets here—and before the sap starts flowing in this heat." He lowered the branches to the ground and brushed off his shirt.

"Yeah," Ned said, "our usual December heat wave is in February this year. Can you believe it? My broccoli bolted to seed. Covered with aphids, too." He pointed to the pile of broccoli plants he had pulled from the ground.

"I'm tempted to put in tomatoes," Jason said. It had been eighty degrees all week.

"Nah, it'll cool down soon. Wait for it."

"Whatever you say, Garden Master. Hey, I got a question for you."

"Sure." Ned took his gloves off and tucked them into his back pocket. He lifted his hat to smooth his gray wisps, set it back on top of the strands.

"Your son's in real estate, right?"

"Why don't you ask him yourself?" Ned turned to Charlie, who was crouched over a mound of weeds in the corner. "Last year he made a ton of money from a couple sales. Boy, if I had been smart, at his age, I would've done that instead of engineering, for sure."

"He exaggerates," Charlie said as he stood and pulled his gloves off to shake Jason's hand. "Are you looking to buy or rent?"

Jason jostled Charlie with his jackhammer handshake. "My girlfriend and I are ready to buy a starter place, if that even exists, but we don't have a clue where to start. If it's not too much trouble, would you mind talking to me for a few minutes? To get me started?"

Ned jumped in. "I probably shouldn't tell you this, but for the right person he gives a big discount, saves you the commission. It's usually people I send to him that account for it." He laughed.

"Slow down, Pop, he's only asking questions." Charlie nudged his father and glanced at Jason. "Seriously, I can't take him anywhere."

"Can't a man be proud?" Ned waved off Charlie's embarrassment. "You're the only son I've got." His eyes dropped, and he pulled his gloves out of his back pocket. "When Charlie came along," Ned told Jason, "he was such a great kid, we thought we'd have—well, we tried to have more, but . . . Well, it didn't work out that way."

Ned smoothed the gloves, blinking back unexpected tears. He could see Miriam's face after the third miscarriage, as if it had happened yesterday. She was so heartbroken from the losses, she couldn't bear trying again. It took him a while to let go of his dream—a house full of rambunctious kids. Over time, though, Charlie stole his heart, overshadowed the old yearnings.

"I'm a lucky kid, Pop." Charlie squeezed his father's shoulder.

"And what a handful, this one. I taught him about gardening, but he had other plans." By seven years old, Charlie had already organized a neighborhood summer theater, figured out how to rig a pulley system from his second-story bedroom window to the nectarine tree in the backyard (for easy access to fresh fruit), and ran the highest-grossing lemonade stand in town.

"Smart, too," Ned said. "Fresh out of college, he started flipping houses, and the rest is history."

Charlie extended his hand toward Jason. "Here's my card. Call me with your questions."

"Thanks, man," Jason said, with another firm handshake. "You've got a good son here, Ned."

"You bet I do. But I wish he'd hurry up and find a gal, so I can get a grandkid." He batted his gloves across Charlie's shoulder, sending up a cloud of dust.

"Jesus, Pop." Charlie laughed and brushed off the dirt.

Jason chuckled and strode off down the path with his armload of branches.

Ned put his gloves back on and bent down to pull a sprig of the devil's grass poking through the compost. Charlie, his only son. Would he live to see Charlie married, or to meet that grandchild? He supported Charlie's focus on his career, understood that he wasn't ready to settle down yet. Ned wished he would get going on it, though. Back in his day, most middle-aged men were well on their way to being grandparents, and Charlie was still dodging love. Ambition's fault? Maybe. Or maybe Charlie was destined to be the last of the family line.

Lizzie sat on the couch in her living room one evening, reading a well-worn copy of Jane Austen's *Mansfield Park*. It was her second time reading the used book she'd picked up at a thrift store—she had found it disappointing the first time. *Surely, I*

must have missed something. Edmund is clueless, and Austen doesn't remotely imply that he loves Fanny, really, until the end. Fanny herself is an insipid leading lady, something Patricia Rozema remedied in her 1999 film adaptation of the book, though controversially modern in its approach. Lizzie wanted to like the book, but as far as romances go, *Mansfield* wasn't cutting it. Her phone pinged.

Jared's words popped up on her screen. I'm a total heel. Sorry I haven't called.

Speaking of romance, or lack thereof . . .

Hi, she wrote back. *At least he apologized.* She withheld a more effusive response and waited for whatever excuse he'd undoubtedly send next.

I had to help my dad sell a property in Seattle. Had to fix it up before it sold.

Oh, so that's where you were. I wondered. She paused, hit the backspace button. Instead she sent: Oh, I guess they don't have phones in Seattle? ☺

Calling you now.

Her phone rang. Her palms grew clammy as she answered it. "Hey."

"Hi, my trip took a lot longer than expected." Jared sounded jovial. "Is my garden still alive?"

Is that why he's calling? To ask about his garden?

She tried to play it cool, to not appear annoyed, saying, "Most of it's bolted to seed, but it's time to pull everything anyway. I'm being lenient in not giving you a citation."

"Well, thanks, Section Rep Lizzie. I appreciate that." He paused, then added, "How are you?"

Okay, that's better. She softened.

"Doing all right. I'm reading a book I wish I liked more."
She told him what she was reading.

"Jane Austen, huh? I didn't take you for a hopeless romantic."

Lizzie laughed, a little embarrassed. "Surprise."

Jared chuckled. "Really? Oh, shoot. I've been doing this all
wrong." He cleared his throat. "Now we really have to schedule this dinner."

"Ya think?" Lizzie teased.

They tossed a few dates back and forth until they landed on
a Saturday evening in March. A ways off, but at least it was on
the calendar. Something to look forward to.

"I'll call Dolly's and see if they have availability," Jared said.
"We're far enough ahead . . . Geez, it has to work."

"Great," Lizzie said. "Oh, I hope they answer the phone. It's
probably busy tonight."

"Why is that?" Jared asked.

"It's Valentine's Day."

Silence.

Jared finally spoke: "Oh God. I'm an asshole."

Lizzie laughed, the only thing covering the awkward silence
on Jared's end. A quote from Ingrid Bergman popped into her
head. "'Happiness is good health and a bad memory,'" Lizzie
said. "Don't worry. This hopeless romantic hates Valentine's
Day."

"Okay, but still . . ."

"Let me know when you sort out dinner."

She hung up and rested her head back on the couch, grinning. Let him stew in his own embarrassment for once.

Mary had spent most of the cool Saturday morning pulling weeds in her plot; one of those rare mornings where she felt a spark of motivation to spiffy up the place. She knew better than to let the moment pass. Who knew when it would strike again?

As she gathered the enormous quantity of devil's grass into a pile, she heard footsteps behind her. When she turned to look, Ralph stood at the entrance with a handful of sweet pea flowers.

"Wow, I can smell those from here," she said.

Ralph handed her a few stems. "I have a lot of them at the moment. I figured I'd put them on the mailboxes of all our section reps—well, the ladies, anyway."

"A little post–Valentine's Day gesture? I'm sure they'll all appreciate it."

"Yeah." He looked down.

"They for anyone special?" Mary leaned forward to try to meet his eyes.

"Yeah. NO! No. Just . . . everyone. I mean . . ." His cheeks began to redden.

She tossed him a rescue question: "How long have you been here, Ralph?"

"A couple hours."

"No, I mean here, in the garden—as a member."

"Oh." He laughed. His eyes shot up to the left, and he squinted as he thought. "Ten years and seven months and thirteen days."

"It's a great place, isn't it?"

"Yeah." His eyes returned to the mulch below.

It took some doing, but with the grace of a seasoned professional, Mary asked Ralph about his work and how he came to Vista Mar Gardens. She coaxed him into a rare moment of self-expression.

"I like it here because . . . Well, I've been coding a new video game . . . It's top secret, though, so I can't talk about it. But because of all the code-crunching, I don't see daylight much. My condo doesn't have space for a garden, so it worked out for me to come here.

"That's how I got here. It started when I met Charlie—Ned's son—'cause he sold me my condo. It's not one of those fancy mansions he usually sells—I guess he did it for a buddy of his—but Ned tagged along once to an open house. We got to talking and he asked me a couple computer questions. We became friends after that."

"I didn't know that. Most people meet Ned here—he's always here."

"Yeah, well, now—me too."

Mary listened as Ralph's life unfolded before her. Vista Mar Gardens had turned out to be the missing piece. The long hours in his dim room surrounded by leftover fast-food boxes wore on him. Ned must have noticed, Ralph said, and suggested he come visit the garden. After a short time on the waiting list (only a hundred or so people on it back then), he got his plot and started growing greens. Being more of a "nuke it" kind of guy, Ralph welcomed the new concept of salads into his life.

"But I give most of it away."

"Oh, you're one of those." Mary rolled her eyes.

"What do you mean?" He smiled.

"People who grow gorgeous crops, but they never harvest them. It drives me bonkers."

"I didn't say that." The corners of his mouth turned up, exposed deep dimples Mary never noticed before. "I leave them as gifts. For certain . . . individuals."

Mary probed further. "Like the ladies?"

He chuckled. His eyes darted down and he shuffled mulch with his toe. "Like the ladies." His face grew so red, Mary worried he might pass out.

"Well, I imagine the women here love your gifts. You're also a homeowner. That's impressive, too."

"That was the plan." His smile diminished. "It hasn't worked out that way."

Mary watched him retreat into inner-Ralph. In a last effort to engage, she added, "You're still young, Ralph."

He shrugged.

She felt the urge to give him a hug, but opted to give him an easy exit. "I'd better get back to this devil's grass. It's got my name on it for the rest of the morning."

Ralph looked back up. "Okay. I'll see you la—" He shifted his focus past Mary's shoulder, up the hill.

"What's wrong?"

Ralph pointed to the hilltop. Mary followed his finger, a straight line to what had caught his attention.

There at the top, outside the chain-link fence, stood two men in black suits. One carried a briefcase; the other spoke into a recording device while taking video footage of the garden. His wristwatch caught the morning sunlight, like the sparkly compact discs that dangled from trellises to frighten birds away from tender crops. Crisp white shirts, solid blue neckties, and polished leather shoes stood in stark contrast to the dust-covered gardeners usually found in the area. The men searched from behind their dark sunglasses for a way through the gate. As with most outsiders who showed up attempting to navigate the vast property, they broadcasted the trademark look of disorientation.

Ralph watched Mary's body tighten. He wasn't sure why. She pulled off her gloves and, instinctively it seemed, grabbed a shovel perched on a brick pile in the corner. For a split second Ralph pictured one of those classic scenes—a rancher standing on the front porch with a shotgun when the traveling salesman pulls up the driveway.

Mary hopped out of her plot, tugged on his sleeve. "Come on," she said and started up the path.

"You recognize them?" Ralph dropped his basket of flowers to follow her. He struggled to fill his lungs and keep up with Mary at the same time.

"I recognize their kind. It's never good when suits show up."

He pushed his sleeves up to appear more menacing, since he didn't have a shovel.

Mary yelled from twenty feet away, "Can I help you?" The men in suits shifted their focus toward the sound, like squirrels. They spotted Mary and relaxed, looking confident in their fancy clothes. One smiled, one didn't. The smiling one slipped his recording device into his pocket.

"Yes, we're looking for the chairman. Is he here?" he asked as Mary and Ralph reached the top of the hill.

"She is." Mary thrust her shovel into the ground in front of her with one hand. She put the other hand on her hip and looked through the fence at the men. "What can I do for you?"

Ralph watched the smiling man step forward. He was willowy, his face young and smooth behind his slick (and probably expensive) sunglasses.

"Good morning, ma'am. May we come in to talk for a moment?"

"You're fine right there." Mary lifted her chin. "And don't call me ma'am. Ma'am is for old people."

Without a beat, he pulled a business card from his inside jacket pocket and curled it with his pointer and middle finger as he fed it though a chink in the fence.

"Sorry about that. We're from DSC and Associates, here on behalf of a private party, with permission from the City of Los Angeles."

Ralph craned to read the card over Mary's shoulder when she took it. She ran a finger over the raised blue letters on the card. Ralph caught the words *legal* and *property* before Mary tucked it into her back pocket.

"It's a nice garden you have here. Most people probably don't even know it exists."

Ralph could swear he saw the man's teeth sparkle.

Mary stood motionless. Ralph noticed that her shoulders were tense, though. He recognized those shoulders.

Oh God, she's ramping up.

"What can I do for you gentlemen?" she said a little louder.

The second man, who did not smile, stepped forward toward the fence. His angular body pushed against his well-tailored suit at the elbows and shoulders, his graying temples beaded with unseasonal sweat. "I'll be brief so as not to waste your time or ours. We've been asked by our client to visit the property to assess the land for possible future use." He produced a document from his briefcase and held it up to the fence. "I'm sure you're aware that the city granted Vista Mar Gardens permission to use the land on the condition that if at any time they found a better or more lucrative use for the land, they reserve the legal right to repurpose the property."

"What?" Ralph leaned in, dumbfounded. Mary put her hand out to stop him.

"Yes, we're aware of that." She smoldered under half-closed eyelids. "And we're also certain that we're on a list of properties protected from sale. That list supersedes our conditional use permit. Unless something has changed, this conversation is over."

The smiling man stepped forward, apologetic. "That has yet

to be determined, ma'am—sorry. We're only here to take a preliminary survey. The client may not be inter—" His partner silenced him with a sharp glance.

Ralph wished he had something quick-witted to say, but he couldn't come up with a thing. He was too busy fumbling over the new information. *How could this be? Will they really repurpose the land? Why didn't Vista Mar Gardens own the land? Why didn't anyone else know? How could these people want to get rid of a garden? It's been here for so long—over thirty years! They can't do that, right?*

His palms began to sweat, and he pictured himself doing something—chasing them off the land, calling the police, anything but standing there sweating. Too many thoughts flooded his brain all at once, and he couldn't slow them down enough to grab on to any one of them. He was so busy scouring his mind for something to say that he tuned out the conversation between Mary and the men in suits. It only occurred to him that he was missing something important when he caught a sudden movement out of the corner of his eye.

He hadn't noticed Mary's voice grow stronger, or that the nonsmiling man had stepped closer to the gate—curling his fingers through the fence, his face almost touching the chain link—until he finally looked up, just in time.

Ralph watched it in slow motion, but it didn't happen that way. Mary clutched the shovel with both hands, lifted it up to her shoulder, and thrust the pointed end toward the face of the nonsmiling man through the fence. Ralph reached forward and grabbed Mary's elbow. He pulled her back from the gate as the tip of the shovel grazed the man's knuckle.

Both suits jumped back from the quivering fence; one clutched his hand, the other stumbled to regain his balance. Mary's voice lowered to a growl. "Get off my property." She might be growing old, but she still knew how to intimidate the pants off anyone.

Shaken, the two men turned, gathered the dusty fallen briefcase, and walked back to their gleaming Mercedes.

"We'll see you soon, ma'am," the nonsmiling man called over his shoulder as he adjusted his jacket. Mary and Ralph watched until they sped out of the parking lot.

"Are we really owned by the city?" Ralph said.

Mary inhaled, as if she'd just been reminded to breathe. "Yup." She picked up the shovel and turned to Ralph. "I wondered whether this day would ever come."

Ralph stood bewildered. "What do you mean? You knew about this?"

"I'm the chair, Ralph," she snapped. "I know some things."

Ralph recoiled and shifted his gaze to the mulch below his feet. "Sorry."

Mary sighed. She rubbed her forehead. "No, I'm sorry, Ralph. Not my best moment. I'm glad you were there to witness it, in case they file charges against me for the . . ." She waved a hand in the direction of the fence.

"Yeah. That was close."

"Was it bad?"

"Well, nobody's bleeding, so it's probably okay."

They started to walk down the hill but recognized Lizzie and Sharalyn running toward them. Ralph's heart picked up its pace. He tugged on his shirt and tried not to stare at Lizzie's long, flowing, and, most likely, silky-to-the-touch hair as she approached.

"Who were the suits?" Lizzie said.

She says suits, Ralph thought. *I say* suits. One more thing they had in common. He smiled, but realized it was an inappropriate time for that.

Still smoldering, Mary said, "You girls saw that, too?"

"We were doing paperwork in the shed . . . ," Lizzie said.

"We heard yelling," Sharalyn said.

"And so, yeah. We saw that," Lizzie said. "Are you okay?" She put a comforting hand on Ralph's arm, and for a moment the earth stopped turning. He looked down at her hand on his arm. She touched him. Lizzie was touching his arm. That had never happened before. Between milliseconds, a chorus of angels began to sing, light streaked from her hand, his heart soared. He could die happy in this moment. Then as quickly as it happened, it was over. She lifted her hand and the chorus wound down like a gramophone running out of juice. Sharalyn's voice punched through his retreating elation.

"Did they threaten you?"

"I guess you could say that," Mary said. "I may have lost my head."

"Understatement," Ralph added under his breath.

"Ralph!"

"Sorry."

Mary sighed. "I probably shouldn't have handled it that way."

Lizzie said, "They both looked like Agent Smith."

"Who?" Mary was caught off guard.

"*The Matrix*, Agent Smith. You know." Lizzie got only Mary's blank stare in return. "Anyone?"

Ralph replied in his best Hugo Weaving voice. "Mr. Anderson."

Lizzie threw her hands in the air. "Thank you."

Mary interrupted. "Kids, we have a problem on our hands."

She explained the conversation to Lizzie and Sharalyn. Their mouths fell agape at the news.

"We don't own this property?" Lizzie looked shocked. "My understanding was that someone gave it—"

"No, we're on borrowed land. The City of Los Angeles dedicated this space some thirty-odd years ago as a public garden, but there's no lease. We only received a written agreement, and if they decide to sell it at any time, we have to return everything to its original state and vacate." Her words sounded so formal, as if she were quoting that long-ago agreement.

Sharalyn asked, with her ever-present southern charm, "But doesn't it behoove the city to keep us here? I mean, we make them look good, don't we?"

"We've given hundreds of people a place to garden," Lizzie added. "They'd look pretty bad if they shut us down."

Mary flicked the dirt from under her fingernails. "I guess we've counted on that the whole time, but the city made budget cuts this year, and I'll bet they're looking to make a buck one way or another. I better pull out the files and talk to Ned."

She left them abruptly, shovel still clutched in one hand. Lizzie and Sharalyn walked in silence to Section Four.

Ralph tagged along behind. Losing the garden was impossible. Denial was easy.

"There's no way they can do that," Lizzie blurted out.

Ralph opened his mouth to say something comforting, but his own shock silenced him. Then Sharalyn said what had come to his mind seconds before: "I can't believe they would. We've got over four hundred people on the waiting list for a plot. They'd be stupid to get rid of this community service."

"What do they plan to build here, condominiums?" Lizzie said. "That would really piss off the neighbors. Especially Kurt the Curmudgeon. He'll go ballistic when he gets wind of this."

"It'll all work out, sugar. It's got to." Sharalyn kept her usual positive lilting tone, but there was something unconvincing about it. They each set off to their plots, leaving Ralph standing alone with his uncertainty. He scanned the garden for the first time as something he might lose, not from his own failing, but from a power completely out of his control.

CHAPTER 9
A Date

March

Jared stared into his closet, tried to figure out what to wear. *Casual yet nice*, he thought. He lifted his favorite pair of khakis off the hanger—the good ones that fit in the waist—and checked them for wrinkles under the dim overhead light. He reached into the closet for a long-sleeved, button-down shirt with maroon and black stripes. *Yeah, this is the one. Women like patterns.*

He hung the shirt and pants on the bathroom door while he ran the shower, to let the steam ease out any wrinkles. In the stronger light of the bathroom he checked for stains—all clear—and tried to recall when he last wore these pants. He looked in the mirror, felt his chin for stubble. In a single sweeping motion, he grabbed the razor off the shelf, stepped into the shower, and closed the curtain behind him.

Jared hummed a made-up tune, though it turned into the Grateful Dead's "Touch of Grey" as he lathered up. It evolved into musical scales. His voice grew louder, searching for the sound of reverberation in the room, playing with pitch until he found the resonant frequency above the shower's din. He raised the pitch until he made the metal air-conditioning vent vibrate.

He smiled. *There it is.*

While he shaved, Jared thought through his evening ahead. Dinner at Dolly's with Lizzie. Finally. **Looking forward to it**, her text had said earlier. He hoped so. It had taken them three months to find a time to get together, between working for his father and his own just plain douchebaggery. *Mostly Dad, though. That guy gets obsessed with a project and the whole family gets roped in. Or at least I do.* The glint in his father's eye when he had played a video of the house he planned to flip was enough for Jared to know his time would not be his own for at least two months. But even with the "family discount," he made decent money on the job, which had worked out great, since the first part of the year had turned out to be quiet workwise. For a second, his father had seemed pleased. Maybe Baba was finally getting over his disappointment.

Speaking of disappointment, how embarrassing was that call to Lizzie on Valentine's Day? *Totally clueless, dude. You'll have to make it up to her during this dinner somehow.*

There would be plenty to talk about. Since that moment when he confessed his garden geekiness, he started making a mental list of questions to ask her: Which is better—stakes or cages? Growing tips for squash? Why mulch? Oh, and how the heck do you get rid of powdery mildew? His anticipation grew. Anticipation. He hadn't felt that in a while. Lizzie intrigued him in a way he couldn't explain. She was so together, yet so clumsy in their personal interactions. He was dying to know why.

He shut off the water, toweled dry, and dressed in five minutes. Sleeves rolled up to the forearm, first and second button undone, shirt untucked—the steam had done its job—brown leather hip/cool oxfords, and just in case, a casual suit jacket. He ran his fingers through his hair in front of the mirror, brushed some lint off his shoulder, and was out the door.

JARED ARRIVED AT Dolly's to find Lizzie stepping up to the sidewalk from the street. He didn't recognize her at first. She wore a dress—a strappy, flowing sundress that revealed her legs—a huge change from her usual baggy jeans and long-sleeved shirts. She looked so svelte without all that fabric covering her up. She also didn't wear her garden hat. She looked different. Good, but different. Completely hot, in fact.

A rush of endorphins swept through when he took in her smooth shoulders. Her skin was probably soft, too. He glanced at a beauty mark on her collarbone, then realized he was staring, so he shifted his eyes upward. *Eyes, look at her eyes.*

They said hello and hugged. Lizzie gave him the type of

polite hug that strangers bestow: upper body only, bent at the waist, patting the back. He, on the other hand, went for one arm around her waist. He shifted one hand to the small of her back, the other over her shoulder. She let out an awkward giggle. Nerves?

Jared was struck by the lingering scent of Lizzie's hair as the hostess led them to their table. He tried to put his finger on the scent. It wasn't perfume or shampoo, it was just clean. She got brownie points for not smelling like the ground floor of a department store.

The hostess led them to a table near a window overlooking the garden that during the day was a wash of green, lush foliage in cheerful ceramic pots, with sunlight reflecting off a small pond and fountain, water lilies bobbing on the surface. At night, however, everything beyond the glass was engulfed in darkness except for a few places that glowed or shimmered in dim accent lighting. They stood facing the window, straining to see out. Lizzie said she could make out a pond with a fountain in the corner, but that summed up the extent of their view. So much for impressing her with beautiful scenery.

"We'll have to come back in the daytime," Jared said, laughing.

She chuckled. "Yeah."

Well, that's a good sign.

The hostess cleared her throat. "Is this table all right?"

"Oh, sorry," Jared said. "Yes, it's fine." He and Lizzie exchanged grins and sat down.

The slinky, model-thin hostess handed them menus. Jared

noticed she struggled to walk back to the podium in her four-inch stilettos. *Why do women risk their lives in those things?* Sure, she looked good, but if the building caught on fire or something . . .

Okay, I sound like Tutu. But I'm glad I don't have to squeeze myself into shoes that make it impossible to walk. Crazy.

He leaned over, pretending to adjust the wallet in his back pocket, to glance under the table. Low-heeled sandals. Smart woman. More brownie points, Tutu.

Lizzie disappeared behind the menu, coughing as she read. "$20 for crostini. I'm totally fine with going Dutch, so . . ."

"No." Jared reached across the table, put his index finger in the fold of Lizzie's menu and lowered it. When she looked up at him, he smiled into her brown eyes. "This is a date. I'm taking you out. Feels like we should splurge, right?"

"Oh, okay, right. I'm . . ." She paused. "Thank you. That's nice." Was she blushing? Hard to tell in the candlelight.

"Can I get you anything to drink?" A dressed-in-black waiter appeared by their table.

"Some wine?" Jared asked Lizzie.

"Sure."

"Red?"

"Definitely."

"Dry?"

"Not so much."

He looked up at the waiter. "How about the V. Sattui syrah?"

"Great. I'll be right back to take your order." The waiter departed, and Jared returned his glance to Lizzie.

"What are you going to have?"

"The vegetarian choices all sound good." She read from the menu. "I'm eyeing the mushroom risotto with a brown butter and sage balsamic reduction."

Vegetarian. Didn't see that coming. Should've asked beforehand.

Jared quickly scanned the menu for veggie options. "Sounds good." He closed his menu and leaned in on his elbows.

The waiter arrived with the wine and a basket of warm bread, poured Jared a sample, then relayed a laundry list of specials. Jared held his glass to his nose, inhaling the fruity aromas. *Always good*, he thought. He lifted a hand toward Lizzie, inviting her to order. As he sipped, he watched her ask whether the mushroom risotto contained chicken broth. The smile that spread across her face when the waiter assured her it was vegetarian put Jared at ease.

"And for you, sir?"

"I'll have the salmon. And may we get some olive oil for the bread when you have a chance?"

The waiter chirped a positive reply and set off to the kitchen.

"So," he said, "what do you do when you're not at the garden?"

Lizzie froze for a fraction of a second. Jared imagined the wheels turning in her head as she took a gulp of wine.

Personal question. Should've started with gardening.

She softened and looked down at her wineglass.

"I mostly watch movies and read gardening books, or the occasional novel. And I cook, to use up what's coming in from the garden. But every once in a while, I feel inspired to try something new. Like *Julie & Julia*, cooking my way through a recipe collection or something." She paused. "Sorry, did I lose you there with the film reference?"

Jared shook his head. "Oh, no. I bought the book for my mom one Christmas."

"Okay, good. Sometimes my cinephile brain forgets to bring people along with me. Anyway, I go on cooking jags every once in a while."

"And you have time for that?"

"I used to have more time, but then I had to get a real job." She laughed. "Now I work and garden and watch movies. That about sums it up."

"What do you do for work?"

"I'm a writer. Well, I wouldn't call it *writing*, exactly. I write copy for brochures at a low-budget design firm. I'm supposed to be a screenwriter by now, but . . . well . . . gotta pay the bills."

"Sounds like a decent gig in the meantime."

Lizzie shrugged. "It's decent enough, though I'd much rather be in the garden all day long."

"Man, I wish." Jared felt a warmth in his chest.

"What about you?" Lizzie asked. "You always seem busy."

"Do I?" Jared laughed. "I'm surprised you noticed."

Lizzie's face flushed in the candlelight. She took another gulp of wine and coughed into her napkin. "Well," she said, "all I know about you so far is your penchant for carpentry, and that you help your dad with repairs in far-off places." Lizzie leaned in. "So enlighten me."

"Why do I suddenly feel like I'm at a job interview?" Jared squinted across the table.

Lizzie paused, then sighed and closed her eyes. "Sorry, I'm not used to . . . I mean, I'm not very good at this."

"Good at what? Talking to people?" He smiled.

Lizzie looked down and slowly inhaled. "Getting to know people. Life is much easier at a distance."

"I see." Jared sensed a vulnerability in Lizzie he hadn't noticed before. "Well, I'll try not to spew my life story all at once, if it makes you more comfortable."

Lizzie laughed. "Thank you."

Jared went on. "I will say that I try to live a simple life, and I've had my fair share of occupations that keep things interesting."

"Like what?" Lizzie asked.

"I surf, did that professionally for a while. And the carpentry, which you already know. I did a stint building sets at Warner Brothers, but the hours were brutal. I discovered I'd rather freelance on smaller projects and get more sleep. That's working a lot better for me."

Lizzie whispered, "Did you ever steal a memento from a set?"

"I might have . . . But I'll save that story for another time." His eyes lingered on her until she grinned and raised an eyebrow along with her wineglass.

She asked Jared more about his life outside of the garden. He took it as a sign that the evening was off to a good start.

"I enjoy these side jobs at Vista Mar, too. Mostly to keep from getting bored."

"What do you mean?"

"I mean, I meet so many people who hate their jobs. They're

not doing what they love, so they're bored. I almost went down that path once."

"The J.O.B.?" Lizzie asked.

Lizzie's words floated across Jared's mind. He remembered the choice he had to make all too vividly. His mind drifted back to a time when he believed he didn't have a choice.

HE WAS STANDING in front of the mirror, holding a tie to his collar. He sighed.

"Is this what he wants?" he said to the mirror.

His father had lined up this perfect job at his accounting firm, the regular-paycheck suit-and-tie job that paid a ton of money.

Is this what I want?

No more sunset bike rides. No more travel on a whim. Sure, a fat weekly paycheck is always nice, but at what cost?

Jared flashed back to the conversation they'd had several weeks earlier.

"You can't always rely on your youth and strength for money, bēṭā," his father had said, as if quoting some ancient Sanskrit teaching. "You need something solid. Don't you think it's time?"

"I love my jobs, Dad."

"What if you saw off a finger? I'm handing you an opportunity here. It won't be that easy anywhere else."

"I know, I know."

"You're not the golden boy anymore."

"What's that supposed to mean?"

Silence.

His father had sighed—the heavy sigh of a disenchanted parent. "I'm only saying that you ought to plan further ahead than tomorrow."

His father's words echoed in his head, bouncing back at him off the mirror. *This is where it all ends or begins. It's hard to tell which.*

Jared looked at the time, then lifted a second tie and switched it under his chin. Neither of them looked good. *"Look good"? Or is it "feel good"?*

He'd never worn a tie for anything other than a wedding or a funeral. It felt wrong.

"I can't do this."

He tossed both ties on the bed, sat down, and pulled out his phone. He stared at the keypad for a moment, trying to formulate the best possible way to lessen the disappointment his father was bound to feel.

There's no other way to say it. It's not for me.

"HELLO IN THERE," he heard Lizzie say.

As he became aware of the tablecloth beneath his hands, he noticed Lizzie watching him intensely. Jared shook his head and came back to the restaurant.

"Sorry. I . . ." He paused, then tried again. "I know myself well enough to understand that if I try anything that I'm not passionate about, I'll lose interest and leave. So I take a lot of jobs to keep life interesting."

"How long do you usually stay with one thing?"

"It depends. Some I've done for years, others a couple weeks. But this gardening thing is weird." He sat up in his chair, pushed his sleeves up. "I can't imagine getting bored with my plot. I honestly can't."

"Well, that's good, isn't it?"

"Except it's never happened before." Jared got excited. His voice rose. He tried not to embarrass himself. He laughed. "I know, I sound like a kid, don't I?"

"Yes, but it's nice. Go ahead." She smiled—the kind of smile he could soak in for hours.

"Well, gardening has infinite potential. You can never get it right every time, right? You'll never learn everything. I can picture myself doing this forever. I've never felt that way about anything."

Lizzie pointed a long finger at him from behind her wineglass. "You've been bitten."

"Bitten?" Jared felt a tingle in his gut.

"You're officially obsessed. Here's how it goes: You'll never give up your plot, and you'll crave more land every year. Next, you'll try to grow rare varieties, or crops that don't grow here. You'll see."

"I guess," Jared said. "But it's a good addiction to have, right?"

"I think so." Lizzie took a sip from her glass.

Jared looked across the table at her. The candle in the center cast a warm glow on her face, her shoulders, her chest. He'd never seen this feminine side of her. Strange. She presented herself as a no-nonsense authority at the garden, but this softer side captivated him. Softer, he thought, and for a split second he almost said, *Let's get out of here.*

Instead, he said, "Let me ask you something," then took a sip of wine.

"Uh-oh, should I be nervous?"

"No, it's nothing too probing, I promise."

She tilted her head forward, invited his question.

"What makes you decide to kick someone out of the garden?"

"That's a loaded question, Jared."

He lifted his hands up off the table, miming surrender. "I'm only asking."

"Well, it's not entirely up to me. If someone doesn't respond to the citations in their mailbox, or my phone calls, notes, whatever, the other section reps and I get together and vote on the plot. If it's overrun with weeds, it's easy." She jerked her thumb over her shoulder.

"I see." Jared contemplated her words for a few seconds. "So the trick is to get in good with the section rep so citations never happen."

Pause.

"Touché." Lizzie squinted, lifted her glass in a toast. Something had shifted in her demeanor though. She looked uncomfortable. "That's your strategy?" She stared him straight in the eye.

Jared lifted his hands up again. "Seriously, I'm only asking."

Lizzie downed the rest of her wine. She pointed her glass at him. "Don't cause me any trouble, mister."

He fought a strong impulse to take her hand and reassure her.

"Okay, forget I said anything," he said through his laughter. "I get it. Don't mess with Section Rep Lizzie."

Lizzie nodded. "That's right." Her words slurred a little.

Jared noticed she'd emptied her glass, but their meal hadn't yet arrived. Granted, there wasn't much in there to begin with. She had stopped the waiter before he'd poured half a glass.

"Are you getting tipsy, Section Rep Lizzie?" Jared leaned back in his chair.

"Oh sure. It takes no time at all; I'm such a lightweight." She wobbled her glass on the table. "I don't drink very often, so when I do, it's remarkably effective."

"Good to know," Jared said, relieved the conversation had shifted away from his flub about the citations.

Their meals arrived. Jared looked at Lizzie and her food. He didn't say it aloud, but he appreciated that she didn't order a salad. She wasn't afraid to eat in front of a guy, by the look of that plate. *She also brought a coat. Smart woman. She's different.*

JARED AND LIZZIE chatted between bites of dinner and dessert until late in the evening. He told her about growing up in Hawaii, then Seattle. How moving to Los Angeles for work was the best thing he ever did. They talked about the garden and their plans for the next growing season. Jared felt alive, electric.

When they finished their meal, he offered to walk Lizzie to her car.

"Oh, that's okay, I'm right outside."

"Really? How did you score a parking space right in front?"

"I have parking fairies who guide me," she joked.

"Well then, I'll take you with me next time I go to Trader Joe's."

"Sounds good." Lizzie gave him a thumbs-up. A little awkward, but cute.

They exited the restaurant still talking and found themselves walking the quarter block to Lizzie's car. She thanked him for a great dinner. Jared said something effusive in reply, but he couldn't concentrate on a word he said, too distracted by the desire to pull her in and kiss her. He tried to figure out the best way to accomplish that without scaring her. *Take it easy, tiger. Not so fast.*

He reached out and slid his hand down Lizzie's arm. "I'll see you at the garden."

He tugged her toward him and brushed her cheek with his. Her shoulders relaxed against his arm. She didn't pull away, a good sign. Before letting her go, he kissed her cheek softly, drawing the moment out as long as he dared.

She looked at him with an alluring smile and said good night. Lizzie rounded the corner of her car to the driver's side and waved as she got in. He stood there, hands in his pockets, until she drove away; then, feeling lighter than he had in a long time, Jared turned on his heel and went home.

As Lizzie drove away from the curb, her mind raced.

Oh my God, he's gorgeous! The touch of his lips lingered on her cheek. She bubbled inside. It had been a long time since she'd felt like a schoolgirl. She waited until she got a block

away, verified that all the windows were rolled up, then let out
a joy-filled squeal.

What a change from the usual. He was emotionally demon-
strative. So different from the guys who didn't find it necessary
to show affection. And he dressed well, not in shorts as she had
predicted. He knew himself. That was good. He had a grasp
on what he wanted—except for that jack-of-all-trades thing—
which wasn't a bad quality, was it? *Oh, stop.*

Her mind scrolled through a slideshow of the evening. She
replayed that kiss on her cheek over and over. She relived the
warmth on her neck from his breath. She sensed his desire,
which mirrored her own. So foreign, yet so palpable. As she
neared her apartment, though, she flashed back on the conversation at the table when Jared joked about citations. Lizzie
revisited that twinge of concern and found herself wondering
if he had a hidden agenda for their date that centered on her
board status. Is it a conflict of interest—again—to be the section rep of someone she was dating? It could lead to unclear
boundaries, namely to him taking advantage of her position.
Not to mention the last time she had dated someone from the
garden, it had ended in prolonged heartbreak. She'd hated the
uncomfortable, awkward, and vulnerable potential of that situation. And she definitely didn't want to repeat it.

At the time, over dinner, she'd put the comment out of her
head, wanting to enjoy the moment and all the attention. But
by the time she pulled her car into her parking space behind
her apartment building, she could focus on nothing else.

CHAPTER 10

Unknowns

Late March

Everyone at Vista Mar Gardens eagerly awaited the arrival of late March: official tomato-planting time. Gardeners anticipated not only tomatoes, but the satisfying transition from cool-season to warm-season crops. Gone were the brassicas and root veggies, clearing the way for summer squashes and pumpkins, melons, cucumbers, peppers, corn, and beans. Lizzie collected her favorite varieties from her seed jar and sowed row after row in the open spaces left behind by spent winter lettuces. She transplanted her tomato and pepper seedlings from their cozy growing greenhouse into their new raised-bed homes. Fingers crossed that they'd survive the crows, rats, gophers, and other critters that had become more active in the garden as of late.

Planting afforded her a distraction from her busy mind. She'd spent the last week or so fighting off worry and the impulse to overthink. The litany of questions running through her mind about Jared and his intentions occupied far too much of her time, especially for something so new. It was ridiculous. Why couldn't she relax and enjoy casual dating? Why did she have to overanalyze everything? Try as she might to let it go, whenever she'd daydream about a possible future with him, his question about citations and terminations nagged her. Was he just using her? Was he testing the waters to see what he could get away with? That was a huge red flag, wasn't it? She had ignored red flags like this in previous relationships, chalking it up to paranoia, only to regret it later. Never again, she told herself.

Plus, what was the deal with when he went incommunicado? *If you like someone, you touch base, don't you?* That behavior pointed Lizzie toward more doubt. She played that scenario through to the finish, imagined Jared manipulating her with his irresistible charm (and physique) while leaving town too frequently to tend his garden. He'd beg her to water "just this once," talk her out of citing him, ply her with his innate magnetism until she would look the other way any time he broke the rules.

But he had sent a sweet message or two over the past weeks.

I had a great time the other night. ☺ I forgot to ask you about timing for planting watermelon. Is it time now?

Lizzie texted back, Too early still. Wait until May at least.

OK, cool. Hey, would love to see you again when I get back in town. Maybe a movie?

She waited to respond, debating whether to make up an excuse or not. A movie, huh? He went for the jugular there.

Keep me posted when you're back was the best she could come up with in the moment.

Mary crumpled yet another campaign flyer that had been placed in her mailbox, obviously by Bernice or one of her minions, and tossed it under Bernice's rose hedge. It landed in a pile with others that she'd thrown there over the last two weeks. She didn't read them, but noticed an increase in ALL CAPS and the addition of color print in the recent flyers. Outwardly, Mary projected an air of indifference over Bernice's attempt to oust her from the presidency. Alone, however, she felt a gnawing dread. Mary prided herself on the atmosphere of inclusiveness she had fostered over the years. And while she didn't take crap from anyone, she welcomed folks with new ideas when they approached her. Bernice would ruin that in a heartbeat. She'd probably kick out half the garden, starting with Mary.

She pondered what she would do if she lost her plot at Vista Mar. Where else would she find a community like this one, one that was solely hers, not entwined with her ex-husband's country club life? A life she never fit into anyway. A square peg in a round hole for sure. Boy, if you want to know who your real friends are, you'll find out quick at the club. Once word got out about their split, the ladies-who-lunch sided with their husbands, who supported Tom. But Tom had never set foot at Vista Mar; there were no memories attached to him here. Mary liked it that way. Nothing to repair after the fallout.

Out of the corner of her eye she saw movement along the pathway. When she turned to look, she spotted Bernice, who stopped short when they made eye contact. Bernice turned to leave.

Well, almost nothing to repair.

Mary rolled her eyes and called after her, "It won't kill us to be here at the same time, Bernie."

"I'd rather not," Bernice shouted over her shoulder.

Mary shook her head. "Suit yourself. But just so we're clear, I'm not stopping you from being here."

"Of course," Bernice yelled back, her voice thick with sarcasm. "It's never your fault, Mary." She continued up the path and out of sight.

CHAPTER 11
The Big "E"

April

"Cast your votes, everyone." Ned waved a handful of paper ballots over his head. "Don't forget, you're voting for president, treasurer, and east section reps. And no write-ins, please."

Mary accepted the stack of ballots from her neighbor. She took one, passed the rest to the next person. She didn't peer over the shoulders of the gardeners in front of her, or next to her, though she was dying to. Would they really elect Bernice over her? After all her time and dedication?

Bernice sat across the way, looking nervous: rigid, tight-lipped, eyes shifting side to side. They both checked half a dozen boxes on the ballot and raised their hands to grab the ballot collector's attention. Mary stuffed her ballot into the shoebox and escaped to her plot, hoping for the best.

By April, the garden was in full swing. Dormant gardeners reawakened to the prospect of fresh fruit, tasty vegetables, and more tomatoes than they could ever eat. Tomato seedlings were knee-high with nary a hint of blossom yet, but each plant was mulched, caged, and wrapped in plastic sheeting to protect it from the ocean air. Every gardener plied their own technique for raising healthy tomatoes. Opinions varied across the board. Ned chose to layer red plastic sheet mulch around the base of his plants, while Jason claimed black plastic worked as good as anything else. Bernice used special watering trays, but Ananda dug swales to funnel irrigation to her tomato beds. New gardeners attempted to secure their tomatoes to simple wooden stakes with green floral tape, while veteran growers learned this would only last until the first trusses of fruit began to weigh down the plants with their maturing bounty.

The birds also reawakened in spring. The neighboring eucalyptus trees vibrated, a cacophony of hungry chicks crying for food. Mothers swooped down into the compost bins in search of grubs. Fathers stood watch over their young and chased away curious crows that circled the nests. The din subsided after about an hour each morning, leaving the garden quiet except for the occasional echo from a mallet driving stakes into the ground.

Weekends were active on the hillside. Recent rain triggered millions of tiny weed sprouts, most of which went unnoticed until they reached a height somewhere between ankle and shin. A few gardeners kept their plots in immaculate condition. Those people were not at the garden this time of year, because they kept up with weekly weeding through the rainy season. It was the negligent gardener who was on their knees in April, pulling out the mass of green that had all but consumed their plot.

Mary, among the ranks of the negligent, found her plot carpeted in weeds. A welcome distraction, thank God. At worst, she'd have more time to weed if Bernice won. She stuffed her hands into a dusty pair of garden gloves and bent over behind a wheelbarrow that was already piled high with dandelions and devil's grass from the day before. As always, she swore under her breath as she ripped out oversized stalks of mallow. Pulling mallow took particular skill—a delicate balance between applying the right amount of force to pull the deep taproot, while at the same time bracing to avoid falling over when it released. Mary stood hunched over a waist-high mallow. Its round, geranium-shaped leaves impersonated other flowers that belonged in the garden. She didn't give a hoot that it was edible or made good tea, or whatever nonsense Ananda went on about. She wrapped both gloved hands around the thick base of the stem and gave it a good tug. At first it didn't budge, so she bent her knees to put more muscle into it. She heard the earth grumble and snap as it began to give up its guest, but the long root held fast. Mary pulled harder, leaning back from the weed. All at once, the taproot shot from the ground and Mary flew back, landed on her rear, and rolled backward.

What she wouldn't give for a third hand right now—that

would've helped her brace for impact. She grasped the liberated plant in both hands overhead as soil rained down onto her face from the thick root. Did this have to happen every time? Thank God Bernice wasn't there to witness.

"Next year I'm going to cut them down. Screw weeding," Mary muttered. But she knew that next year she would repeat this painful process. She was a fighter. She had proved her mettle long ago, during the hardest days of her life, fifteen years ago.

That was when fights with Tom had become more frequent. These were not the usual disagreements they'd always faced through the years. Innocent bickering about toothpaste caps evolved into full-blown screaming matches about not spending enough time together. Mary's temper flared every time they argued, exasperation seeping from every pore as she fought to save their marriage. She exhausted every option, insisting on counseling, and even help from the temple they rarely attended. It could have been yesterday; she pictured the ridges of the corduroy couch in the rabbi's office as she dug her nails into it, while Tom sat silent next to her, pressing his thumbs into the bridge of his nose. The rabbi urged him to say he would try, that he'd work with her to save their marriage, but nothing. Only silence. Was he already gone?

In the midst of Tom's midlife crisis, no one had seen it coming. Not Tom's friends, not their family, and least of all Mary. She hated surprises, and he hit her with the surprise of a lifetime.

SHE HAD OVERHEARD him on the phone in the den from her overstuffed brown lounge chair in the living room.

"Hello? . . . I can't talk . . . No, I'll call you."

"Who was that, pumpkin?" she called to Tom.

"Uh, Jerry," he called back. "We're trying to schedule a round of golf for tomorrow."

"What time? We have the shrink tomorrow."

A pause.

"Can you . . . go without me?"

She stewed for a minute. Her throat tightened around words she hesitated to say. Her teeth ground together as heat built in her chest. Mary thumped down her copy of *Seed to Seed* and marched into the den, leaned up against his desk. "This is important, Tom."

"I know, but so is Jerry. Just this once?"

She stared at him, folded her arms, and slid back farther, nudging a pile of receipts out of place with her backside. She reached down to straighten them, but Tom grabbed them and stuffed the rumpled pile into a drawer.

"The Fairmont?" Mary said, registering the letterhead on one of the receipts.

"Yeah, business lunch."

"That's a pretty expensive lunch, Tom." She waited for an answer. Ideas rolled through her head, raced toward one conclusion. "It isn't lunch, is it?"

She went numb when he slowly pushed himself back from the desk, stood up, and, without meeting her eyes, announced that he had fallen in love with a woman at the golf course. At first, she couldn't track his words. Then she started to recall his odd behavior. How had she missed it? The late nights and long weekends away were obvious calling cards of an affair. How could she have been so stupid?

And this woman. Was it better or worse that she hadn't met her? What was she like? When did they meet? She started to ask Tom how long ago it had started, but emotions overcame her, and she found herself vomiting into his office wastebasket instead.

Befuddlement turned to fury. Mary raged. She broke every dish in the house. She threw furniture across the room, anything she could lift. She even threw his TV out the window. Tom was lucky to get out with only a bruised knee, which happened when he leapt for cover from a flying Cuisinart.

He yelled from the street as he limped to his car, "And you wonder why I'm leaving you!"

MARY SAT UP now from where she had fallen, mallow in hand, spat the dirt from her lips, and tried to shake off the memories of her old life. Was she about to lose everything again, here at Vista Mar? Would Bernice take it all away?

She heard shuffling behind her coming down the pathway. She twisted around in the mulch to find Ralph rumbling toward her plot like an oversized toddler with a basket full of flowers. He looked up from the ground and noticed her sitting there. Smiling, he reached into the basket and lifted a gerbera daisy from the top of a bouquet.

"My, Ralph, those are beautiful."

"Here's one for you . . . Madame President." He held out the gerbera while Mary struggled to her feet. He tried to extend his other hand to help her up, but she was out of reach and, instead, he leaned too far and tipped his basket. Colorful flowers tumbled out. Ralph grunted as he bent down to gather them, his thick hands fumbling with the stems. When he stood up and regained his composure, he held three gerbera daisies in one hand, so he handed the whole bunch to Mary.

"Wait, they've counted the ballots already?"

"I did, yes, ma'am."

Mary cringed. "And was it close?"

"You won by a landslide."

Mary's shoulders dropped a few inches and she released a deep, pent-up sigh.

"Mazel tov," he said.

"Thank you." She twiddled the daisies in her hand as she let it sink in. "I didn't expect to be so relieved."

"Did you really think Bernice would win?" Ralph asked.

"I don't know. People complain all the time. It's hard to know how they really feel about . . . about the work we do here."

"They obviously chose the best person for the job."

Mary breathed another deep sigh and nodded. "Damn straight." She looked up at Ralph and smiled. "My kids will be relieved, too. They said I'd be a pain in the tuchus if I didn't have all you folks to boss around."

Ralph laughed. "Your kids are smart. It's Benjamin, right? And . . . ?"

"Sarah. Yeah, they know me pretty well." Mary held up the flowers to admire. "I don't suppose you could spare a couple more of these? I'd like to give them to my grandkids when I see them this afternoon."

"Sure thing." Ralph handed Mary the entire bundle of gerberas.

"The little one likes to play he-loves-me, he-loves-me-not." Mary looked over the flowers, then suddenly had a realization. "You know what this means, Ralph?"

He looked at her, perplexed. "No."

"It means that Bernice is going to be a royal pain in my ass, worse than before."

Ralph asked, "Has she always been like this?"

"No." Mary blew through her lips. "Bernie and I used to be friends. But I guess she didn't like me as president. Things changed after that. I don't know why."

"Well, maybe you two will work it out someday."

Mary laughed. "I doubt it, but it's a nice thought, Ralph."

Ned poured himself an afternoon cup from the decrepit coffee machine in the main shed. He put the lid on the pot, careful to hold the cracked pieces together while he wiggled it back in place. Ned ran a finger over the tattered masking tape to smooth the twenty-year-old label.

"Still makes a good cup of coffee." He closed the door of the shed, then stepped into the pathway to look out over the garden. His straw hat shaded his eyes against the sun, still lingering above the ocean. Five thirty P.M. and no sign of sunset.

As he zipped up his jacket, he thought, *Gotta love these midspring days.* His Champagne grapes would be setting fruit soon.

His thoughts were interrupted when he heard the clank of the gate at the top of the hill. He spotted two men in dark suits, one smiling, one not. Someone had left the gate open, so they walked right in. Ned's coffee kicked in; his heart raced. He set his mug down on a tree stump by the pathway and trekked up the hill to meet them.

They looked over the vast expanse of the garden, unsure which way to go. One of the men saw Ned hurrying toward them and reached into his briefcase.

Ned struggled to catch his breath. "Can I help you?"

"We're looking for the garden master—Ned Flossman, I believe."

"That's me." Ned adjusted his straw hat.

"Sir, we're here to deliver this on behalf of our client." The smiling man stepped forward. Despite his smile, he seemed reluctant as he extended a blank manila envelope toward Ned.

Ned reached out to take it, then stopped. "What's this all about?"

"We're not at liberty to say. We're only required to deliver the document."

Ned took the envelope and peeked inside; he noticed legal-looking numbers on the page. "Hang on. If you have official business, you should give this to our chair."

The stern-faced man stepped forward. "We've already . . . spoken to your chair. We decided you were a suitable replacement, as it stands."

The look on the man's face triggered Ned's memory. He recalled Mary's story about two suits who had shown up at the garden earlier in the year. This didn't look good.

"We'll see you soon, Mr. Flossman," the stern-faced man said before he turned to leave.

The smiling man lingered. His smile faded. "I'm sorr—"

His partner called to him from the gate. The smiling man gave Ned a sober look, then walked through the gate, leaving it standing open. Ned pulled a single sheet of paper from the envelope.

"What the heck?" Ned scanned the paper flapping in his hand, trying to piece it all together. After he had filtered through the legalese, his eyes went back up the page and settled on the title of the document: NOTICE OF EVICTION.

He didn't need to keep reading to get the gist: the city had revoked their protections and reclaimed the property to sell it to a prospective buyer, Kurt Arnold. Effective December 31, end of this year. At least he was giving them plenty of notice.

Vista Mar Gardens had made a few enemies in its day, and plenty of people filed complaints. The board had always tried to work out disagreements with neighbors in the past. Ned knew Kurt wished the garden had never existed in the first place, but he didn't realize the man would go to these lengths to get rid of it.

Ned felt the blood drain from his face; his hands tingled. The truth penetrated through to his bones. *It's happened. After all these years, they're taking it back.* He reached out toward the chain-link fence, but it moved away from him. He fell forward a few inches before his hand hit the fence. His trembling fingers clutched the familiar crosshatch of galvanized wire.

Ned turned toward the sun, toward the acres of garden plots sloping down to the street below, toward his second home for over thirty years. He tried to picture it as it looked when this all started: barren land with a few enthusiastic volunteers growing their first crops; the hope and excitement when they mapped out those first plots with pieces of scrap wood, when they determined where to put compost and garden waste bins.

We've come so far. Now it's over.

He couldn't imagine a day without coming here, having nothing to do that made a difference. Without the garden, the meaninglessness of day-to-day life would brush him away, like eraser dust swept off a page. And no more tomatoes. He looked down at the fluttering piece of paper, so sterile and unsympathetic. How could something so flimsy deliver such crushing news?

A moment later, Ned felt light-headed and disoriented. *Are we having an earthquake?* His knees gave out and he teetered off balance, lurching face-first into the fence, his hand still clutching the wire. He struggled to open his heavy eyes. His body slid to the ground as the paper in his hand fluttered away into the bushes. He watched it disappear as he drifted into unconsciousness.

CHAPTER 12
Citations

Late April

Blustery wind pelted Sharalyn's blue Bronco with rain as she drove up the hill. Windshield wipers slapped back and forth to clear her view of the dim, drenched landscape ahead. Driving up to the garden at sunset in rare but precious wet weather inspired both dread and excitement—dread because the biting hillside winds threatened to tear through the one winter coat she owned and chill her fingers until they were numb and fumbling; and excitement because she knew storms did wonders for garden produce. Though frost never swept the coast, this storm was the closest thing. She ran down the mental list of crops in her garden that would thrive in this weather.

The high-pitched howl of the wind intensified as she crested the hill. She felt goose bumps rise under her coat. Dread, definitely dread. Sharalyn turned the corner and confirmed that, sure enough, the gate had blown open. She cursed her rotten luck, volunteering for gate closing during the rainy season. Figured the rains would be over by April. Though she supposed she should be grateful for the rain, and that there was still a garden to check on, after all that business with Mary and the lawyers a couple months back.

She sat for a few minutes in the warm—well, warmer—car to wait for a quieter moment in the storm.

Might as well check on my garden since I'm here.

She pulled her industrial rain slicker up one arm over her coat. Before wrapping it around her body, she paused, steeling herself for the great outdoors. *This is no worse than any storm on the sea, plus I'll have my feet on the ground.* She spied another car in the parking lot. Dang, she'd have to hunt them down and kick them out. *It's sunset, people. Garden closes at sunset.* She pulled up the other sleeve, flipped up the hood, and slipped out her car door.

Sharalyn entered through the open gate, closing it behind her, and crossed the hill to her plot. She walked between a row of broccoli and her cabbage patch. Rain beaded up on the waxy leaves, weighing them down. The pea trellis still stood upright, but gusts of wind sweeping from the west thrashed her tower of peas from side to side. She inspected them, decided they were secure enough to last out the storm. She wrestled a few pods from the vine and stuffed all but one in her pocket for later snacking. Rain-drenched peas tasted different at sea, not at all as satisfying as this. The crunch would be deafening were it not for the wind.

She surveyed other nearby plots and noted a few trellises blown over, but for the most part, the garden was handling the storm well. Sharalyn fished shears out of her mailbox and snipped a handful of broccoli side shoots, sprouted after she'd harvested the main head last week. She held the shoots together in a bouquet, put her drenched shears back in the dry mailbox, and left to inspect the perimeter gates.

After checking the padlocks on each gate surrounding the garden, Sharalyn sent a quick email to Ned about a malfunctioning lock. She walked up the hill to secure the office and main shed. As she reached up for the roll door at the shed's entrance, the unmistakable stench of urine and filth wafted past her.

"Aw, hell," Sharalyn muttered under her breath. She crept up the ramp to lean through the doorway. Sure enough, there in the back corner, fast asleep under a layer of tattered blankets and cardboard, lay that homeless man. *Not again.* Standard procedure was to call the police. She hadn't expected to have to call today.

She reached into her pocket to extract her cell phone from the clump of cold, wet pea pods. The number for the local police was printed on a laminated card on the shed wall next to the emergency number for the plumber, in case anyone broke a water line. The sleeping man snorted when she leaned over him to read the number. The odor was so strong, she swore it changed the temperature of the room. She stepped outside, around the corner to stand underneath the eaves and dial. She put on her "white lady" voice, hoping that would get them there quicker, or at all, for that matter. From her vantage point, Sharalyn glimpsed someone else in the distance—a woman in a white raincoat, bent over a plot under the wobbly shelter of an umbrella—but she couldn't discern who it was in the dim light. Must be the same person who was parked in the lot. Hopefully she would leave without needing a talking-to. The rain eased up as the operator answered the call.

HALF AN HOUR later, the police arrived to escort the homeless man to a shelter. Sharalyn was chilled through by then. Arthur, they said his name was, gathered his belongings while he mumbled to himself, or possibly to someone else. The police officers wore blue surgical gloves that stood out against their standard-issue rain slickers. They were patient as the man collected his things. Sharalyn stepped outside to get some fresh air and spied the woman in the raincoat approaching to investigate. It was Bernice, clutching the raincoat closed under her umbrella.

"Is everything all right?" Bernice said.

"Yes, ma'am. We'll be out of your way in a minute," one of the officers looked up long enough to say.

Sharalyn said, "The gate's unlocked, so you can go on out the way you came in."

The officers continued to gather up the man and his belongings, while he struggled to appear sober.

"I got it, I got it," Arthur slurred, trying to fold his blanket.

One officer reached in to speed things up, but Arthur held up his hand. "I do this all the time, Officer. I got it all figured out." A rumbling belch escaped his lungs as he bent forward to pick up his cardboard and blanket.

"I'm tryin' to help," Arthur continued. "These people, they don't take care of their stuff. They let things die. They don't water, so I do it for them." He went on. "I found a hose doohickey in someone's mailbox once. I use it when I come here, and not just to shower, okay?"

Sharalyn dropped her head, mortified by the image of this man hosing down her tomatoes from overhead. That would explain all the early blight last year.

Without warning, the homeless man choked up. His eyes softened, grew watery. "There's a spot in the corner, up by the Andy Gump . . ." He leaned in toward the officers. "I found some flowers laying around, so I planted them near the john to make it prettier. They oughta thank me."

Sharalyn debated whether to say something about the watering. *You're trespassing, Arthur*, came to mind, but she watched the man's face light up when he described his makeshift beautification project. She almost thanked him. The porta-potty did look nicer these days.

After twenty minutes spent waiting for him to gather up his meager possessions, Sharalyn watched the police officers walk the homeless man along the pathway, past Bernice, toward the exit. Bernice lowered her eyes.

As he shuffled along, Arthur looked up and smiled a toothless grin. "Bye, Bernice."

Bernice stood with her umbrella tucked into the crook of her arm. She waved a few fingers at him and wedged them back into the fold of her elbow. Arthur and the officers turned up the hill, went through the gate, and disappeared over the crest.

Sharalyn wondered what that was all about. Minding her own business, she turned back to ask "Friend of yours?" but Bernice had vanished.

When Sharalyn left through the gate, she noted the police car still on-site. Bernice stood next to the squad car talking with the officers as they jotted down notes. Did Bernice have more than a casual acquaintance with that homeless man? The icy wind nudged Sharalyn toward her truck, deciding for her that now was not the best time to find out.

Mary stared into the eyes of the twentysomething office receptionist, looking for an in. "I need to speak to the mayor," she said, shaking her dripping umbrella onto the carpet.

The assistant held up a hand to block water from splattering her paperwork and let out an exasperated sigh. "Do you have an appointment?"

"No, but he's going to sell my garden out from under me, and I'm here to stop him."

The receptionist plucked several tissues from a box on her desk corner and blotted a stack of papers. "The mayor is very busy. I'm sure you understand."

"It's on a list." Mary leaned over the desk. "He can't sell it. Do *you* understand *that*?"

The receptionist glared. "I'm calling security if you don't lower your voice."

Mary drew a long, slow breath and said in a whisper, "Is this better? Maybe you can help me. I'm trying to figure out why the city would sell off a property that's on the no-sale list. It's very important to about a thousand people and the mayor is obligated to help me. Now."

The receptionist blinked twice and gave Mary the look of someone humoring an old lady. But it was edged with fear. "Let me see what I can do."

When Mary had found Ned lying slumped against the fence a couple weeks back, awake but dazed, she knew change was coming. Ned had insisted he was fine, and instead of allowing Mary to call an ambulance, directed her attention to the hedge where the eviction notice sat wedged in between two branches. She'd read the document, swallowed hard, and made a pact with Ned that they would keep it to themselves until they resolved the issue. There had to be a way out. After several failed attempts to secure an appointment with the mayor, she had opted to try a different strategy.

The receptionist picked up the phone, dialed, and waited. She covered the mouthpiece. "What's your name?"

"Mary Burcham from Vista Mar Community Garden."

"Hi. I have Mary Burcham from Vista Mar Community Garden here? It's about a property on the no-sale list? . . . Wait, what? . . . Okay."

She brandished her bleached-white teeth at Mary and, before she even hung up the phone, said, "The mayor is unavailable, but he did give me a message. He said, 'You're lucky we're not pressing charges.' So here's what I'd suggest"—she handed Mary a business card—"email a message to the office and we'll make sure he gets it." She poised her finger on the phone's red security button. "Have a nice day."

Word gets around, Mary thought. *Best not to throw a fit here. It won't help my cause, and I'll probably get arrested.* She gave her umbrella another good shake and nodded to the girl.

"See you soon."

After the rain stopped and the storm clouds receded inland toward the mountains, gardeners came out with the sun to inspect their plots. Cars full of anxious members crested the driveway, all craning their necks to see whether their tall crops and trellises had withstood the storm. Lizzie had a clear view of her plot through the fence as she drove in. Her tomato cages hadn't taken flight, as they had in the last storm. She sighed with relief knowing she wouldn't have to search for the plastic-covered cages in the nearby field.

The garden smelled of sweet earth. The scent of rain-drenched soil drew Lizzie in, gave her every reason in the world to forget about the rest of her dreary day. She stepped up into her plot and set her harvest basket and tool bag next to a patch of Swiss chard. How happy the plants looked. Their bright leaves sparkled in the sun, squeaky clean from nature's shower. This was the best time to harvest, right after a rain. Lizzie felt the damp mulch saturate her jeans when she knelt to pick bright yellow and pink stems.

Tempted by everything she saw, she picked crisp vegetables to her heart's content. She gathered her treasures in her harvest basket, brushed mud off her knees, and stepped out of her plot. As she walked back to her car, the idea struck her: *When's the last time you did a walk-through?*

Calculating that it had been at least a month, she returned to her plot, set down her basket, and pulled her yellow booklet of citations from her tool bag.

She walked along each row, checked pathways and plots for weeds or other infractions of the rules and regs. It wasn't the kindest thing to write a citation after a storm. After all, everyone assumed a rainy day meant a free pass. She entered the row near Jared's plot and noticed tufts of shin-high weeds off in the distance. The closer she got, the worse it looked. His pea trellis was improperly installed—right up against the border between his plot and his neighbor's. Her stomach knotted when she located the pile of wood and tools in the corner, also against the rules.

"Giving rats a perfect place to live." Too many infractions to choose from, she didn't know where to start. Did he not read the *Rules and Regs*? Or was he pushing the boundaries because he'd taken his section rep out for dinner? Memories of that moment during their date flashed through her mind.

"*. . . the trick is to get in good with the section rep . . .*"

"That's your strategy?"

She walked past the plot, scribbled a note on the back of her citation booklet to email him about the mess. Then she stopped.

No, you can't make exceptions. This is exactly what you didn't want to deal with.

He had said something about going up north for a few weeks to work on a kitchen installation, but he'd been gone much longer than that. Sure, she missed him, but he didn't call during his travels, and it was obvious he hadn't arranged for anyone to tend his plot when he left.

The whole thing left Lizzie heavy with dread. Was she supposed to let this go? It wasn't fair to the other gardeners, who would suffer when his dandelions burst into seed, to make excuses for him. *Well, this would make it clear, wouldn't it?*

She backed up to Jared's plot and flipped over her citation booklet, pulled a yellow slip of paper to the front over the fold. She sighed and stood for a moment, pen poised over the page. *Don't mess with Section Rep Lizzie.* His own words.

Pen met paper, checking boxes down the page. Weeds, check. Improperly stored tools, check. Other, check. She wrote on the line that followed: "Trellis too close to neighbor." Below it she added, "Don't make me do this again."

She tore the page from the booklet and jammed it into Jared's mailbox, which overflowed with gloves, hose nozzles, who knows what else. She closed the mailbox and flipped up the red flag. Every nagging thought from that night after Dolly's came flooding back.

Why didn't you listen to yourself? You knew this would piss you off. Keep the lines drawn; it's the only way you'll be happy.

She played the scene in her head: They would fall in love, he'd take advantage of her position, they'd break up, then she'd dread coming to the garden. She'd spend all her energy there avoiding encounters with Jared. He'd make it impossible for her to feel comfortable. He'd ruin everything. The only solution was to not get involved at all. Simple as that.

Disappointed and suddenly tired, she returned to her plot to gather her things and head home. When she neared the top of the hill, the sound of voices grew louder. A heated conversation? For a second, she strategized how to cut across a row of plots and exit through a different gate, but she recognized the voices of Bernice and Ned. Bernice was doing most of the talking, her British cadence crisp as a frosty morning.

"It simply isn't fair, Ned." Her frustration built on each word. "If everyone in the garden is expected to use the compost we create, everyone must have access to the compost! It's gone before anyone is notified of a fresh bin, and those of us who don't think to check daily would rather go to the nursery and buy bags of compost than settle for the dregs that are left. I'll tell you something else. People don't necessarily buy certified organic compost. I've watched some awful stuff come through that gate, sewage sludge and all."

Ned couldn't get a word in, though he tried.

"We were promised years ago that finished compost would be announced via email, but that never happened. It's been over three years since that thin proclamation was made, and I don't mind saying that it makes you and Mary look ridiculous that you can't fulfill a simple promise to this community." Bernice was on a roll. "Well, Mary looks ridiculous all the time, but that's another matter.

"It's bad enough that I have to make excuses every time someone asks me when the broken locks on the gates will actually work. People keep coming in here to steal citrus off my trees. How hard can it be, Ned, to keep a store of working padlocks in the office for expressly this situation?"

She paused for a second, time enough for Ned to rev up his Boston drawl.

"Now, Bernice, I need you to be patient. There are more important issues going on right now."

"Like what?"

Ned opened his mouth to say something, then hesitated for a beat. "Never mind. We've done our best to replace the locks as they get reported, but if no one says anything, how do I know they're broken?"

"That's the point, Ned. If you had installed those additional floodlights that the board approved back in November this wouldn't happen. I'm sick and tired of playing this lengthy waiting game with every request. Leaving notes in mailboxes only works if you check your mailbox, Ned, and not everyone does. Can't we implement a phone tree or something more effective? If Mary isn't going to take the initiative, we must elect someone who will. This cannot continue."

Bernice's fiery gaze shifted toward Lizzie, catching her eye. Ned turned to see where Bernice looked. This was the last thing Lizzie wanted to get involved in today. *Where's an invisibility cloak when you need one?* Lizzie scanned Ned's furrowed brow from where she stood. She couldn't tell whether she should rescue him or not.

"Lizzie! Come here a minute." Ned reeled her in like a life raft.

Ugh. She took a deep breath and smiled. "Sure, Ned."

Ned's strategy didn't go unnoticed. Bernice folded her arms and let out a gruff sigh. She looked as though she was trying to regain her composure in case Lizzie hadn't witnessed their argument.

"What's up?" Lizzie pretended she hadn't just walked in on *There Will Be Blood.*

Ned appeared less than his usual enthusiastic self. "I've been meaning to ask you: Have you noticed any broken locks in your section of the garden? We're trying to figure out how nonmembers keep getting in."

Lizzie shook her head. "As far as I can tell, they're all in working order. I'll double-check though. Was there another break-in?"

"Well"—he waved his thumb toward Bernice—"it appears that Bernice's orange trees were cleaned out again."

"Isn't the gate closer supposed to report any broken locks?" Lizzie said.

Bernice jumped in, all composure abandoned: "Yes, that's exactly what they're supposed to do, but they're lazy! We should dock their community hours if they can't complete that simple task."

"Hang on a second," Ned said, propping his hands on his hips. "Sharalyn reported a broken lock just a couple weeks ago. She emailed me a letter."

Bernice hammered on. "Then what happened, Ned?"

Ned scowled. "I need to remember to forward those emails to the repair guys. I'm having trouble keeping track of things lately, to be honest. There's a lot going on."

Lizzie had an idea. "Maybe the gate closers should carry a clipboard they pick up in the office before doing their rounds. If we make a diagram of all the gates, they can mark an 'X' for any gate with a tricky lock. It will also keep people from bailing on their shift. Make them sign in and out on the same clipboard. Then the repair guys can just check the clipboard and you don't have to worry about it."

"Finally, a voice of reason." Bernice let show the slightest hint of a smile.

"We'll try it." Ned nodded at Bernice. "I'll draw something up today. We'll make an announcement in the newsletter."

"You're not off the hook yet, Ned. You still haven't answered me about the compost and the floodlights."

"I'll make sure the floodlights are up by the end of the month, okay? Then we'll tackle the compost. There's a lot on my list, Bernice. Be patient."

Lizzie bowed out, saying, "I'm going to put this Swiss chard in some water."

Ned thanked Lizzie, giving her a look of relief.

"All in a day's work," she said to him under her breath.

She opened the car door, set the harvest basket on the floor of the passenger side, and settled into the comfort of the sun-warmed seat before driving down the hill.

It was nice to feel appreciated. It almost made up for the citation burning a hole in Jared's mailbox.

CHAPTER 13

Spring Fever

May

Lizzie couldn't ignore her heart pounding in her chest as she clambered up the hill from the street. Was it anxiety? No, but whatever it was, she fervently wished it away. She scanned her body for a sliver of calm to grab on to but found none.

No matter how much the pollution or stress of living in a big city affected her, Lizzie could always count on a picturesque sunset from Vista Mar Gardens to ease her mind. Outsiders also came up at sunset to take in the view. Typical Angelenos, they sat in their cars to watch the sun dip below the horizon. After the show, they'd start the engine and pull out of the dirt field, on to the rest of their evening. Lizzie never had the heart to tell them they were trespassing. Everyone should be allowed to stop and enjoy the sunset.

On this clear evening in May, Lizzie desperately needed that sunset's calming effect. She sat on the edge of her plot's retaining wall, planted her boots in the layer of pine mulch, and took a deep breath. The sun's warm rays shone red orange through her closed eyelids.

After counting to five, she exhaled and opened her eyes. It was longing, this feeling, she realized. Desire. And for no good reason, except that it was May. Spring fever. It had been so long since she had felt anything resembling passion, she didn't recognize it. Out of the corner of her eye, she identified a familiar car leaving the garden. *Jared? Just missed him. Probably better that way.* She wanted the garden to herself. She hadn't talked to him since the citation, but he'd sent an email painting himself as awkward and embarrassed, which in turn, had the same effect on her. Sometimes avoidance was best.

As colors deepened in the sky, she understood the grim truth: the sunset wasn't working. Her walk to the garden from her apartment hadn't calmed her down. And now this. The air in her lungs thinned out, her heart rate climbed once more. Inexplicable desire? *Damn hormones.*

Her mind turned to the classic 1995 BBC production of *Pride and Prejudice*, which she had stayed up late watching the night before. She replayed the moments between Elizabeth Bennet and Mr. Darcy—Colin Firth's smoldering passion restrained behind his prideful, upper-class demeanor. Despite his repulsion at Elizabeth's family and station, he can't talk himself out of his desperate love for her. The tension between them is so delicious, entwined with desire—he's undone by it all. Watching it, Lizzie swooned.

The residual emotions lingered all day, overtaking her at odd moments. At lunch, she'd found herself breathless. Then it occurred to her that she was fantasizing about being swept away by some version of Mr. Darcy. Oh, how she longed for someone to profess passionate proclamations of love to her, how she longed to indulge in that kind of passion herself. She was suddenly Elizabeth. There was Mr. Darcy taking her in his arms, his fingers tangled in her hair, staring into her eyes and confessing his love for her despite all attempts to quell it.

When has that ever happened? Not with Dylan, or anyone else for that matter. Sure, it had been a passionate affair, but she worried the whole time and couldn't enjoy it. She ached to experience total abandon, to shut off her brain and savor love's reckless excitement.

Lizzie choked down the thick lump in her throat, pressed her hand to her chest to calm her galloping heart. She looked down at her feet and forced them deeper into the mulch. *Stay grounded. Stop feeling sorry for yourself. That's only a story. This is reality. Be present.*

Just when her resolve had begun to strengthen, she saw someone walk up from the gate at the street. Jared. Her heart sank. Or was that elation? She wasn't sure which she wanted to feel. Her pulse quickened; the frivolous exercise of digging her feet into the soil had accomplished nothing. She scrambled to stop herself from floating. She pretended she hadn't spotted

Jared until he waved. What was he doing here? Hadn't he left? Her inner battle continued like a tennis match.

I've got to go. No, you don't.

I'm defenseless. It's okay.

Oh God, why now? This is perfect timing.

His smile exhausted her. Not really, but she felt her insides tighten when his lips parted.

"Hey there!" He swung his backpack over his shoulder to free up his hands for a hug. When she stood up, he wrapped his arms around her, gave her a solid squeeze.

"Hey," she said. He smelled of fresh laundry. She wanted to curl up into a ball. "Did you forget something?"

"Oh, I was just moving my car—makes watching the sunset easier without the gate closer breathing down my neck. I hoped I'd run into you, but I didn't see your car."

"I walked," she said.

"Perfect." He slid his backpack off his shoulder. As they sat down, Jared slid his hand down her spine, coming to rest above the two dimples at the small of her back. Lizzie scooted over to make more room for him.

The hair on her neck stood up when his thumb brushed across her shirt. She tried to stay in the moment—not let her mind run away. "You might want to water your plot before the sun sets. The gate closer is lurking nearby."

"That's been taken care of." He smiled. "I came back for the company."

Lizzie's stomach squeezed. The voice in her head said, *You are so screwed.*

They sat in silence, watching the sun sink toward the ocean.

He cleared his throat. "I cleaned up my plot."

"I saw that. Thank you." *Keep the lines drawn, mister. You: gardener; me: section rep.*

Hard to rationalize with that warm hand on her back, though. The bottom edge of the sun's glowing orb met the horizon.

"Have you ever come here at night?" Jared said.

Lizzie smiled. "No, it's illegal."

"Oh come on!"

"Oh come on, what? The garden closes at sunset. You know that. It's in your *Rules and Regs*."

"Yes, but haven't you ever come here after dark? I mean, we all have a key."

Lizzie pursed her lips and paused a second before she nodded. "Yes. But only to pick one of my lemons for dinner. Once."

He pointed an accusing finger. "Aha!"

Lizzie shot him a flirty glance and shrugged.

"What's it like?" he asked. He leaned over to nudge her shoulder with his.

"Very dark. The ambient light from the street doesn't reach the plots at all." She searched for the right words. "It's a different world. Strange noises. The familiar is unfamiliar. It was a little scary."

"I've always wanted to be here to see what goes on." He paused.

Lizzie said nothing, but in the silence her mind spun out of control.

At last, Jared spoke up: "Let's stay here tonight."

"What?"

He grabbed her hand. "It'll be fun."

Lizzie tried to argue, but as much as she compelled herself to put on her section rep hat to follow the rules and regs, she could only focus on Jared's hand holding hers. She wished her whole body was inside that hand. Yearnings for her Mr. Darcy came rushing back. Besides, she had always wanted to experience the garden after dark. Her brief visit for a lemon years ago was exactly that—brief. She had run in and out, hoping not to attract attention, her car parked right outside the driveway gates. This time she had walked; no car to worry about.

"Come on." Jared stood up, picked up his backpack, and pulled Lizzie to her feet. He led her by the hand down the hill. "We'll hide behind the compost until the gate closer's gone."

Lizzie's legs moved of their own accord. She found herself sitting behind the compost bins when the sun finally dipped below the horizon. Jared nestled his backpack between his legs and unzipped the main pocket, pulling out an ultrathin, high-tech camping blanket. No, two.

Lizzie's mouth dropped open. "You totally planned this, didn't you?"

Jared grinned and reached into the bag, pulling out two plastic cups and a bottle of wine.

She burst out laughing, but managed to sputter out, "Double infraction! No alcohol on the premises."

"I know." His grin widened, accented by a raised eyebrow.

"You're such a scofflaw." She laughed.

Jared uncorked the bottle with a flourish. He handed her a clear plastic cup and poured until she motioned him to stop. He poured his own drink and tucked the bottle into the dirt. They leaned against the wooden wall of the compost bin. The smell of fecund earth surrounded them, and warmth from decomposing organic matter emanated from the wood, taking the chill off the evening.

"Cheers," he said.

Lizzie shook her head. "To scofflaws."

Jared laughed. They drank.

The garden came alive at night with a new cast of characters unseen during the day. Birds retreated into the trees, while crickets ventured out. A few bats swept the sky in search of wayward insects, and Lizzie swore she could overhear snails make their slimy procession across a nearby lettuce patch. The sounds of traffic dwindled, and a calm descended over the garden. Streetlamps along the road cast an orange glow into the sky, but the plants in the garden were engulfed by the murky black of night.

"It's strange not to be able to see anything. I'm used to knowing where everything is," Lizzie said.

"You have to trust that it's still there." Jared rummaged in his backpack for something.

"What are you doing?"

"Hang on . . . Aha!" Lizzie heard a click. Jared dangled a headlamp from his raised hand. "Wanna explore what's out there?"

"Nice," she said. *Impressive*, she thought. They stood and

shuffled toward the orchard. "Maybe we'll catch the horn-worms decimating my tomato plants."

As they passed through the orchard, Jared triggered a security floodlight. Darkness vanished in an instant and they both froze. She wasn't sure if it was just a floodlight, or the new light with a camera Ned had mentioned. Lizzie pictured their shadows being captured on the live security feed. They darted out of the light and stopped, safe in the darkness once more. Lizzie exhaled with relief. A few steps farther toward Lizzie's plot, something scurried across their path.

Jared grabbed Lizzie's arm. "Holy crap!"

While they searched the darkness for whatever it was, the floodlight behind them tripped on. One of the resident feral cats skittered through the light beam and bolted for a hidden target.

Lizzie patted Jared's hand, which still gripped her arm. They both burst out laughing, then proceeded down the path.

The nightlife of insects was much more active than she had imagined. It was almost meditative to watch these movements. Sow bugs crawled over plants in vast numbers, scurrying to the underside of the leaves to avoid Jared's beam of light, or rolling up into tiny armored spheres. Other bugs didn't mind observation. Jared and Lizzie stood over her plot, staring at a patch of calendula flowers where they found two ladybugs mating. Two red dots stacked one on top of the other, rocking back and forth. The event ended quickly, but it left a lingering impression on Lizzie.

"Sex in the garden." The words came out of her mouth unguarded. "They've got the right idea."

Jared's hands encircled her waist. He turned her body toward him and took off his headlamp, leaving them in darkness. Lizzie's heart raced. She ran her hand along his chest, felt the heat of his neck when she brushed her fingers through his hair. Jared pulled her in and pressed his cheek against hers. She felt his lips on her neck, her cheek, her lips.

Hormones overtook reason. Lizzie's logical brain told her that she should keep him at a distance, keep the garden as her safe refuge, but her body had been without touch for so long, she couldn't stop herself.

She dove in, tugged at his T-shirt, pressed herself to him. They made out like teenagers. She pulled Jared's shirt over his head. He did the same for her.

Lizzie stopped, breathing hard. "Wait a second."

"What's the matter?"

"I need that blanket."

Jared chuckled. He kissed her while laughing and nudged her backward down the pathway. She stepped back as he shuffled his sneakers forward between her feet.

"Come on. We'll find it somewhere." He stretched out his arms mimicking a sleepwalker in the dark, entwining Lizzie's body, sweeping her along with him.

Lizzie giggled and almost fell to the ground. His humor relaxed her.

After a few steps, he picked her up. She wrapped her legs

around him and he found his way back to the blankets behind the compost bin, where they were alone together, like the other creatures of the garden.

As THE FAINTEST touch of pink began to color the morning sky, they awoke. Dew had settled over the garden, leaving the plants and grasses fresh with the heaviness of moisture. Under the blanket, arms and legs tangled, they stayed warm and dry, but Lizzie's damp hair made her shiver with a chill. Jared stroked her arm.

"I've always wanted to do that," she said.

"Which, stay here at night or . . . ?"

"Have sex in the garden."

"Really?" He propped himself up on one elbow. "And here I worried I was turning you into a scofflaw."

She laughed. "Well, you are. But I guess there's some of that there already."

They sat up, wrapped the blankets around them, and took in the view of the garden. The cool morning air gave way to the sun's warmth as the day began. Lizzie reached for her clothes. Then she tasted her stale wine mouth.

"I'd better get going." She scanned the main entrance for anyone arriving to open the gate.

"Don't want to get caught, right?" Jared said.

"Yeah. That would look—well, not good."

They dressed, gathered their things, and said their goodbyes behind the compost bin. Jared breathed in as he held Lizzie in one last embrace before departing. He kissed her and smiled. She smiled back, but anxiety pulled her away.

"I'll go first, okay?" she said.

Jared let out a laugh. "You're kidding, right?"

"No, it's better that way. In case someone's here." She already regretted saying it.

He shrugged. "Okay. We'll talk later?"

She nodded.

Lizzie looked around for gardeners before she walked the path to exit through the gate at the street. A small part of her didn't care. In fact, that part wanted everyone to see her. She glowed, she felt free. She walked toward home, still light from the evening. Her feet hovered above the ground at first, but as her brain kicked in, she began to settle back to earth.

Memories of Jared's touch lingered; she imagined his hands roaming across her body. But other, more rational worries interrupted. Would the garden feel different? Would she look for him every time she went there? Would he be there even when he wasn't there? *What if it all goes wrong?*

Her skin had goose bumps, her body pulsing alive in stark contrast to the indecision in her head. With each step, she felt more of the sidewalk through her shoes, every rock, every grain of sand. She passed a sketchy-looking shop that bore a nondescript name: the Past's Future. She'd noticed it on her way home for years and always wondered what went on in that ramshackle store, but she had never had the courage to go inside. Could be a palm reader; could be a drug den. Not going to find out which.

The earlier throes of passion began to feel misguided as reality set in.

What am I doing? This is crazy. One mixed emotion led to another, and negative thoughts started to snowball. The sweet sense-memories from the night before drifted further away, leaving behind twinges of panic, seeds of doubt. Lizzie put her hand to her head. *What if he loses interest and dumps me? What if I humiliate myself again?*

She attempted to slow the avalanche of doubts, of regrets piling up in her brain. *Stop, you're overreacting. It's going to be fine. You can do this. You can have a normal relationship and still keep clear boundaries, right?*

No, if something went wrong, she wouldn't be able to show her face. She would dread going to the garden, her one place to get away from everything, everyone. Going there would no longer be about the garden, but about this guy. Vista Mar would no longer be her sanctuary.

But what if he's the right guy?

Was it worth the risk to find out? She was used to being alone—comfortable with it, in fact. Did she need a relationship? Did he even want one? Good God. She couldn't lose the garden. Her refuge mattered more than companionship.

Her mental chatter was less convincing, though, while endorphins still coursed through her body. His hands on her hips, his breath on her neck, it had been such a long time since . . . But it wasn't worth it. Maybe if he left Vista Mar she could do this, but it wouldn't work otherwise. Personal life and garden life are separate. *It was a nice romp, but don't do that anymore. Too much trouble.*

An old but potent memory struck her. She flashed back to

high school and college, watching her friends pine for boy-friends; they believed they'd be miserable without a guy. She had found it sickening, really.

"If anyone can go through life without a partner, I can. After all, relationships get in the way of ambitions. Honestly, they're unnecessary." She bolstered herself, murmuring these familiar words while she crossed the street to her apartment building. *Time to pull that screenplay out of the drawer and get to work*, she thought.

By the time she reached the door of her apartment, she'd made her decision. She had gone from elation to caution to certainty in one quick mile. In the end she'd be happier. Now to figure out how to tell Jared there wouldn't be another garden rendezvous.

Not long after their night in the garden, Lizzie spied Jared in his plot. He bounded up the hill to greet her, unguarded in his enthusiasm. She braced herself through her smile. She had uncomfortable news to deliver.

"I had a nice time the other night," he said.

"Yes, it was nice."

"And I want to see you again." His voice rang with sweet confidence.

She let out a nervous giggle. "I do enjoy your company."

Get on with it, girl, her brain urged her as he reached out a hand toward her.

"Look, Jared . . ."

Whatever words she was about to say washed away in that

moment with the sensation of his skin against hers. He brushed her arm in the same way he had that night. She scanned the garden for anyone who might be watching them. They appeared to be alone.

Maybe this is okay, she thought. She was so confused. Her mouth wasn't doing what she wanted it to do. She had it all worked out, bullet-pointed and outlined. She'd almost brought a copy of it with her so she wouldn't screw up the delivery. Damn. Suddenly all her arguments for cutting off this affair, relationship, tryst, whatever it was, seemed stupid.

"You're too nice" was all that came out.

"You got a problem with that?" Jared stroked her hair.

Kryptonite. I'm butter. She reached up and kissed him. This hadn't gone at all as planned.

CHAPTER 14

Tomatoes

Late June

"Hey, Ned, I left you something in your mailbox." Ralph tried to subdue his excitement, but it was futile.

Ned looked up from his clipboard at Ralph's smug grin. "Already? You little son of a gun. You win every year."

"Aw, it's nothing."

Ned walked to his mailbox, eyes cutting back to Ralph the whole time, and pulled down the door to reveal a ripe Yellow Pear cherry tomato inside.

Ralph couldn't help himself. "First of the season. Well, second. I ate the first."

"Now you're bragging." Ned shook his head and smiled. "I'm sure I'll enjoy it. Now get out of here."

As summer approached, gardeners' anticipation shifted to full-tilt production. Most tomatoes were still green, the vines heavy with unripe orbs. Squash plants began to crowd out their neighbors, competing for space in the pathways. Yellow squash blossoms hummed each morning as worker bees flew from flower to flower, sticky with pollen, bringing life to the garden.

Beans reached toward the sky, sent out new shoots with tiny white flowers every day. Corn patches towered above other plantings, bringing symmetry to an array of eclectic gardens. Gardeners who planted their entire plots with corn did so in designated areas along the edges of each section. Long ago, the Vista Mar Gardens Board had quelled complaints that cornstalks shadowed neighboring gardens (as well as complaints from Kurt Arnold about the effect on his view) by creating these special growing areas. People could grow all the corn they wanted without blocking their neighbors' sun exposure.

Ralph spotted newfangled tomato cages dotting the landscape as well. Each year, a new trellising invention premiered in seed catalogs, and the newest gardeners at Vista Mar were first in line to test them. But he and other seasoned gardeners used traditional cages, a tried-and-true method. No experimentation necessary.

Peppers of all shapes set fruit. Slender chilies stood next to round bell peppers. It would be a while before they'd turn colors, but the hint of change already blushed the shoulders of some of the fruits. These were the benchmarks of summer. Gardeners came daily to observe whether their first tomato would be ready to pick.

They held an unspoken first-harvest competition each year, and Ralph would watch it unfold. Lizzie's reliable favorite was Stupice, a red heirloom salad tomato, always the first to produce in her plot, so she said. She had bragged to him once when she passed by with her basket. Would she flaunt her tomatoes past his plot this year? Okay, even in his head that sounded weird.

Mystery tomatoes sprouted from willful seeds in pathways, corners, or crevices. These volunteer tomatoes often produced early fruit. Ralph happened to notice that Lizzie had one in the corner of her plot. A cherry variety with marble-sized tomatoes that burst in your mouth with flavor, though he had to take her word for it; she never shared one of those. It ripened long before Stupice.

"Ha, take that, Stupice! Dethroned by a volunteer."

Ned swore by his Brandywines. Mary grew Jaune Flamme every year, knowing those orange beauties would grace her garden early in the season. Sharalyn didn't play the game at all, reminding the braggarts that good things come to those who wait. *Yeah, whatever.* She said her favorite was a tie between the good old Italian paste tomato, San Marzano, the only tomato used in Italian kitchens for sauce, and Prudence Purple, the pink beefsteak with purple-streaked shoulders.

Ralph reveled in his yearly victories. He relied on his Yellow Pear tomatoes to be the first to take the summer stage. The cheery teardrops were melted sunshine on the tongue. He anticipated the look on Ned's face every year, when he'd stash one in Ned's mailbox, just to tick him off. This unofficial competition meant he was unbeatable at least once per year.

Vista Mar's official tomato-tasting contest each August told a different story. Everyone got serious once Mary announced the contest date. There was much to do before then, before anyone brought a tomato to the table for judges to decide who, indeed, secured the coveted title of Tomato Champion. August was more than a month away, but gardeners planned ahead. They watered and fed, weeded and mulched their plants with the attention of experts. Though members typically maintained a strong sense of camaraderie, a routine secrecy developed among them as summer set in.

Sure, neighbors shared tips for how to keep lettuces from bolting to seed in the heat, and when to pick the first beans of the season. But everyone kept their tomato-growing secrets to themselves. Ralph hid his kelp emulsion in a paper bag so as not to reveal which brand he used. Ned had tried on numerous occasions to get Ralph to divulge his secret. No dice, Garden Master.

Gardeners tipped one another off when a new pile of compost opened for use. If word got out fast enough, the pile would disappear within two days. Ralph overheard Bernice complain to Ned one day about a lack of forewarning. He decided to spare Ned the trouble and help Bernice at the same time.

"Bernice, give me your cell-phone number. I'll text you when we open a new pile."

"Text? What is this text business?"

"Come on, you know what texting is, right?"

Bernice sighed. "Of course I do, dear. It's just a ridiculous form of communication. I could say a hundred things in the time it takes to type one sentence."

Ralph chuckled. "Don't you have a smartphone?"

"Heavens no, my phone is idiotic. I barely understand how to use it."

Ralph laughed. "I mean, can you check email or get text messages on it?"

Bernice fished her flip phone out of her pocket and handed it over. "You tell me, dear."

"No wonder you hate texting. This thing's a relic." Ralph analyzed her phone. "I'll show you how to check for messages. And I'll give you a heads-up when the compost is ready next time."

"You're a saint, Ralph. Maybe you should be garden master."

"Oh, no, Ned's doing a great job."

"That's a matter of opinion." Bernice paused, squinting at Ralph. "You remind me of my son when he was younger, dear."

"Oh, was he dorky, too?" Ralph dropped his chin and gazed toward the ground.

"No." Bernice became suddenly somber. "He was gentle and kind. But he's not anymore."

When he looked up, he saw Bernice sink into an emotional void, like she might start crying in front of him. He'd never seen her that way before. She was always so serious and, well, angry most of the time.

Ralph didn't know what to say. He felt sorry for Bernice,

but words fell short of expressing it. Instead he managed to say, "Anytime you need tech support, you let me know."

He handed back her phone and watched her wander off, distracted by old memories she didn't deem fit to share.

Ned stepped into the office in the main shed to find Mary squinting at the computer monitor. She appeared to be scrolling through the member roster.

"Whatcha looking for?" Ned bent forward to squint at the screen himself.

Mary replied, "Checking occupations to see if we've got any lawyers among our ranks." She jotted a few names down on a scrap of paper.

"Maybe we should look for paralegal folks, too," Ned added.

"What about Charlie? Would he know how to deal with this?"

"It was the first thing I thought of when I came to, that day." Ned scratched his head. "He's looking into it, but at first glance he said we probably can't fight it."

"Well, we owe it to everyone to try." Mary leaned back against a bookshelf and sighed. "I was thinking of going door-to-door to start rallying support from the neighborhood, but I don't know what good it will do."

"We've always kept our nose out of their business, so they may not care what happens to us."

Mary shrugged. "Worth asking?"

"Worth asking," Ned echoed.

Mary swiped the piece of paper from the counter and left.

June gloom: the gray marine layer that blocks out the morning sun, then evaporates after one o'clock. The moist, salty air often brought with it diseases, such as blight, wilt, or leaf spot, that wiped out a hopeful tomato grower's crop. Gardeners kept a watchful eye as the month progressed. They met any sign of disease with force—either drastic pruning, or spraying with an organic control. Some made their own homemade concoctions from stinging nettles or dish soap, while others relied on horticultural remedies that were approved for use in organic gardening by OMRI (Organic Materials Review Institute). Lizzie took a biological approach: become a steward of the soil food web. Feed your soil, and the soil microbes will take care of your plants. The right balance of microbes fights off blight and many other diseases nature throws in the mix. She had discovered years ago that fungal-dominant soil contained good fungi and bacteria to combat leaf blight, powdery mildew, and verticillium wilt. While others sprayed neem oil, she sprayed homemade compost tea, brewed in a five-gallon bucket with an air pump overnight. She didn't care if her neighbors thought she was weird. It brought her garden soil to life.

Impatience followed a gardener around in June, with its exciting yet frustrating sense of "we're almost there." Since Southern California gardeners had finished spring gardening in May, a month earlier, June—when the rest of the country harvested results from their spring crops—simply launched the long, hot journey toward fall.

Lizzie often wondered what would happen if she had to survive only on what she grew, without reliance on the grocery store to fill in gaps of the garden harvest. Since she had never figured out reliable succession-planting techniques to extend her harvest over a long period of time, weeks or months went by during the year with nothing to harvest. In June, she'd eat a handful of haricot vert beans, some Swiss chard, green tomatoes, and that was about it. She wanted, once and for all, to assemble a journal of charts, a clear plan for planting a few seeds at a time throughout the spring season, but every year, she panicked and planted every square inch of space all at once.

You'd think I'd have this down after twelve years.

She, along with many gardeners, felt a strong case of senioritis coming on. She knew it would hit Vista Mar soon. Kids were out of school, families were headed off on vacation, but this was no time for a gardener to leave. Still, Lizzie longed for a vacation and time away from garden duties. She wanted to ride a bicycle along the beach, or spend two weeks writing in a cabin in the Sierras, but her plot wasn't yet ready for her to leave. She became impatient for that time when she could put it on autopilot and disappear for a while.

How many times have I felt this way? A quick trip out of town would fix it all.

Then she thought about Jared, and how each encounter with him plucked her out of her daily routine. It was an escape, but one that nudged her ever closer toward emotional vulnerability, and therefore, disquieting fear. On any given day, she vacillated between the high of this new . . . whatever it was, and the terror of exposing her defects to another human being.

Jared enticed her over to his place with the promise of a freshly cooked meal. His invitation, while casual in its delivery, set a precedent for something new and different in their courtship.

"Door's open. Come on in," he shouted from inside when she knocked.

His apartment was nice, but definitely a bachelor pad: chin-up bar across the door, surfboard hung on the wall over the television, and a pantry filled with oversized boxes of cereal. Something straight out of *Dogtown and Z-Boys*. He kept it clean—no toothpaste caked on the drain in the bathroom sink, anyway. She noticed a light trail of sawdust from the doormat to the kitchen: a clear sign of the woodshop being tracked indoors.

"What have you been making?" she asked as she crossed the threshold.

"Veggie lasagna," Jared called from the kitchen.

"No," she said, laughing. "I mean in your shop?"

Jared poked his head out to see where Lizzie was looking and acknowledged the trail of sawdust.

"Oh, right. I'm working on a cage for one of my raised beds. I'm adding doors tomorrow. When it's done, the rats won't stand a chance."

"And once everyone sees it in action, you'll be selling them like hotcakes."

"Is that legal?" He dried his hands on a towel as he approached.

"Nothing in the *Rules and Regs* that says you can't."

"You're so handy to have around." He smiled and kissed her.

"That's me, the walking rule book." She hung her purse carefully on the back of one of two mismatched kitchen chairs, which creaked as she sat down. The aroma of simmering tomato sauce caught her attention.

"That smells fresh."

"I wish," Jared said. "My tomatoes won't be ready for a while. These are from a can, but I did add basil from my plot in here. Most of the sauce is in the oven, but this is for the top." He stirred the sauce and invited her to taste it.

"Mmmm"—she slurped the steamy tomato sauce—"you're handy to have around."

Moments later, Jared plated the lasagna, and they sat down to eat. To Lizzie's surprise, his cooking was more than decent. In fact, it was delicious. He must have culinary experience along with the mishmash of other skills. Why hadn't he mentioned that before? She scrutinized the meal as she cut into it, took a bite. Something didn't make sense. The layers were consistent, the noodles perfectly al dente. The sauce balanced the flavor of the filling. She'd made enough lasagna to know that people don't get it right the first time, not like this. Normal people burn the edges, or don't use enough sauce, or the sauce is too watery, or . . . something. Was it the recipe, or was he hiding another skill set, another facet of his personality from her? Or was this meal from a box, passed off as his own?

"Do you always cook for the women you date?" The words came out before she could edit them.

Jared grew contemplative. "I . . . don't think so. But then again, I never had a garden before. This is all pretty new to me."

Lizzie's suspicion grew. "So where did you learn to cook like this?"

"I guess I'm just lucky, or I know how to follow a recipe, at least."

She doubted that. "You just whipped this up, no problem?"

Jared's tone turned defensive. "Yeah, lasagna's not that hard. Noodles, veggies, cheese, sauce. What more do you need?" He paused, brow furrowed. "What's up with you?"

"Nothing." She chewed another bite, but her wariness triggered more questions. "It's hard to believe you've never cooked before this."

"I didn't say that," Jared retorted.

"You just did."

He studied her across the table. "What's going on, Lizzie?"

Lizzie set her fork down, searching for the right words. She suddenly felt the urge to flee. Her throat closed up, her heartbeat pulsed in her neck. "I . . . Nothing." She pushed her chair back. "So you have made this before." She started to spin out, searching for the logic to cut through the distrust.

Jared looked exasperated. "Yes, I've made food before. I live alone."

"Why won't you tell me where you learned how to do this?" She pointed to the specimen lasagna on the table. "I don't know anything about you. You're being evasive."

"*I'm* being evasive?" Jared said. "Who's the one who 'doesn't like to get to know people too quickly'?"

Lizzie stood up. Her fight-or-flight response took over and time sped up. "I need to go."

"Lizzie, wait." Jared reached out to touch her, but she had already grabbed her purse and hurried toward the door. "You didn't give me a chance to answer."

"I have to go." Lizzie was already out the door and down the stairs by the time she comprehended the last words Jared had said before she slammed the door. It was too late to go back for his answer, and way too embarrassing. She ran to her car and sat, unmoving, for a good five minutes. Once again, she had screwed everything up. Then her phone rang. It was Jared. She reluctantly answered.

"My mother taught me how to cook when we lived in Hawaii. I was her sous chef for like five years," Jared said. "There, I admit it. I was a momma's boy." He paused. "I guess I was embarrassed to say so."

Lizzie sighed. "Go on."

Jared rambled on. "She taught me how to make poi, which is disgusting, by the way. And I helped her cook an entire kālua pig once. Plus, she didn't have a daughter, so she wanted me to know how to make a complete Indian meal for my dad. He didn't appreciate that. Said it was a girl's job, but Mom didn't care. And hey, now I know how to make chapati."

Lizzie released a slow, deep breath. "I'm sorry I bolted."

She recognized his vulnerability, and the opportunity he

was giving her to be equally vulnerable with him. She felt tears well and blur her view of the street in front of her. It took her a few breaths to be able to speak through her fear. "I guess I want to get to know you more quickly."

"Then come back and finish your lasagna."

CHAPTER 15
Everything in Its Place

July

Lizzie inhaled the sea-scented breeze as she positioned a blanket on the Venice Beach shore. Jared sat to kick off his shoes, then huddled over his collection of goodie-filled tote bags. Lizzie noted that hopeful light in Jared's eye as he, with a flourish, opened a sealed container and placed it on the blanket in front of her. This time he'd made lentil curry with fried okra from his garden. She couldn't help but be impressed. She grabbed a fork and sampled the curry.

"I know what you're up to," she said between bites.

"I've always been clear about my intentions." He reached over to steal a piece of okra from her plate for his own. "I make you dinner, I invite you to stay the night. And I define 'stay the night' as falling asleep until the sun comes up, just to be clear."

Lizzie let out a combination laugh and sigh. "I'm sorry."

"It's okay. I mean, I don't get why you don't want to sleep over, but it's okay. I'll keep asking until you decide to stick around."

"It's not that I don't like your place, it's just . . ." She watched Jared draw a square in the sand with two fingers.

"I know," he said. "Boundaries."

He was right. She held clearly established—you might even say rigid—boundaries. Yet it sounded stupid when he put it that way. Her reluctance made sense when she wasn't with Jared. But when she sat across from him in this beautiful setting, those pesky fears shrouded what could be blissful happiness.

Lizzie squinted. "I'm being ridiculous, huh?"

He smiled. "You'll get over it when you're ready."

She finished her curry, licked her fingers, and shifted over to Jared's lap. She leaned in and kissed him. "We'll see."

He pulled her closer and returned the kiss, long and slow. The breeze grew stronger as the sun disappeared beyond the horizon. Lizzie felt goose bumps rise on her skin, a combination of chill from the air and the building passion between their bodies. She leaned away enough to say, "Let's get out of here."

AN HOUR LATER they lay tangled in Jared's sheets. Lizzie stroked his back and waited for his breath to even out before she reached for her shorts. The bed creaked when she bent forward to put on her sandals.

"But I made curry," came Jared's muffled voice from the pillow.

Lizzie smiled in the dark. "And it was delicious, but I have to go."

He groaned.

She kissed his head. Jared reached out and took her arm, tried to pull her back to bed. "You don't have to."

She lifted his sleepy hand off her arm and gave it a squeeze. "Yeah, I do."

"I'll try chocolate next time." Jared rolled over and pulled up the sheets. "Maybe that will convince you."

Lizzie stood for a moment watching Jared drift back to sleep, then picked up her purse and exited quietly through his apartment. She exhaled as she closed the door and descended the stairs, eager to go, but feeling pulled back to his bed at the same time.

Bernice knelt over a perfect row of potatoes. Their foliage formed neat mounds twenty inches tall. She pulled on her brand-new pair of gloves, bent her fingers, and marveled at the way the gloves hugged every curve of her slim fingers. These were a smart purchase.

She pressed her fingers into the soil in search of young tubers. The curved outline of one Russet Burbank revealed they were still small, not yet ready.

She stood up, knees crackling, and rested at the entrance of her plot to survey her day's work. All the years of grooming her garden to perfection had paid off. Not a weed in sight—she prided herself on that fact. If she didn't set an example for her gardeners, who would? Bernice's roses formed a low hedge along the perimeter of her plot; crisp white blooms—only white—put on a show worthy of a ribbon at the Chelsea Flower Show. Her candle larkspurs, *Delphinium elatum*, flowered in true form, exploding skyward in rich shades of blue. She glanced at a patch where she had planted foxgloves, *Digitalis purpurea*, last year. Even after the devastation one morning when gophers confiscated half of them, she had sallied forth and replanted twice as many in the fall. She surveyed the reward for her efforts—speckled pink and white bells deepening in color as they rose from the earth.

Her eyes fell on a small corner where a mix of hollyhocks, *Alcea rosea*, and Canterbury bells, *Campanula medium* var. *caly-canthema*, were planted. She spied a weed poking out from behind the lush foliage and gasped.

"Not in my garden." She marched over, bent down, and with one quick motion, ripped the tuft of lamb's quarters, *Chenopo-dium album*, from its hiding place.

Bernice dusted off her hands and returned to the entrance of the plot. Noticing some soil on the center urn, Bernice pulled a hankie from her garden bag to wipe away the gritty blemish. She paid particular attention to cleaning under the lip of the urn as well, since spiders were prone to take up residence there. She glanced up to find Ralph standing in the pathway at her plot entrance.

"I don't care for the webs," she said to him. "So messy." She rubbed the polished stone, scrubbing the crevices between the detailed scrollwork where dust collected. Ralph invited her to come dust his plot anytime.

"Your roses are on par with mine, Ralph. You've developed quite a green thumb over the last few years."

Ralph blushed and said, "Well, yours remind me of some royal garden in England. Mine will never come close to that."

"It does remind me of home." Bernice grew melancholy.

It felt so recent and yet so long ago, she told Ralph, coming to the United States at ten years old. Her father was discharged after the Malayan Emergency and had brought his family stateside. Their new life had begun with a challenge: to make new friends and decipher the oddities of American culture. At the time, she longed for the familiarity of her backyard in the outskirts of London. The trickling stream that ran through, the lush flowers, the perfect canopy of climbing roses overhead on the porch—her secret garden.

"I spent so many hours of play in that garden as a child." She had layered rose petals in the hollow of the large stone under the holm oak tree, *Quercus ilex*, her special rock where she left gifts for the fairies she imagined came to visit. On many a cold, rainy morning, she had sneaked out into the garden to search for any gifts they might have left her in return.

"Mum never comprehended my secret offerings, and it infuriated me to find that she often swept away the petals from the stone. One day I overheard her saying, 'I wish those bloody birds would stop ruining my sculpture garden.' I wanted to shout at her, but I was too embarrassed to tell her I believed in fairies."

Ralph chuckled. "I would absolutely believe fairies were living behind your house in England."

"I miss the fog floating through the garden. It's different from this"—she waved toward the ocean—"marine-layer business." She told Ralph she didn't miss the cold, but part of her missed her childhood belief of fog's magical powers. She had fantasized it healed broken flowers. Bernice laughed aloud, recalling her naïveté. "What a silly girl."

"It's not silly," said Ralph. "It sounds like an awesome fantasy world you created. I'd read that novel."

"I thought you might appreciate that, Ralph."

Bernice looked around. This plot was different from her childhood imaginings, she thought. It served as a standard of excellence for other gardeners. This was how a clean and tidy Vista Mar garden should look. No rambling vines, no dead foliage, no rubbish piled in the corners, and no weeds. As long as she kept her garden in perfect condition, she justified writing citations for any plot that didn't measure up to hers. When Bernice introduced new gardeners to her section, her own plot was first on the tour. She told her gardeners they should strive for order of a higher caliber and warned them that a deviation in the direction of what she considered to be messy—namely, wildflowers—would be cited.

"Bernice, why don't you ever pick your roses?" Ralph asked.

"That would spoil their beauty. I deadhead spent blossoms,

and cut them back each January, but I wouldn't dream of picking the flowers or taking them from the garden."

"But why?" he asked again.

"They belong here, and I come to the garden every single
day to observe them. Rain or shine, holiday or not. Norman
may well brand me obsessed, but he doesn't complain. And it
gets me out of the house." Bernice acknowledged, with only
slight agitation, that Norman appreciated her absence. After all
their decades of marriage, she knew when to leave the house,
and the garden provided a much-needed escape for them both.

She explained her reasons to Ralph. For years, Norman had
given her a bare-root white rose bush on their anniversary. *De-
voniensis* 'Magnolia Rose': a hybrid cream, double tea rose from
1938.

"Every year, bless his heart. Until I ran out of room, that is."
She had brought each one to Vista Mar Gardens to plant them
side by side. This garden demonstrated fortitude and commitment. And tolerance. Abundant tolerance. Only this morning
before she left for the garden, she'd been sorely tried. She relived the conversation she'd had with her husband.

"NORMAN, WHY DON'T you write something for *The New Yorker*?
You still have a contact there."

"No, it's too stuffy. I'd rather write for *The Onion*."

"*The Onion*? That rubbish? What a colossal waste of time."

"You have no sense of fun, woman."

"I certainly do. I very much enjoy reading your articles in

distinguished magazines. I don't understand why you want to write for journals best read while on the toilet."

"There's nothing wrong with those."

"I beg to differ."

"Beg all you want. It doesn't change how I feel."

"What a waste, Norman."

BERNICE REALIZED RALPH was watching her as her mind wandered. "How rude of me. What brings you here, my dear?"

"Nothing," he said. "I was passing through and thought I'd say hi. In case I didn't mention it before, sorry the election didn't go your way."

Bernice rolled her eyes. "It appears nothing with the board goes my way."

Given that she didn't know exactly where Ralph's loyalties rested, Bernice kept her feelings about Mary to herself. But inside, she fumed.

In her first years in the garden, Bernice took pride in her role as section representative. She often argued they should make special badges for themselves, but the board shot that idea down in a meeting long ago. She still harbored resentment over that incident, come to think of it. Mary, of course, had probably instigated the peals of laughter at her expense.

Mary, that hateful woman. It was all her fault. Since Mary had become president the garden had all but disintegrated. There were dozens of people—more than she could count on her fingers—who should have been kicked out of the garden, but Mary made too many exceptions. It was abominable that these lazy louts retained membership with a waiting list of over four hundred people.

Bernice asked Ralph, "Have you noticed Mary's been acting strange lately, like she's hiding something?"

"I don't know. She's been carrying a shovel with her more often, if that's what you mean."

"No, it's something else . . . Never mind." She didn't want to burden Ralph, but she speculated that Mary was keeping secrets the rest of the board should know.

Though she questioned Mary's methods during board meetings, no one knew Bernice's true opinions about Mary and her supposed leadership. Bernice may have lost the election in April—by only a few votes to be sure—but she still had plans.

"If I were in charge, things would be different," she told Ralph. "No second chances. Gardeners would be allowed exactly one citation and no more. Only the best, most dedicated gardeners would be permitted to stay. No more reprieves for frequent travelers either. If they can't tend their gardens, they should do us all a favor and leave so someone else can have a chance."

Ralph squinted, deep in thought. "Yeah. Maybe someday. Hey, I have to get going."

"I imagine I've bored you silly, haven't I?"

"No, don't worry about it. I just need to get back to work. By the way, we're opening up a new compost pile later this week. I'll text you the night before."

"You're a sweet boy."

He wandered off down the path.

He was such a helpful young man, Bernice thought. Not like Mary at all. If Bernice were president, she'd run the garden with a firm hand on the tiller. No, not if. When. She'd amassed a number of complaints from fellow gardeners, those who shared her concern about the woeful state of Vista Mar. She'd try harder next time; she would be elected president next term. Once victorious, she'd kick Mary out for throwing snails into her plot.

It was obvious. She never had a snail problem before Mary became president. It didn't go unnoticed, either, that if ever they engaged in heated discussion at a board meeting, Bernice found her plot full of snails the next day. She simply didn't understand how someone with such a lack of moral character could hold a position of authority at the garden. Did no one else notice?

Before Mary was elected, they were amicable neighbors. Friends, even. They had shared recipes and gardening tips across their trellises. In fact, Bernice had encouraged Mary to run for a board position. Had she known it would backfire so appallingly, she never would have suggested it.

Luckily, she had another refuge where she went to forget about Mary. No one knew—nor would they ever—about Bernice's Sunday afternoons at the St. Matthew's shelter. It was the only way she could keep track of him; know whether he were alive or dead. She nearly held her breath waiting for him to show up each week, hoping he'd remember her. She hoped he'd be as happy to see her, her Arthur, as he was during their encounter at the garden.

She spent those Sundays serving ladles of oatmeal to hungry regulars and rehearsed what she would say when he turned up.

Finally, she had spotted him at a table one week.

"Hullo, Arthur. It's nice to see you."

"Hi, Bernice."

"I wish you'd call me Mum."

He rotated his tray away from her.

"I'm concerned about you, Arthur. Where have you been?" Arthur looked up from his bowl, disorientated. Oatmeal dripped off his beard, but his face softened into a smile when he made eye contact with her this time.

"Hey, Bernice," he said in a gruff voice. He hadn't been drinking yet this morning, she noticed. His voice, in this instant, sounded the clearest it had in ages. Ten seconds ago he was someone else.

"How ya doin'?" He twisted on the bench toward her.

These precious moments of lucidity were so fleeting. She tried to relish them as they came, fought her urge to grab him and hold him tight.

Arthur looked up at her. "I'm sorry about that time at your garden. I didn't mean to stay there that long. But in the rain and all, I didn't want to leave."

She was relieved. "I understand, Arthur. And you understand you can always find me there. Right?" She reached out to touch his grimy sleeve. His expression shifted as he looked down at her hand. She pulled away and added, "But next time, be more mindful, yes? Did the police treat you well?"

"Oh, yeah. They're always nice to me. I don't mess with them. I go with 'em. They took me to the shelter. I got a new shirt out of it, so it's all good."

Oh, yes, that day in the garden during the rain. Sharalyn had called the police, and Bernice watched them take Arthur away. She had been so conflicted, but she checked her behavior in that moment because she didn't want Sharalyn to know. By the time she ran to the squad car, she'd only had a minute to attempt a conversation before they drove off with him.

"Well, I'm glad you're all right, Arthur. Your father and I miss you." She scanned the room as she pulled a prescription bottle out of her pocket. Bernice cautiously opened it and closed her hand around Arthur's wrist, pressing two pills into his hand. His eyes widened.

"Please, take these. They will help you think more clearly, dear." His hand felt so rough, so damaged. She couldn't see him for the tears in her eyes. "Come back to us, darling. We can help you."

Arthur's eyes grew vacant; he sat motionless while Bernice's heart pounded.

"No!" He knocked the prescription bottle out of Bernice's hand. Pills scattered across the cold steel table. He swept his meal tray on to the floor along with the pills and lunged toward her. Shelter security guards descended upon the table and pulled Arthur away from Bernice, while other guests scrambled to pick up pills off the floor.

She couldn't do anything. She couldn't hold him, and she couldn't help him. God knows they tried, for years. When it began, Arthur simply acted out at school. Over time, he turned more serious, more dangerous, more disconnected from reality. After a diagnosis, they tried to get him proper medical attention. Everything they did drove him further away. She found a journal in his closet filled with disturbing letters and drawings, and that broke her spirit.

How could he want to hurt his parents? His words were too severe to be ordinary teenage angst. She called the police and the doctor she had consulted at the county psychiatric ward.

But Arthur ran away from the hospital. He disappeared for four years. They thought he was dead. By the time he surfaced—disheveled, drunk, and drugged—he was a legal adult. He refused help from anyone, refused medication, refused his parents' offer to come home. It took a decade, but Bernice finally tracked him down at St. Matthew's and started volunteering there to keep an eye on him. For the past sixteen years, that was her only way to connect with Arthur.

BERNICE TOOK A deep breath and tugged on a rose petal. She had gotten used to feeling helpless. But not here. Here at the garden, she was anything but helpless. She was in charge, in control. She dusted off her linen pants, slid off her new gloves, and reached into her garden bag to trade the gloves for a thin booklet of citation forms and a pen. Writing citations always made her feel better.

CHAPTER 16
Locks and Keys

Late July

Catholic schoolgirls go one of three ways: they either end up pregnant, go to jail, or carry the mantle of Goody Two-shoes into adulthood. The latter develop a lifelong fear of getting into trouble, and that fear dictates most, if not all, of their decisions. Lizzie fell squarely into that category, try as she might to relax. Stick to the path, follow the rules, and nothing bad will happen. Or so they said. Long ago she had ditched the straitlaced life, but she couldn't shake off at least one indelible lesson: follow the rules.

This relationship business, however, presented a problem. Lizzie had yet to experience relief from anxiety and distrust by following any prescribed Rules of

Relationship thus far. To her disappointment, the guidelines she established for herself did nothing to ease her way.

She found it easy to leave Jared's each night after their time together. That kept the boundaries clear, defined their spaces, made everything clean and simple. But to stay? That would muddy the path.

If I stay, I'll have expectations. Of him, of me. Of us. Expectations lead to disappointment. We don't want that, do we?

Jared may have said he accepted her desire for clear boundaries, but, nonetheless, he continued to tempt her with reasons to stay.

"Wake up with me tomorrow," he said one night, after plying her with yet another dinner. "I've got waffles in the freezer and fresh plums from the orchard to go on top."

"What, no chocolate?"

"That's for right now." He jumped up, opened the freezer, pulled the lid off a carton of double chocolate chip ice cream, and returned to the table to slide a spoon toward her.

Lizzie took a spoonful straight from the carton. "Why do you need me to stay?"

"My neighbors are starting to ask questions."

"Seriously?"

"No, but I do get the stink eye from the old lady downstairs."

Lizzie laughed. "She thinks you're sending me home?"

"And that I'm a jerk, probably, but none of that is why I want you to stay over." He paused. "God, you're going to make me say it."

"Say what?"

Jared closed his eyes and inhaled. "That I like you, okay? I want to wake up and see you, to know how you look in the morning."

Lizzie stopped with the spoon in her mouth.

"Sorry, does that sound creepy?" Jared said.

She pulled out the spoon and swallowed her bite of ice cream. "No. It's sweet. But you already know how I look in the morning—out in natural sunlight, no less."

"I mean here."

Was it his patience? His cooking? Or the fact that he had, so far, respected her boundaries? Lizzie thought back to a couple of weeks ago, when he drew that square in the sand. He understood her; that made her feel safer than she ever had before. His display of vulnerability helped, too.

So she stayed.

That night, she settled into bed and draped her arm over Jared's chest. He wove his fingers through hers. The smell of fresh laundry she always noted on his clothes surrounded her in his bed. Sleeping over might prove easy, after all. Before she drifted off to sleep, she wondered if he would like her apartment.

Eventually Lizzie found out, but not before processing her pesky expectations first. Inviting him over didn't have to mean anything. It didn't mean she was giving up her personal space, or blurring boundaries. Right? She could invite a guy over and maintain detachment. She proposed the idea of him coming to her place under the guise of showing off her new mini home theater system (found secondhand at the local thrift store). Just to watch a movie.

But they watched *He's Just Not That into You*, which completely backfired as a "let's just see a movie" choice, and they ended up having the we've-been-dating-for-four-months talk. Lizzie started the conversation, despite her better judgment. To her surprise, they were on the same page: both wanted exclusivity. They celebrated their newly discovered monogamy with sex—a lot of sex.

Amid the free-flowing oxytocin, she rationalized her fears. She would invite him in as long as she held two criteria in place: time alone and assurance that the garden was her private space. If she stood by those two standards, everything would be fine.

ONE NIGHT AS Lizzie came through Jared's door, her purse slipped off her shoulder and spilled onto the floor. He knelt to help pick up the contents and noticed a dull metal keychain in the shape of a watering can. It encircled three small keys. Jared plucked it off the ground.

"What's this for?" he asked.

"Those are my garden keys."

He looked them over. "Keys, plural? Oh wait, of course. You're a section rep." He thought for a second, then asked, "Does one of these open the toolshed?"

Lizzie paused. "Yes. Why?"

"That would've been handy last week. I had to wait an hour until Ned showed up to let me get a posthole digger."

Lizzie smiled. "You should've called me."

"Well, maybe I'll just borrow them when I—"

"No. Sorry. I can't loan you my keys."

Jared looked at her, struck by her seriousness.

She softened her tone. "But call me, I'd be happy to open the shed for you. I do that for all my gardeners."

His expression was one of disbelief, as if he were waiting for her to say she was joking. She wasn't. Gibberish from the TV in the apartment next door pierced through their silence.

"You're serious," he said.

Was she being too stringent with her boundaries? She felt awkward, but there was no way she could lend out her keys. She offered a solution.

"Maybe when you've been around long enough, and if you keep busting your butt to help, Ned will give you a toolshed key. A few trusted non–board members have them."

"I've been there nine months." He looked bruised, but waved the idea aside. "You know what, don't worry about it. It's not a big deal."

DESPITE THE OCCASIONAL awkward moment here and there, they had developed a comfortable domestic routine—watching movies and taking hikes. *Breakfast at Tiffany's*, Mandeville Canyon Trail, *Swingers*, Paseo Miramar hikes, *The Red Violin*. They took turns cooking dinner. Lizzie began to accept the idea that she had a boyfriend. Comfortable, but not certain. She frequently reminded herself that the whole thing could end at any moment, so she never allowed certainty to settle in.

She tried not to leave anything behind at Jared's when she spent the night, but one morning she'd forgotten her razor and hairbrush. She didn't want to inconvenience him, but she asked Jared to return the items to her mailbox at the garden if they weren't going to meet for a while. He left a note rubber-banded to her hairbrush: "There's this place called Rite Aid. Supposedly, they sell duplicates for your BF's apartment."

Boyfriend. The words on the page conveyed permanence.

Over and over, he invited her to keep a set of toiletries at his apartment. She warmed to the idea, but still hadn't done it. Why this resistance laced with doubt? He liked her now, but how long would that last?

An all-knowing voice echoed in her head, *He's a keeper. Don't screw it up.*

He was. She didn't want to screw it up.

LATE ONE SATURDAY morning, Lizzie showed up at the garden and, to her surprise, could not find her keys. She dropped her sun hat on her head to free up her hands to rummage through all the pockets of her purse. They weren't there. She played back the last two days in her head. Where did she leave them? At home? No, she'd stayed at Jared's the other night, and that's the last place she pictured them. In fact, she was sure of it. She had taken them out of her jacket pocket and dropped them on the end table next to her purse. Her mind lingered a moment on what had happened next, when Jared reached up from the couch and pulled her on top of him, buried his face in her neck. She relived the goose bumps from the touch of his lips on her skin, and the passion that followed. Sex with Jared was the best she'd had in years.

Keys! Right. They must still be there. Or maybe he'd brought them here to her mailbox.

She approached the entrance, expecting to wait, to beg someone to let her in, but instead she found Mary standing at the open gate, arms folded and face tight with concentration.

"Waiting for someone?" Lizzie asked.

"The police," Mary said. "We've had a break-in."

Not again. "What did they get?"

"Nothing appears to be missing, but it's too early to be sure." Mary rubbed her forehead. "We found some of the most expensive tools scattered throughout the garden. They've already started to rust. A few wheelbarrows are upended in the compost pile; someone punched a hole through one of the plastic ones. Somebody tried to jump in it, I guess. But most of the damage happened in the plots."

Lizzie groaned. "How bad?"

"Trampled artichokes and a few crushed tomato cages, a kicked-over mailbox, and someone took a nap in Ralph's asparagus patch. Everything is snapped off at the ground."

"That's terrible."

"The thing is, Lizzie . . ." Mary fell silent.

"What?"

"We found your keys at the site this morning." Mary eyed Lizzie with equal parts suspicion and concern. "They were hanging from the padlock."

Lizzie's mind started to race. How could her keys have been

there? If she'd left them at Jared's— Did he have something to do with this?

She couldn't wrap her head around it.

"Can you explain any of this?" Mary's voice took on a tone Lizzie recognized—one reserved for outsiders.

Lizzie couldn't answer. She shook her head, unable to breathe. Her heartbeat pulsed in her neck. *They couldn't possibly think . . .* No one had ever accused her of breaking and entering before. It gave her chills.

"I must have dropped them in the parking lot or something."

The lie came out so effortlessly it scared her. She scolded herself. *That is not what happened, and you know it.* Why was she protecting Jared? Why did he do this?

"It would help if you retraced your steps, for the police report."

Lizzie's stomach twisted into a fist. She shuddered under Mary's gaze. "It wasn't me, Mary—you know that." She reached out and touched Mary's arm.

"I do, sweetie, but I need to cover my bases."

With chills running down her arms, Lizzie crossed through the gate, past Mary. She couldn't meet Mary's eyes, could only watch the ground beneath her. The blur of mulch underfoot made her dizzy until Mary's call froze her in her tracks.

"Lizzie!"

She turned up the hill, forced herself to look at Mary. "Yeah?"

"You probably want these." Mary held out Lizzie's keys.

"Shouldn't they dust for prints or something?" She turned back up the hill and reached for her keys.

"They're probably clean." Mary didn't let go. "We'll figure this out." Her warmer, more mothering tone pushed through her somber expression. She must have noticed Lizzie's furrowed brow, etched with embarrassment—no, humiliation. Mary gave her hand a squeeze before she let go.

As soon as Lizzie stepped into her plot she reached for her phone, but stopped short of dialing Jared's number. If he'd done something here, then a call, a text, could be used as evidence. How had her keys gotten into the hands of criminals? She tried not to jump to conclusions, but without the truth, those conclusions pushed other explanations out of her head.

Lizzie put her phone away. Her breathing was labored, her hat uncomfortably tight. *Busy hands, busy mind.* She set to work in her plot. But thoughts of betrayal seeped in as she trimmed away dead tomato leaves. Intermingled scenes from *Jagged Edge* and *Kill Bill* pushed to the fore, fueling her ever-more-plausible theory about what had happened.

Icy prickles of confusion grew into anger as the hours passed. She distracted herself by pulling weeds, waiting for her brain to work out a more rational explanation for all this.

Jared appeared at the foot of her plot.

"Hey." He was cheerful.

"Where are my keys, Jared?" Her eyes bored into him while she tried to stay calm.

"Um, probably at my place. The guys came over last night, so my mind's still cloudy." He sounded nervous.

She told him about the break-in, how Mary found her keys on-site.

Jared's chest sank, his eyes glazed over. He lowered himself to the edge of Lizzie's retaining wall.

Lizzie stood over him. "What's going on, Jared?"

He didn't speak at first, but rubbed his forehead and ran his fingers through his hair.

"I didn't anticipate that," he said, looking up at Lizzie.

"What happened?" Her calm drained away. In its place, the black bile of fury took hold.

He closed his eyes and shook his head.

"Jared!" Lizzie's voice rose.

"The guys were making fun of me, tossing your keys around at my place last night. They were curious about this garden I'm so obsessed with. They said they'd bring them right back."

She shouted, "And you let them take my keys?"

He tried to explain. "They were only going to take a look. I had no idea they would break anything. They were drunk, but they're not stupid."

"Why didn't you go with them? With my keys!" Lizzie was beside herself. She put her trembling hands on her head, dropped down onto the pathway, paced in front of him.

"I did," he said.

"What?" Lizzie whipped around to face Jared.

He looked down, embarrassed. "Tequila is really not my drink." He stifled a chuckle. He relayed as much of the story as he remembered, but none of it made sense. Lizzie was so dumbfounded, it stopped her for a second, but her anger swelled, washed over his words.

"I can't believe you. No. I don't believe you. You couldn't have let this happen."

"I'm sorry, Lizzie."

She paced even faster. "How could you even let them touch my keys? Why didn't you call me right away?"

He cringed. "Apparently, I was busy?"

Lizzie lunged toward him, her face inches from his. "You think this is funny? I lied, Jared. How does this make me look?" She needed to leave.

Jared reached for her hand as she passed, but she yanked it out of his grip.

She shouted, "This isn't some adventure of yours, this is my life!"

"I'm sorry." He stood up. "I'm going to beat the crap out of all of them."

"Them?" she yelled. "What is wrong with you? And no, being blackout drunk is not an excuse."

"I . . ."

Lizzie felt herself come unhinged. "What about you! You were there. You participated. They'll terminate you for this!"

"I'll fix it." He tried to put himself in front of her, but she swerved to avoid him. When he reached out to touch her shoulder, she recoiled.

"I trusted you. How will you 'fix' that, Jared?" She stopped pacing. In that moment of stillness, a chasm cracked open between them. Betrayal and doubt flooded into the space she had finally carved out for trust. Regret oozed into every cell of her being. If she told Mary what had happened, they'd kick Jared out of the garden, maybe even her, for being so irresponsible with the office keys.

Why did he do this? He's ruined everything.

As tears stung her eyes, she saw her mistakes laid out before her. She had let her guard down, let the lines blur between her duties to the garden and her personal life. She should never have let him in. If this had been any other person, she would think nothing of signing the termination letter on the spot.

Her voice choked through tears. "I knew this would happen."

"I'm so sorry."

That's all Jared could say. It didn't help.

Lizzie sat down on the edge of her retaining wall, unable to speak. Minutes passed like an afternoon. Then the word came. "Go."

"Lizzie, don't—"

"I said go." She stared him down.

Jared looked distraught. He pleaded with her, saying that he would make everything right, but his eyes showed pure disappointment, the kind of look that knows nothing will ever be the same. He apologized repeatedly while he stood there, but Lizzie didn't respond.

She couldn't look at him anymore. Was he waiting for something from her, some kind of acceptance? She couldn't give it.

Dejected, Jared said, "I guess I'll see you around."

She kept her head down as the sound of his footsteps faded into the distance.

CHAPTER 17

Dog Days

Late August

Must be August. It's hotter than Pa's gumbo, but drier than jerky." Sharalyn offered her opinion to whoever might be listening—nobody, at the moment.

Never thought I'd miss those hot, soggy August days back home.

At this point, she'd take soggy over this dry heat anytime. There wasn't enough lotion in the world to keep her hands supple. The sweat she wiped off her forehead stung the cracks on her thumb.

This time of year, gardeners focused on staying cool and out of the sun. They chose from any number of pergolas and trees under which to take refuge, including the spot at the bottom of the hill near the bountiful fig tree. Only a handful of people got to the figs before the squirrels did, which made this summer fruit a prize. Sharalyn sat down in the shade near the fig tree and mopped up the sweat trickling down her neck. She bit into the succulent sweetness of the Brown Turkey fig; it was a ritual for her, and for the gardeners with plots near the tree. Her fingers were sticky with sugary juice. She could hose off her hands at the nearby spigot, but she paid it no mind.

Late August qualified as the dog days of summer in Southern California's blistering, arid weather—though according to the Roman calendar, the dog days ran forty days from early July to only mid-August. Sandy soil dried out two hours after sunrise. Vegetables curled inward to protect themselves from the sun's beating rays. Rain, not seen since April, had become a distant notion. Despite that, the coastal air coated every squash leaf with powdery mildew, and Sharalyn cut away sickly stalks and leaves to help extend the life of wandering vines. Her pumpkins had already turned orange, and she was sick of zucchini. She'd long since run out of friends to burden with the extras. Her tomatoes were still going, but other plants had given up the ghost early, from either disease or negligence. Late August was a time of abandonment.

Her gardeners went on vacation for weeks at a time and didn't arrange for a neighbor to water. They figured nature would take its course, and they'd return to either a dead garden or a flourishing one, depending on how well the summer crops did without irrigation. In the middle of the drought, state officials restricted the water supply, as well as the times and days they were allowed to water. If someone missed the window of time, their plot had to go all day without it. Some people gave up. Others got clever.

Sharalyn walked down each row of plots and discovered, tucked into the soil, a few fancy drip irrigation systems, installed to make the most of the rationed water. Other gardeners buried ollas, ceramic jugs used by the Spanish settlers and Native American people to irrigate crops in the deserts. Gardeners would fill these jugs in the morning, and the moisture then seeped through tight ceramic pores all day—a slow-release underground watering system with direct access to the plants' roots. No evaporation there. It made Sharalyn smile.

She observed other smart ideas at work, too. Since the rules and regs prohibited timers or electric sprinkler systems, gardeners added mulch. They covered their planter beds with wood chips, compost, or cardboard, allowing soil to retain moisture better than if left exposed to the summer's scorching heat. Sharalyn's approach? Take advantage of the longer daylight hours while the sun's intensity waned. She soaked her soil as the sun set, when plants and gardeners alike breathed a collective sigh of relief from the heat of the day.

Despite the sense of desolation in the late-August garden, board activities had kept Sharalyn busy lately. She had been surprised by a call to attend a "closed" board meeting several weeks ago, and it surprised her further to discover that Lizzie wasn't there. Turns out, the meeting was all about Lizzie and Jared.

What a mess that was, and she sympathized with Lizzie. All

those years of commitment upturned in a moment of stupidity. Not Lizzie's; Jared's. She said as much to the board in Lizzie's defense. Everyone seemed to agree in due time, except Ned. He defended Jared, too. That was heated. The board needed someone to blame, and Jared was the obvious choice. But Ned stood up for him on account of Jared being dedicated to the garden, working hard to rebuild retaining walls, building the shed, offering to help out wherever. Ned didn't want to lose a re-liable worker. Though Sharalyn wanted Jared out for her own reasons—seeing as Jared was fooling around on Lizzie with someone named Bunny and all that none-ya-business—she understood Ned's reasons. She didn't blame Ned for trying to strike a deal with the board. In the end, the board terminated Jared's membership, with a plan to reinstate him a week later as a show of goodwill because of his extreme efforts to make amends . . . and Ned's persistence. On top of that, they gave Jared a citation for uncivil behavior. More for show than any-thing, because by then the board understood his actions were uncharacteristic, never to be repeated. A tidy end to it all, or so it seemed.

Mary billowed her blouse and glanced down at the petition on her clipboard before taking a deep breath. She stepped up to the front door of what must have been the thirtieth house in the neighborhood that day. She knocked and waited. So far, her petition listed only two other signatures besides her own. The list of those who shut the door in her face, however, was much longer. *What's wrong with these people? Why don't they care?*

The door opened to an older woman, maybe around Mary's age. Mary put on a smile and introduced herself, pointing across the street to the garden.

"Do you know about the eviction?" She started in.

"Of the community garden?" the lady said.

"Ah, so you do know." Mary nodded. "It's a terrible shame, and we're fighting it. But so far, it's been a challenge. We're asking our neighbors to show support for Vista Mar by signing this petition. You don't have to do anything else, but I'd really appreciate it if you could sign—"

"I'm sorry, I can't help you." The lady started to close the door.

Mary put her hand on the door. "Wait, why? What is going on? Does this guy have you all under his thumb or what? Everyone is telling me the same thing."

"I'm sorry, I . . . Kurt's a friend. We have to keep the peace around here. I can't sign your petition." She shut the door.

Mary's hunch that Kurt had a strong influence over the neighborhood turned out to be true. If the neighbors didn't care what happened to the wide-open space in front of them, who would?

Lizzie descended the hill to water her plot late one afternoon. She scanned the garden for other people—for one person in particular. While grateful for the board's decision to let her stay, her stomach knotted up knowing they had done the same for Jared. Her irrational fear had become a reality. Every time she visited, she wondered if she would run into him, what would transpire between them. In all honesty, she wanted to hide, but she had to be professional. She rounded the corner to her plot and spotted Jared a few rows down, busy tilling the soil. His bronzed arms flexed as he lifted the shovel into the air and drove it down to loosen the earth, compacted from summer's baking heat. She tried to ignore the flutter in her stomach.

I should leave, but I have to water.

The flutter quickened when Lizzie arrived at her plot to find a small coffee mug filled with cut roses at the entrance. She bent down to pick them up. Their fragrance was tremendous, the colors exquisite. Deep corals, reds, and whites graced the petals, with beautiful yellow centers. She nestled her nose inside one of them and took a deep breath. Complex floral notes filled her head. Her heart suddenly lightened.

Over the past month, she hadn't answered Jared's calls and had made sure she never visited the garden when she anticipated he'd be there. If she did spot him, she left. She tried to restore the boundaries between personal life and garden life. With renewed parameters in place, maybe she could heal.

He left voicemails for a while. One said that he had turned himself and his friends in to Mary, made them pay for the damaged property. He said he'd marched them all over to the garden to apologize for their actions. Another message said Mary wrote a character reference letter to the judge, convincing him (to Ned's delight) to give Jared and his friends community service for their crimes—digging trenches for new plumbing at Vista Mar Gardens. She'd smiled when she listened to that message. Touched by his effort to keep her abreast of the news as it happened, she appreciated that he'd tried to set everything right, but it didn't change the fact that Jared had betrayed her trust and put her in a compromising position. Sweet messages or not, she wasn't about to trust him again.

Once Jared had come forward, everyone came to the natural conclusion as to how her keys could have gotten into his hands, and Lizzie's lie was uncovered. Her own penance to the board and garden was embarrassing. They documented Lizzie's formal reprimand in official meeting minutes, which were posted on the website for everyone to read. While no one questioned that she'd had anything to do with the break-in, the board still gave her a dressing-down for lying to protect Jared. Exposure topped her list of humiliations once everyone found out about their relationship. Despite a few concealed nods of approval from Ned for "scoring a handyman," as he would later congratulate her, Lizzie was mortified that her colleagues now saw her with fresh eyes, as someone so easily swayed by a tender touch and charming personality. The embarrassment, the vulnerability made her sick each time she relived it.

Her office and toolshed keys were confiscated for a month (Mary gave them back after three weeks, though), and she received a citation for uncivil behavior. Mary withheld the details of Lizzie's lie from the police, kept the matter internal, but it had changed the way Mary looked at her.

When Lizzie found out about Jared's termination and re-instatement, she'd had mixed feelings. The board had shown more understanding than she did.

In Jared's recent messages, his tone had changed. Instead of apologetic, he sounded frustrated. He'd say hi, then ask why she didn't call him back. "It's been a while," he'd say. "I miss you," he'd say. "Please, Lizzie, call me. We need to talk." In the last message, he sounded angry. And then he stopped calling. Now these flowers. Well, flowers or not, she wasn't going back. She would thank him, though.

She looked down to Jared's plot, where he continued to dig away at something. She tucked the mug of roses into the crook of her arm and set off in his direction.

"Jared?"

He didn't look up. He continued to force the shovel into the soil, chopping up clods of dirt. When he thrust the shovel into the ground, he threw out a "hi" but kept digging.

"Thank you for the flowers."

Jared stopped. He looked up at Lizzie, eyed the flowers, and wiped his face on his sleeve. "They're not from me."

His expression confused her with its mixture of anger and sadness. She didn't know how to respond.

As if in answer, Jared said, "You must have a new admirer."

Lizzie surmised where this was going. The words sputtered out of her mouth. "Not that I know of. I don't— I'm not dating anyone, Jared."

Jared's face softened the slightest bit, but his eyes still burned with anger.

Neither said anything. Jared went back to tilling.

Lizzie started in. "Look, I appreciate what you did to help, but—"

"Why isn't that enough?" He took the shovel in one hand and thrust it into the ground. It stood up on its own as he walked toward Lizzie.

Her heart and head scrambled for purchase as he came near her. The question threw her. She couldn't speak, but Jared had plenty to say.

"I've apologized a hundred times. I tried to talk things through. I even turned in my friends. But you still won't talk to me. I screwed up and I did everything to fix it." His voice rose as the words poured out of him, a long-awaited volcanic eruption from the pressure of silence. "You think you're the only one who cares about this garden? I care, too. And I care about you. I hoped if I fixed everything, we'd go back to the way things were, but you won't let that happen! What more do you need from me?"

She wanted to die, to curl up in a ball and disappear into nothingness. A mangled wad of shame, obstinacy, and fear crawled up from her stomach and clogged her throat. She managed to get out a few words. "I trusted you."

Jared paused for a second, glanced down at Lizzie's feet. "It's not fair. I can't get you out of my head"—he looked back up, peered into her eyes—"and you won't even try. You aren't willing to let go of all your stupid rules and regulations for one minute to"—he searched for the words—"to actually live, Lizzie. This is not about trust. This is about life. It's messy sometimes. There's this world outside that little box you live in, and you don't want to explore it." He lifted the hem of his shirt to wipe a rivulet of sweat away from his temple. The sight of his muscled torso inundated her sense memory. Her gaze lingered there after he pulled his shirt back down.

Oh God, get a grip. There suddenly wasn't enough air to breathe. She felt woozy. Jared was still talking, though, and his words brought everything back into focus.

"I mean, maybe I'm a total dumbass for believing there was something real here." His finger flicked back and forth between them. "But you tell me. Am I wrong?"

He stopped speaking. Lizzie's head reeled. She had nothing to say. She wanted to throw down the flowers and wrap herself around him. Instead she stood perfectly still.

When she didn't respond, Jared exhaled. "I guess I am."

He walked to his shovel and pulled it out of the ground. He turned his back on her to resume his task.

Lizzie watched him slip away from her. It was for the best. She wanted to say, *I wish you understood where I'm coming from, Jared,* but it wouldn't help. His body said it all. After this, she imagined he would understand: they shouldn't be together. It was a bad idea all along.

Lizzie stepped away from his plot and was making her way up the hill to leave when she realized she still hadn't watered. The sun dropped toward the horizon and she didn't have much time. She couldn't get out of there fast enough, but her thirsty garden forced her to stay. *Is this how it's going to be? Constant anxiety?*

She put the roses down in the pathway and absentmindedly hosed down her raised beds, all the while struggling not
to look down toward Jared's plot. She noticed too late that
she'd watered her tomatoes from overhead. It didn't matter—
the summer was almost over and they would die soon, anyway.

She turned off the hose and picked up her flowers. Then she
turned to look at Jared's plot. He was gone.

Well, if that didn't put an end to it . . .

Everything slowed down for a moment, and something
broke inside. She expected relief, but she found no comfort in
this conclusion. Instead it felt as though her blood had drained
from one spot deep in her chest, turning to vapor in the afternoon air, never to return.

It's going to be okay.

She didn't believe it for one second.

Lizzie once more began her ascent up the hill toward the
gate, passing a few gardeners on her way to the top who were
finishing up their chores. She hoped they hadn't witnessed her
showdown with Jared.

"Those are pretty flowers," came a voice off to the right.
She turned to find Ralph standing waist-deep in his rose garden. His T-shirt extended away from him, caught on a thorny
cane. It took only a second for Lizzie to notice that he was surrounded by the same roses she held in her hands.

Oh God. Quick, say something.

"They are beautiful, aren't they?" She tried to smile.

Ralph's shy demeanor bumped up a notch toward confidence. "Someone must think you're pretty special."

"Yeah, I wonder who?" She decided to play dumb. "Your roses are pretty, too."

Is that all you can say? Her mind raced. But her mouth wouldn't open to say anything else.

Ralph continued to stare at Lizzie.

"Well . . . ," she said, "I'll see you later, Ralph." She turned and hurried up the hill through the gate, wishing she could erase this day and start over.

CHAPTER 18

Disclosures

Early September

Sharalyn couldn't help noticing Lizzie's lack of enthusiasm every time she laid eyes on her these days. Ever since the board decision, Lizzie behaved as if she wanted to be anywhere else but here. If it weren't for the heat and the fact that plants would die without irrigation, Sharalyn wouldn't be here herself. Lizzie's reasons, of course, were different.

Lizzie passed Sharalyn's plot with her umpteenth wheelbarrow piled high with blight-infested tomato plants bound for the dumpster. Sharalyn called to her.

"What's your trouble, sugar?"

Lizzie set down the wheelbarrow. "Take one guess."

"Your heart's still wrapped around that man?"

Lizzie walked to the edge of Sharalyn's plot. "I thought it would be easier now that it's over, but it's not over, not really. I mean, it feels awful, not over."

"I hear you."

"I want to be done with it," Lizzie added. "I wish I could delete my memories like what's-her-name in *Eternal Sunshine of the Spotless Mind*."

"It's never that easy." Sharalyn turned her empty tool crate upside down and motioned for Lizzie to take a seat. Lizzie joined her under the shade of late-blooming climbing roses.

Lizzie sat in silence for a moment. She pulled at a loose petal on a nearby rose. "It would be easier if I hated him."

Sharalyn reached into her garden bag for a towel to mop the sweat off her brow. Lizzie's words prompted the memory of the dubious moment she'd witnessed of Jared on the phone. "Really?" she said. She was never one to pass up a chance to help a friend with insight and information when such an occasion arose. "Are you sure?"

"Yeah, I wouldn't miss him if I hated him."

Sharalyn contemplated the best way to relay such information to her friend in need. "Well, in that case . . ."

She unwound the story of Jared's phone call with "Bunny" and the flowers he'd picked from his garden for this mystery woman. Lizzie listened, speechless. Her expression went from confusion—eyes darting side to side to mentally connect the dots—to wounded and angry.

"Who the hell is Bunny?"

"I take it he never mentioned her?" Sharalyn said.

"No. God, I'm so stupid." Lizzie dropped her head to her knees.

"That wasn't the reaction I was hoping for, sweetie." Sharalyn rubbed her hand across Lizzie's hunched shoulders. "You're supposed to get angry. It'll help you get over him."

Lizzie groaned into her own lap.

"Oh, honey, I'm sorry." Sharalyn imagined Lizzie's mind whirling. Awkwardness, sadness, and pain must be running through her heart. Top it off with being cheated on. Poor thing.

Sharalyn tried to make up for the damage done. "I presumed it would help."

Lizzie sat up and slid out from under Sharalyn's comforting hand. "I know. It should. But please don't help anymore."

She stood up and began to turn away; Sharalyn called after her. For a second, it looked as though Lizzie wanted to stay, to talk it through. But something shifted and she broke into a sprint. Lizzie ran past her wheelbarrow, piled with the remains of her tomatoes, left for someone else to deal with.

Mary had spent the summer exploring tactics to stop the eviction. She and Ned researched their rights as conditional-use permit holders, only to find they had few to none. They could file a lawsuit to slow things down, but could they afford it?

"Maybe it's time to tell the board," Ned suggested.

"No." She was president; the responsibility landed squarely on her shoulders.

"More heads could help solve the problem, Mary."

She sighed. He was right, but who on the board could they trust to keep it quiet? "Lizzie can keep a secret," Mary said. "I mean, we hardly know anything about her life, she's so private. What do you think?"

Ned mulled it over, then nodded. "She's had good ideas in the past. Let's bring her in."

The following Saturday, Mary and Ned squeezed into the main shed with Lizzie, each perched on a metal folding chair. Lizzie looked worried, questioned why she was there.

"Don't worry," Mary said. "It's not about Jared. It's . . . bigger than that."

Lizzie did not look reassured. "I'm being kicked off the board?"

"No, sweetie," Mary said, chuckling. "We asked you here because we need a board member we can trust."

"Oh." Lizzie was visibly relieved. "Okay. What do you need?"

Ned relayed the details of the eviction notice while Lizzie listened, slack-jawed. They told her about Mary's attempt to connect with the mayor and explained the results of their research on legal action. Lizzie sat absorbing the data with a furrowed brow, then interrupted Mary. "Wait, we were served five months ago?"

Mary glanced at Ned. They nodded.

"And you haven't found any loopholes to get us out of this?"

"Not so far," Mary answered, reluctant to admit it.

"And we have until December 31 to stop it?"

"Well," Mary said, "end of November, technically. At that

point we have to pull everything out to be ready to turn over the land by the end of the year."

Lizzie sat frozen, eyes darting around as she processed what they had told her. "So you're keeping chaos to a minimum by not telling the membership. Is that the plan?"

"All hell would break loose," Ned said. "We'd have gardeners running off with everything worth anything on this property."

"Don't you think they might try to help instead?" Lizzie posed the question.

Mary and Ned looked at each other. Ned replied, "We've already wrangled all the legal experts in the garden. They confirmed we don't have much legal standing with a conditional-use permit. Not without a ton of money, anyway."

Mary added, "We also talked about asking the membership for money, but we weren't sure how to do that without telling them why."

"Shouldn't we tell them what's happening?" Lizzie reiterated.

Mary shook her head. "If we can prevent the sale from going through before anyone finds out, that's the best solution."

Lizzie went quiet, furrowed her brow again. "What about doing a fundraiser for legal fees or to try and buy it ourselves? Like a crowdfunding campaign?"

"This is why you're here," Mary said. "We need ideas."

"With a fundraiser, you can keep it vague, or say we've been sued by a former member, which has happened before."

"As much as I'd like to fabricate a motive, we can't lie when asking for money," Mary said. "Although I can't imagine we'd raise much if it sounds like we're having a bake sale. It needs to sound serious."

"Right," Lizzie said. "Let me write a draft. I'll come up with something. How much money do we need?"

Mary shrugged. "I have no idea. I can't get anyone from the city to tell me diddly-squat, so it's probably going to take a lot of digging to get answers. Lawyers are expensive."

They bounced around a few numbers and landed on a starting point for the fundraiser. Lizzie nodded and typed a few notes into her phone. "We should also contact the local papers to try and get some attention. Maybe TV news outlets, too."

"Lizzie, we need to hold off on publicity. For now, no one else can know. Understood?"

Lizzie hesitated, disapproving, but then nodded in agreement. "Got it."

CHAPTER 19

Bolting to Seed

Last Day of September

Mary finished pulling weeds in the orchard for the third time this month. It calmed her nerves, gave her something to do besides worry about the eviction. She gathered the giant bundle of seedy grasses and tucked them under her arm. An unoccupied wheelbarrow stood a few rows down, one of the rusted metal rejects, not the lightweight, newfangled plastic wheelbarrows that were easier to push uphill. A few of those that had survived "the incident" sat somewhere farther off. Not worth getting for the armful of weeds she intended to take to the composting area. She stood at the edge of the orchard to review her work.

Much better. The orchard, nestled at the bottom

center of the gardens, held Mary's attention with every waxy leaf and fragrant blossom. Forty fruit trees, ranging from three-year-old peaches to fifteen-year-old citrus, made up the ramshackle collection that provided fruit to garden members through most months of the year. Figs, plums, and nectarines fell from the trees in September's heat, and she eyed the persimmons farther up the hill—they'd be ripe early this year. *Thank God. If Kurt Arnold has his way, we won't be here to eat the late fruit.*

Despite Lizzie's secrecy, hushed rumors had begun circulating when she posted the fundraiser to every bulletin board in the garden. The newsletter had announced the crowdfunding campaign: a general request to support the VMG legal defense fund, an insurance policy against future lawsuits. The money would go into an investment fund to provide financial relief for the garden in case of emergency. But the rumors indicated that people were catching on. Mary knew she couldn't keep it a secret much longer. They had to stop this eviction from going through, and soon. The end-of-year deadline was fast approaching.

What would happen to her pet project? Each tree in the orchard, whether young or old, grew in the center of a circle of fecund soil amid the grass, weeded and mulched by volunteers. Well, most of the time. Mary spent her spare moments keeping grass and weeds from trespassing across these well-defined borders. She smiled as she inhaled the earthy musk of fresh mulch beneath a row of apple trees.

Mary stuffed her pruning shears into her back pocket with

her free hand and walked across the path toward the compost piles. She took a roundabout route to the garden waste area, past her own plot, where she paused a moment to inspect her tomatoes. The last few days had been hot as hell. She wondered how her plants had held up in the sudden abundance of ninety-degree days.

She confirmed what she'd expected: tomato leaves curled inward to protect themselves from the burning sun. Mary resisted the urge to drench the plants. She understood nature's defense mechanisms. By the end of the day, those tomato leaves would unfurl and return to happiness once more, as if nothing had bothered them in the first place. She squeezed the bundle of weeds closer to her chest to adjust her grip.

Mary had become so absorbed in her tomato plants that it wasn't until she stepped up into her plot to pop a Sweet 100 into her mouth that she noticed the flurry of activity coming from the garden plot next door. She looked over and under the grapevine at the edge of her plot when the unfamiliar noises intruded on her thoughts. There, she saw Bernice hacking away at her roses.

What in God's name?

Bernice held aloft a rusty set of loppers. She thrust them into each white rosebush, twisting and severing thorny canes at random. Mary overheard Bernice grunting, muttering something under her breath, but couldn't make out the words. Still holding her bundle of weeds, Mary stepped down into the pathway to investigate.

"Whatcha doing, Bernice?"

The loppers froze for a second, then plunged back in. "None of your business."

"It's not the best time to prune roses." Mary tucked her weed bundle under one arm and shifted it to her hip.

"Leave me alone," Bernice barked over her shoulder. "Don't you have something better to do than pester people in their own plots?"

Mary clenched her jaw. "Suit yourself. For a second there I thought you'd gone batshit crazy, but it's clear you're only being yourself."

"Oh, shut up, Mary." Bernice snapped the loppers into the roses to punctuate her words.

Mary's blood bubbled up. *Where's a bucket of snails when I need one?*

"What's the matter? You're a little more 'stick up your ass' than usual."

Bernice whipped around to face Mary, her eyes full of tears, her face puckered red as though she'd been crying for hours. Mary was stunned to find Bernice's usual disagreeable resolve had evaporated. Bernice clutched a set of rusty loppers in both hands, gripping them with bloody knuckles. Her scratched, bleeding hands shook as she pointed the blades at Mary.

"What's the matter?" Bernice shouted with a shaky voice. "What's the MATTER? He's leaving me, Mary. That's what's the matter. Are you happy now?" She fell to her knees into the soft mulch beneath her feet, dropped the loppers on the ground, and dissolved into convulsions of tears.

Mary's mouth went slack. Her heart dropped into the pit of

her stomach, and she instantly felt like an ass. Bernice's husband, leaving her? How on earth? They were the classic enduring couple. Forty-five years of come-what-may marriage. She'd only met Norman once, but she knew him from the stories Bernice had often told years ago. Stories that had, on rare occasions, exposed Bernice as a human being. The sound of Bernice's sobs pierced through Mary's clouded mind.

She dropped her bundle of weeds and stepped up into the plot. "Oh, Bernie, I'm so sorry."

She sank to her knees and took Bernice's quivering shoulders in her hands. Bernice heaved with sobs and leaned into Mary's arms. They sat together like that, Mary cradling Bernice.

"That's what he said," Bernice blubbered.

"What, that he's sorry?"

"No, that I've got a stick up my ass." Bernice strained to compose herself through sobs and hiccups.

"Oh, Bernie. You know I'm messing with you." She squeezed Bernice's shoulders. "Nothing would get done if you weren't nagging me all the time."

"Well, apparently he's tired of it." Bernice leaned forward to reach into her back pocket. She pulled out a monogrammed handkerchief to sop the tears from her eyes.

"What happened?" Mary asked.

"I honestly don't know. One minute I was at the table clipping coupons, telling him our plans for a trip back home. The next, he made some ludicrous suggestion"—she spat out the words—"about writing jokes for late-night television. He snapped, Mary; came completely unhinged.

"I only said, 'What a waste of your talents, Norman.' Next thing I know, he's stuffing cardigans into a suitcase, yelling that I don't understand him, I don't celebrate him for who he is." She tried to quell her hiccups but instead lapsed into another bout of tears. "And he blames me for Arthur."

"Arthur?"

"My boy," Bernice sobbed. "My poor boy. I lost him . . . so long ago. He wouldn't stay, and I couldn't fix him. We couldn't fix him."

Bernice plunged into the depths of her memory, recounting it all. The story sprang forth like a blast from a fire hose, too many years restrained. Mary was taken aback by her sudden openness, but listened as Bernice wove her tale. She told Mary about Arthur's mental illness, how heartbroken she'd been when he ran away. How Norman had told her to keep the matter internal, that they could handle it themselves. His sense of betrayal when she made that call, when Bernice signed Arthur over to the hospital.

"I had no idea . . . ," Mary said.

"Norman blames me. All these years, he's held it against me. He says it's my nagging, why he's leaving, but that's not the reason. I know why." Bernice's tears streamed down her face. "Now he's gone, too. I've lost them both, Mary. What am I to do?"

Mary held Bernice in her arms and sat with her as she cried. She felt the sting of tears in her own eyes. Memories of her own divorce bolstered her empathy.

Bernice sniffed. "Why am I telling you this?" She blotted

her tears on Mary's shirt. "You'll probably print it in the news-letter to humiliate me."

"Nah. I couldn't possibly make you feel worse than you do now." Mary patted Bernice's trembling shoulder. "Besides, we've got a lot more in common than you think." Mary lapsed into silence as the sting in her eyes grew stronger. She cleared her throat. "It's going to be okay. You'll go through hell for a while, but you'll be okay."

Bernice looked up. "How did you manage when Tom left?"

Mary took a deep breath. She hadn't exactly stayed quiet about that, but she didn't expect Bernice had even noticed when her life had come crashing down. She exhaled and looked out toward the ocean.

"It nearly killed me. At least, I thought I was going to die. But I got so angry at that bastard, I didn't notice I was a wreck for at least a few months."

The sweltering heat bore down on the two women. Mary's shirt clung to her skin where Bernice's tears had left soggy stains.

"Don't take this the wrong way"—Bernice wiped her nose on her already wet hankie—"but I never imagined I'd end up like you."

"Well, you're a pain in the ass, but I would never have wished this on you." Mary stroked Bernice's hair and lifted her upright by the shoulders. She reached down to peel her blouse away from her sticky skin. "Here we are, two flawed old ladies, melting together in the baking sun."

Bernice nodded and sniffed, beginning to regain compo-sure. "Who would've thought?" She looked down at the cuts on her hands, the blood already dried in the sweltering heat. Then, she surveyed her garden, the butchered roses. White petals from a late-summer bloom lay everywhere. Canes hung broken and twisted.

"Oh God," Bernice wailed. "What have I done?"

"He gave you those, didn't he?" Mary said.

Bernice let out a chuckle despite her sorrow and nodded. "That is correct."

"Well, let's finish the job, shall we?"

Mary got to her feet, picked up the loppers, and extended them to Bernice with a smile. Bernice sighed, then stood up to accept them. She turned to face the disheveled roses, snipping the loppers in the air a few times. Then, without a word, she picked up where she'd left off. She hacked away at the roses, taking out her aggression on the once-beautiful garden that reminded her of Norman. Mary pulled her pruning shears out of her back pocket and joined in. The satisfying sound of cutting out old plants drifted over the garden and out to sea.

As the two women did their best to demolish the past, Ned came walking across the path. He was talking to himself; he must not have seen or heard them. Bernice stood up straight and shuffled some mulch on the ground to make noise. Ned raised his head, revealing a perplexed look. His eyes glistened.

"Everything all right, Ned?" Mary recalled his fainting spell earlier in the year. She was concerned it would happen again.

"Uh, hi, ladies . . ." His eyes darted around. "I'm all right. I came down to check on the compost piles."

He stood, immobile, staring out to the ocean.

"You okay?" Mary guessed it was the eviction, not his health, that was troubling him.

Ned's face was still hidden. He reached up to wipe his eyes before turning to Mary. "I'm okay. I got some bad news, but it'll be all right."

"Is it about the notice?" Mary probed.

"No. I mean, yeah." He nodded, eyes searching for a place to focus. "The notice. But I'll tell you later, Mary. When there's more time . . ." Ned waved weakly and wandered down the path.

Bernice and Mary looked at each other. Bernice asked, "Notice?"

She shook her head. "You don't need any more bad news today."

"Don't you dare pull rank on me. I have pruning shears." Bernice stepped forward, brandished her rusty loppers. "What's going on?"

"Okay, but you better sit down for this."

They sat at the edge of Bernice's plot, where Mary told her about the eviction notice Ned had received months earlier. She told her about the property list and Kurt Arnold's plan to buy the land.

Bernice leaned away, shocked. "You've kept it secret all this time?"

Mary looked out at the ocean unfazed. "We're working out a strategy to present to the board."

"And?"

"Nothing yet."

"Good God, Mary!"

Mary rolled her eyes. "No kidding." She turned to Bernice. "Look, you can't tell anyone until we announce it to the board. I'm scheduling a closed meeting tomorrow. Okay?"

Bernice was silent.

"Bernie!"

"All right, all right! I'll keep quiet until the meeting, but you'd better have devised a plan by then."

"I've got one more trick up my sleeve. I don't know if it will work, but it's all I've got," Mary said. "Just don't tell anyone."

"Of course not. Silent as the grave."

CHAPTER 20
All Good Things . . .

First Day of October

Word spread through the garden like pernicious weeds. The property was on the market with a solid pending offer. Gardeners whispered over wheelbarrows of compost, through rosebushes, and under trellises. Soon, the whispers became grumbles, which erupted into roars from the membership. They demanded that all members be admitted to the emergency meeting the next day.

The meeting area overflowed with members. People lined rows of benches; they spilled into the pathways and grassy corners. Some voiced their anger about not being told when the eviction notice first appeared.

Others wrung their hands with helplessness. Mary did her best to field questions about the pending sale, tried to bolster confidence with assurances.

"I want to thank those of you who have made calls to the city already. If you responded to Lizzie's flyer without knowing the reasons behind it, well . . . now you know why. The board is doing everything in its power to investigate the situation and put a stop to the eviction."

Jason rose to his full height in the first row of benches and proclaimed, "Hey, if you want Kurt the Curmudgeon taken care of—I know someone. Say the word."

Mary recognized it as a joke but clearly some members didn't. Someone from the back yelled, "I'll do it myself!" The crowd's volume rose as others blurted out their own two cents.

"Thank you, Jason," Mary said firmly. "I'm sure we all want to string the guy up, and I'd be the first person to kick the chair out from under him, but we can't do that. We must fight the right—legal—way. Everybody, please!" She held up her hands for quiet.

The dissonance of many voices simmered to a dull chatter as Mary gained control. "Now, where are my members with legal experience?"

A few hands went up.

"Great. Please talk to me after the meeting to discuss our next steps. According to the eviction notice, we have until December 31 to either take action or vacate. Our agreement with the city says that we promise to put this place back the way we found it."

Groans and cries lifted from the crowd. Mary put her hands up to calm them.

"That means"—she raised her voice to be heard—"that means we're required to remove all retaining walls, all plant material, and all irrigation aboveground and belowground."

"They can't do this!" someone yelled.

"Please, people, calm down," Mary said. "Let's prepare for whatever happens. As I said, the board is going to meet with the city, and we're trying to get a meeting with the mayor's office this week to sort out the issue. Those folks who raised their hands, if you can, please plan to attend as legal counsel. We'll update you as soon as new information becomes available. But in the meantime, every member must participate." Mary took a deep breath. "I'm going to hand it over to Ned to give you instructions about what to do. Ned?"

Quiet settled over the group.

Ned stepped up from behind Mary. He wobbled as he approached the PA system. Mary moved out of the way to let him pass. Their eyes did not meet. Ned reached up to hold the microphone steady and missed. His hand thumped against the mic and the sound reverberated through the speakers. Ned blinked and suddenly looked more alert. He reached into his shirt pocket to pull out his notepad. His hands shook while he flipped over a page of his notes.

He cleared his throat. "Okay . . . First of all, we're asking all gardeners to take home any furniture or decorative items you keep in your garden, this week. That will make it easier to tell what we'll have to remove with equipment."

Ned looked distracted, or unable to focus; Mary couldn't tell which. He searched up and down his notes.

"Sorry, hang on." He flipped more pages. Mary stepped forward to look over Ned's shoulder. She pointed to the page with his list of to-dos, but Ned still looked confused. Mary put her hand on his shoulder and reached out for the notepad.

"I've got it, Ned."

Ned looked up at Mary with blank eyes. He nodded and released the notepad to Mary. She returned to the mic and read off the list of tasks for members to do.

"We'll send regular email updates and announce emergency meetings as the situation develops. That's all for the moment."

"Can we protest in front of this guy's house?" someone called out from the crowd.

Mary looked at the other board members and took a quick silent vote based on the looks in their eyes.

"As long as it's peaceful and you stay outside his property line, I wouldn't be able to stop you."

With that, the members dispersed to their gardens, perhaps to look at their plots in a different light for the first time since joining VMG. Fear of termination for weeds or overgrown gardens was a thing of the past. One realization filled each of their minds: plot ownership was temporary. Any crops gardeners planted now would be their last—some vegetables might not be ready to harvest by the time they'd have to be pulled.

A sadness blanketed the garden. There was always a risk of losing crops to inclement weather or pests, but to lose their garden wholesale was altogether different.

Lizzie and Sharalyn separated from the group to join Mary and Ned. Mary held Ned's elbow and whispered into his ear. She lifted her gaze to Lizzie and Sharalyn when they approached.

Lizzie blew air through her lips. "That was rough. You handled it well, though, Mary."

Mary wasn't listening. She focused on Ned, who stared at the ground ahead of him. His eyes were wet.

"It'll be okay, Ned." Sharalyn stroked Ned's back. "Do you want to sit down?"

"What?" Ned looked dazed. "Oh. Yeah. That's . . . a good idea."

Lizzie grabbed a chair from a nearby table. Mary guided Ned into the seat.

Mary knelt in front of Ned and squeezed his hands. "Come on, Ned, we'll figure something out. You won't lose this garden."

He sniffed and wiggled his hand free from Mary's, reached into his shirt pocket for a handkerchief to run across his nose. His hands shook.

"You gals are great. I'm sure we'll come up with something. It's just bad timing for me."

Lizzie and Sharalyn crouched down beside Ned. Lizzie smiled. "Did you plant asparagus crowns or something?"

"I wish that was it." He paused, swallowed hard. "No, I got a call yesterday—" He squeezed Mary's hand. "I'm having trouble . . . My son . . . Charlie was in a car accident. It was bad. He's . . . he's . . ."

Ned pressed his handkerchief over his eyes. Lizzie and

Sharalyn watched Ned shrink in his chair. Mary reached up to wrap her arm around him.

Ned sensed Mary's arm surrounding him. He felt Lizzie and Sharalyn stroke his back. But he was somehow detached from this swirling comfort. He floated inside it, not sure what to do. He could only focus on Charlie. The garden meant everything, but Charlie meant more. Especially since Miriam was gone. Charlie was all he had left. *Had.* Every hope and dream came true through Charlie. His life had blossomed because of his son, and he'd looked forward to enjoying what the future would bring. But yesterday, that future drove off a cliff.

The voice on the phone said Charlie was driving in Topanga Canyon, coming home from an open house. The roads in the Canyon twist and turn, notorious for accidents. Two kids on motorcycles rounded the corner on the wrong side of the road. Charlie swerved to avoid hitting them but didn't recover the wheel in time to make the next turn. He crashed through the guardrail, down the slope, into a bramble of cactus, but not before flipping the car twice. He'd put the top down that bright, sunny day, celebrating a successful showing that morning.

The paramedics said there was nothing they could do. His skull was crushed on impact when the car rolled; he died instantly.

The three women listened as Ned repeated the cold, lifeless

words from the phone call. He heard them talking around him but couldn't make sense of their words.

"No wonder he couldn't find his place in his notes. I'm amazed he showed up for the meeting at all, let alone to speak," Mary said.

Lizzie and Sharalyn asked how they could help.

"Find people to bring hot meals to Ned's house for a few weeks," Mary said. "He won't have much of an appetite for a long time, but we have to try."

Ned wanted to thank them, but he couldn't move. All these things coming to an end. The garden, and now Charlie. *Enough, already!*

Ned realized Lizzie and Sharalyn were talking to him. They wanted to help him to his car. Mary would drive him home, they said, to make sure nothing happened.

Good old Mary.

Gardening was the last thing on Lizzie's mind after she escorted Ned to his car. His sorrow unsettled her, shook her out of her rut. She had never lost anyone important. Her parents were still alive. Life was moving forward as planned, for the most part. Except for the Jared thing, which felt suddenly irrelevant. She made a mental note to stop at the market on the way home to pick up an extra meal for Ned. In the morning, she'd send out a sign-up sheet to her section to ask for volunteers. That was more important than wallowing in her sorrows about a failed romance.

She had managed to avoid encountering Jared on most days, though she observed occasional traces of him at the garden. A new retaining wall here and there, new cool-season plants in his plot for fall despite impending eviction. He must have been doing pretty well. Probably wasn't suffering at all, in fact. *Damn him.*

Lizzie decided to check in on her garden after all. She needed to shake off thoughts of Jared, and Ned's son. Pulling weeds would help. Sharalyn had gone ahead of her to do the same. As Lizzie approached the path, Sharalyn caught her eye from afar, waving her arms through the air. She gesticulated toward Lizzie then pointed down the hill. Was Sharalyn going to "help" her again? Lizzie traced the trajectory of her gestures, at the end of which she spotted two figures off in the distance. One was Jared, the other was a woman. He appeared to have his arms around her.

Anxiety washed over Lizzie. She told herself to go to the car and leave before she witnessed anything else, but Sharalyn's frantic gestures intensified.

Don't go down there? Is that what she means? Or is it something else? Lizzie squinted across the distance to Sharalyn's corner plot and shrugged her shoulders. Sharalyn's signals increased in strength and velocity. *Come over here? Is that it? Ah, yes, that's it.*

The second she arrived, Sharalyn grabbed her and pulled her down behind a short trellis.

"What are you doing?" Lizzie whispered.

"Just watch." Sharalyn couldn't keep her voice down. She pointed down the hill to where Jared and the woman stood.

From their vantage point, Lizzie tried to decipher the woman's features. She stood encircled by Jared's arms. No, wait. Not encircled, supported. Jared held her up. She was older, a lot older, and she appeared to be wearing a bathrobe, a tropical print bathrobe.

"What the heck?" Lizzie said. "Who is that?" She stood up.

Sharalyn tugged at her arm, whispered, "What are you doing?"

"This is ridiculous. I'm going down there." Lizzie stepped out from behind their impromptu cover. Before she could fashion what to say, she was already halfway down the hill, her feet way ahead of her brain. She had no idea how to mask her curiosity, how to justify this random inspection without reason or purpose. *He's not breaking any rules*, Lizzie reminded herself. *He's here with a friend . . . a woman . . . in a bathrobe.* Time was running out and still nothing came to mind. And then he saw her. She panicked.

"Howdy," she shouted, a skosh too loud for the distance between them. *Ugh, kill me now.*

Jared smiled and tried to wave, but his hands were full. He twisted toward the woman and spoke to her in a low voice. She nodded, then Jared helped lower her into a nearby chair in the corner of his plot. Once settled, he turned back to Lizzie with less of a smile than before, more tentative and guarded like hers probably should have been. His eyes showed no sign of the anger he'd unleashed the last time they spoke.

"How's it going?" he said, after the traditional male chin-lift greeting.

"I came down to make sure your guest is current on her tetanus booster. You know, safety first." It was all she could come up with. "It's highly recommended with all this horse manure."

Just when Lizzie was certain the moment couldn't get any more awkward, the woman reached up toward her from her chair and said, "Oh, there you are, Wila. Hand me my shawl."

Lizzie froze with a stupid grin on her face, eyes locked on Jared. She scanned for answers in his eyes. What was she supposed to do?

Jared reached down into his backpack and withdrew a purple knitted shawl. He turned to the woman, squatted in front of her, and draped her shawl across her shoulders. "This is Lizzie. She's in charge here at the garden. I guess she looks a little like Mom, doesn't she?"

The woman gave Jared a disoriented glance, then shifted to Lizzie. "She's not Wila?"

"No, that's Lizzie, a friend of mine."

"Oh. She seems nice."

"She's all right." He drew her shawl closer to her neck. "Is that better?"

She nodded. Jared stood to face Lizzie, gestured back to the woman in the chair. "This is Bunny, my grandmother."

Of course that's Bunny. Who else would it be?

Lizzie struggled to hide her embarrassment. She planned to strangle Sharalyn when she got back up the hill.

"Nice to meet you, Bunny."

Jared explained that Bunny had been sick but had improved enough for him to bring her outside. He wanted to show her where he picked the flowers he often brought to her, especially since the garden might be gone soon.

"She seems to like it here," he said.

"What's not to like?" Lizzie replied.

He paused and looked down. "Apparently there are a few things." Jared's tone shifted. When he returned his gaze to her, Lizzie perceived a glint of fire in his eyes.

She stepped back. "I'd better go." Memories of their last fight, his accusations, telling her to let go of her stupid rules and live—they all came back with stinging acuity.

Jared shook his head. "You don't have to."

You don't have to? What's that supposed to mean? Coming from anyone else, it might sound inviting, but from Jared, it hit her as another judgment, that she should let go and relax. That she was too rule-bound to "go with the flow." She wasn't, and she didn't appreciate his accusations.

"Yeah, I'm gonna go"—she tightened up—"back to my box, where it's safe. Nice meeting you, Bunny." She turned on her heels to propel herself up the hill as fast as she could without running, which is what her body longed to do.

Sharalyn was waiting at the top for her. Lizzie blazed past

her as Sharalyn poured out a stream of questions. Lizzie ignored all but one.

She reached for the gate, threw it open, and barked back at Sharalyn, "Bunny is his grandma." Then she stormed through the gate, leaving Sharalyn standing in her plot, most likely confused and still full of questions. As Lizzie reached for her car door, she heard Sharalyn call out, "Isn't that good?"

CHAPTER 21

The Service

October

A week later, the board hosted a memorial service for Ned's son, Charlie. Vista Mar Gardens' meeting area under the magnolia tree served as the perfect location, spacious enough to hold Charlie's friends and Ned's fellow gardeners. Members had gathered flowers of every color from their plots—late-blooming roses, nasturtiums, paper-white narcissus, borage, lavender—and handed them over to Ananda to arrange in small vases. Using a knack for elegant flower arranging that was not apparent to critics of her plot, Ananda had transformed the main meeting space into a colorful, perfumed sanctuary of solace.

Friends of the deceased who approached the meeting area looked out of place in suits or high heels. Several women struggled down slopes, sank into the soil, their patent leather stilettos coated with a fine layer of dust. A few men leaned against nearby trees to shake pine needles and pebbles out of their pant cuffs, only to find sap sticking to their hands.

Gardeners, on the other hand, treated the memorial as a come-as-you-are occasion. The most important thing was to be there for Ned. Most of them knew Charlie only through Ned's constant stream of praise. They attended the service as strangers to Charlie, but heartbroken mourners for Ned. Many passed Ned and touched his hand, draped lifeless over the armrest of the green deck chair. He looked up on occasion to greet whoever touched him. "Thank you" was all he could say.

Mary approached the portable PA system to start the memorial service. She had enough on her mind already without having to plan a memorial, but in a way, this was easier than the endless hours spent trying to save the garden.

She'd come straight from the city council and the mayor's office, where she'd gone to beg for help. The mayor remained aloof and unsympathetic toward her pleas—he couldn't get her out of his office fast enough. The crowdfunding campaign to raise cash for a counteroffer had come up short of pledges by several million dollars. Lizzie tried to add the land to the National Register of Historic Places, to ensure that if they lost the garden, no one would be allowed to build on the parcel. But since the property had become a garden less than fifty years ago, it didn't qualify.

Mary was struggling with defeat, but this memorial functioned as a welcome, though somber, distraction from all that. She tapped the mic and cleared her throat.

"We're here to say goodbye to Charlie in the company of friends. Those of you who don't know Charlie's father, Ned, might wonder why Vista Mar was chosen for the service, instead of a church or someplace more familiar to Charlie. I've always said that funerals are for the living, and I'm sure those of you close to Charlie understand that this place is Ned's second home. So in addition to honoring Charlie, we're here today to offer support for Ned, who continues on in Charlie's absence."

Despite the crowd that had gathered, Ned felt entirely alone. He heard the words "in Charlie's absence" and thought, *What am I without Charlie? He's all I had.*

He lowered his head and let tears fall onto his lap. The sound of others crying caught his attention. Lizzie sat next to him and reached out to take hold of his hand. She sobbed harder than he did, so he slid his hand out from under hers to pat her shoulder. The act of comforting her somehow soothed him.

Later in the ceremony, Ned gathered enough strength to stand up to speak. He thanked Charlie's friends for coming and asked them to share some of their favorite memories of Charlie with those assembled. One by one, the guests walked to the microphone.

A middle-aged man in a black pinstriped suit buttoned his jacket and shifted from foot to foot in front of the crowd.

"Charlie and I have been friends since his family moved here from Boston. I remember this one time when Charlie called me up to tell me that he'd gotten in trouble at home."

Quiet groans drifted up from the audience.

"One time?" somebody said.

The man chuckled and brightened. "Yeah, he said, 'I blew it this time.' He told me how he found his dad's collection of pruning shears and decided to take them all apart to study how they were constructed."

Ned looked up, smiling for the first time in ages. "He told you about that?"

"He told me you were pretty ticked off. That you made him clean, sharpen, and oil every single one of them before putting them all back together."

The crowd of gardeners laughed and shook their heads.

"Nice job, Ned," someone said from the back.

Ned turned in his seat to respond. "I also made him ride his bike to the store and buy me new washers, because he lost a bunch of them. That kid . . ."

More chuckles bubbled up from the group. A steady stream of guests came to the microphone to share stories from Charlie's life, and Ned felt lighter by the time Mary closed the service.

"Thank you all for coming. If you want to sign up to help Ned with meals or shopping, please talk to Ananda." Mary pointed to Ananda standing nearby, who waved and rocked back and forth in her Birkenstocks.

The final gesture came from an unknown woman. The shiny rectangular badge pinned to her suit lapel read "Winston Mortuary." She approached Ned and held out a marble urn. Ned accepted Charlie's ashes and sat with them in his lap for a few minutes as someone played a song on a guitar. Guests filed past him to say a few words before leaving.

The group thinned out while Ananda and some other gardeners gathered the flower arrangements. Lizzie squeezed Ned's shoulder as she stood up to help stack a few chairs. She took the list of volunteers from Ananda and said goodbye to Mary. Lizzie spotted a familiar blue shirt out of the corner of her eye. Jared stood at the base of the magnolia tree with his hands in his pockets.

She felt his eyes on her, but when she met his gaze, he turned and walked away.

CHAPTER 22
A Bud

The Next Day

Lizzie walked through the garden in a daze, still pre-occupied with the memorial service the day before. She found herself back at the meeting area under the magnolia tree, without knowing how she got there. The space that pulsed with life and community yesterday felt empty and forgotten today. Empty tables, scattered with traces of yesterday's flowers, looked abandoned and lonely. Pink and red rose petals here, a sprig of fern there—no doubt Ananda had left them behind for the birds to use to build their autumn nests. A surge of tears filled Lizzie's eyes as she pictured the abundance of flowers. What a wonderful gesture to support Ned in his grief. Ned was lucky.

His son just died. Of course he's not lucky. God, what am I think-ing? But, yes, lucky in that so many people showed up to support him.

She stood there reliving the ceremony. The people who had come from outside the garden to pay their respects were so gracious. It gave her the impression that Ned's life through Charlie was robust. What else didn't she know about Ned, or anyone else at Vista Mar, for that matter? The garden's borders enclosed this world, and since people came there to recover from their day, most gardeners didn't talk about their lives outside the gates. The whole notion suddenly felt duplici-tous, to gather in a common place and socialize with people every week yet learn nothing about them. It was so incom-plete. So sad.

How have I known Ned all these years and never met Charlie? What else am I missing?

Faces of friends, colleagues, and fellow gardeners came forward in her mind, each with questions she couldn't answer about them.

Then it hit her. Jared was right.

She did keep everyone at a distance. Especially Jared. Lizzie thought it was self-preservation, protection from getting hurt, but it was just fear. *I'm missing so much of life.*

Lizzie flashed through memories, scenes of when she could have inquired, learned more about her neighbors, when she could have shared some of her own life with them. She really was living in a box, safe away from people and connection. Safe from the terrifying exposure that came with it. Exposure that would make her life much richer. Her head started to spin—dizziness nearly overwhelmed her.

She sought refuge in a chair for a moment and heard voices coming toward her from the south pathway. Two gardeners—a husband-and-wife team—appeared in the open space of the meeting area carrying stacks of dripping-wet seed flats. They didn't notice Lizzie sitting in the corner. The woman was burdened with a large tote bag slung over one shoulder, nasturtiums dangling out the back. She lost her grip on the seed trays, heavy with waterlogged soil, and stopped at a table to recover her hold. Her tote bag slid off her shoulder, jostling her forearm. One of the trays toppled and plopped upside down in the weeds. The woman let out a yelp as the tray upended, but her husband turned too late to help. He set down his trays, and the woman took off her bag and set it on the table.

Get up and help them.

But Lizzie couldn't lift herself from the chair. She drifted, detached from her body. Her mind swirled with images of all her missed opportunities. She recalled Ned holding his son's ashes in his lap. A lump formed in her throat. She pictured Ned going home every night, picking up the phone to dial Charlie out of habit. It was heartbreaking, how alone Ned must feel. How he would always have this empty space in his heart he could never fill.

She sensed an empty space in her own heart, the great solitude that propelled her forward through her day. Most of the time, the ability to be alone was a strength—and she was comfortable with it—but today it was a suffocating lie. She sat hidden in the shade, her eyes fixed on the couple who worked to solve their problem, together. *Together.* By comparison Lizzie's supposed strength—her isolation—shone through for what it really was: pure loneliness. Her eyes blurred with tears. Her stomach tightened into a knot.

Focusing on the woman's canvas tote bag on the table, Lizzie blinked away her tears. She hadn't noticed the words printed on it before. Suddenly, like the profound messages from films that had so often reached her at just the right time, the words on the novelty tote sprang toward her from across the distance: "AND THEN THE DAY CAME WHEN THE RISK TO REMAIN TIGHT IN A BUD WAS MORE PAINFUL THAN THE RISK IT TOOK TO BLOOM." —ELIZABETH APPELL.

Lizzie felt the earth drop away from her. She tried to stand up, but fell back into the chair, hand clasped over her mouth. She couldn't breathe. The couple gathered their trays and meandered toward the north pathway, but they didn't move fast enough.

I've got to get out of here. Too many people.

She somehow pushed herself out of the chair and ran out of the meeting area. She tried to sprint up the hill to a private spot, but instead broke down sobbing and dropped onto a bench at the edge of the main pathway. She fought the urge to throw up—her body couldn't contain the emotions spilling out of her. All the years of strength in solitude fell away, leaving her naked in isolation.

She chose to ignore the footsteps coming up the path. She couldn't stop crying, but she didn't care anymore. Everyone had cried yesterday at the service, so it shouldn't look too out of place.

The footsteps came to a stop in front of her. She knew before looking up that she'd find Jared standing there. She lifted her eyes and held his gaze. A sigh shuddered out of her before she dissolved into tears once more. Without a word, he slid onto the bench and enveloped her in his arms. She sobbed into his soft cotton T-shirt.

"It's okay," Jared said into her ear.

That only made Lizzie cry harder. *Ned, alone. Me, in my fortress. Jared, right this whole time. It's not okay.*

She struggled to form words through her tears. "I thought being alone was right for me, that vulnerability is weakness, but . . . that's not true."

He whispered, "You're not weak."

Her body tremored with a muddle of shame and relief. "I know. I'm sorry."

She wrapped her arms around his chest and breathed him in. She buried her face in his neck. Her breath quivered, hesitated, but slowly evened out.

Jared stroked her hair, then after a moment, leaned back to look at her. She imagined her face was swollen and red, but she smiled anyway. Despite the bloodshot eyes and runny nose, she felt beautiful when he took her face in his hands.

He brought his lips to hers and kissed away the past.

Wiping tears from her cheeks with his thumbs, he said, "I was hoping you'd see things my way."

"Don't get used to it," Lizzie said.

They chuckled and held each other, not yet willing to let go.

After what seemed to Lizzie like hours later, but was probably fifteen minutes, Jared broke the silence.

"By the way"—he reached into his pocket—"Ned gave me these." He held up a key ring with two shiny keys attached. "Now I don't need to steal yours to break in."

Lizzie's reaction blended a groan and a laugh. She squeezed him tighter and patted his chest. Her tears were gone; she felt lighter than she had in years. Completely wrung out, but lighter—and lucky. For once, her brain didn't try to talk her out of feeling what she felt, and being where she was. Right where she was supposed to be.

CHAPTER 23

Compost Happens

November

Vista Mar members spent the rest of fall in limbo, never sure whether to pull up plants or sow new seeds. In an ordinary Southern California November, gardeners planted seeds up through Thanksgiving, and even into December. With the prospect of bulldozers arriving to demolish the property in a month, everyone hesitated to start new crops. Instead, they harvested lettuces and kales, and some gardeners fertilized their pea plants with extra worm castings in hopes of speeding along the process. Perhaps those vines would bear fruit before the delicate tendrils had to be torn down.

The tenuous outlook drifted across the garden on

the fall winds. With it came anger and, for some, resentment that they would have to leave. A steady stream of protesters took turns picketing in front of Kurt Arnold's house. Kurt came home to the sight of hand-drawn signs lining the sidewalk across the street, accompanied by the sound of angry gardeners shouting, "Food, not condos!" Ralph and Bernice spent part of each day staked out at Kurt's house, trying to coerce Kurt to reveal details about the pending sale. Kurt was close-lipped every time, with one exception. One day, when he pulled into his driveway and stepped out of his Cadillac, Ralph shouted from the street, legal distance from the property.

"What will you build on our land, Mr. Arnold?" Ralph stood as straight as he could. He felt Bernice's reassuring hand on his shoulder. It helped him feel stronger.

Kurt ignored Ralph on most days, but today he stopped. He turned toward Ralph, scanned his sturdy frame, and came to rest on Ralph's belly. He lifted his eyes to meet his adversary's.

"I'm not sure yet. Maybe a lawn, but I might pave the whole thing for supplemental beach parking, start a shuttle service. That's a great idea, don't you agree?"

Bernice muttered under her breath, "Pompous, contemptible wretch."

Ralph gave Bernice a sideways glance with a hint of a smile. He didn't want to break the stern veneer he'd put on for Kurt, but he did wish Bernice had said it loud enough for the guy to hear her flowery insult. Instead, Kurt stood prideful in front of the protesters, above it all.

"How much will that cost, Mr. Arnold?" Ralph tried to sound sophisticated.

"It doesn't matter, does it? As long as that mess is gone." Kurt turned toward his house, ignoring the jeers of protesting gardeners. One voice pushed through.

"You! I know you!" Sharalyn, who had joined them on the picket line for the first time, stepped out into the street.

Kurt appeared to tense at the sound of her voice, turned to find the face that matched it. Ralph wasn't sure what was going on until Sharalyn prodded his arm.

"This is Kurt Arnold? Are you kidding me? I've seen him before—in my garden, ripping off my roses." Her voice boomed loud enough for Kurt to hear.

She turned to the crowd of protesters and yelled, "This is the swamp rat who keeps stealing my roses. Who'd 'ave guessed this guy needed to steal anything? But he's going to steal the whole garden. Get outta here, you swamp rat!" Sharalyn shouted. She jabbed her picket sign overhead and chanted, "Stop Kurt Arnold! Rose thief! Garden crook!"

Ralph watched Kurt try to stand tall amid the echoes of Sharalyn's chanting, which built as more protesters joined in. Kurt's indifference faded in light of this new information. Stoicism turned to anger. In that moment, Ralph identified Kurt's anger for what it was: power. Somehow the protesters' cries fell flat against that power, and Ralph recalled Kurt's last words to him moments ago.

He probably has an unending supply of money. That's not good. Ralph slumped under the weight of this new hypothesis. He turned back to the group and dialed his phone to relay the message to Mary.

"We're pretty screwed," he told her.

Mary sat at the office of the county clerk's archives in search of any available information on public record about the property that their lawyers may have missed. She combed through boxes of microfiche looking for loopholes, scanned through copies of newspapers and city documents that detailed the history of the land upon which Vista Mar Gardens had been established. Mary's eyes had begun to blur after hours staring at screens filled with small print. She was about to call it a day when a paragraph caught her attention, something that confirmed the garden indeed was at one time on a short list of properties to be sold off.

"Complaints from neighboring residents with regard to potential developments, followed by the threat of a lawsuit, caused the city to remove the property from the list of sellable parcels."

So what changed? She leaned in on her elbows toward the screen. Digitized pages fluttered by as she scrolled forward in time. Nothing. She found nothing. Kurt must have had some inside connection.

Mary stretched her arms back, then turned off the machine. She gathered the files, returned them to the counter, and thanked the clerk for his help. As she left, one notion burned in her mind. Kurt must be paying the city—and his neighbors—a lot of money.

A WEEK LATER, the weekend before Thanksgiving, gardeners harvested more than they would have preferred to pick. With the promise of future celebrations on hold indefinitely, they opted to use most of their produce for their Thanksgiving feast—a last supper, so to speak. Salads weren't part of a traditional Thanksgiving dinner, nor was Swiss chard. But baby greens and colorful stalks made an abundant offering this time of year. Along with winter squashes stored for the holidays and some very young garlic, the celebration of the garden's bounty took on new meaning this year.

The board members had tried to return as much of the garden to its original state—a slope of bare dirt—as they could without destroying any plots. They were still holding out for some miracle, hoping to find a flaw in Kurt Arnold's plan to raze the land.

"Can't we rally his neighbors to speak out against him?" Lizzie asked Mary as they rolled mulch-filled wheelbarrows down the hill.

"I tried that. No one would talk to me. It appears our friend Kurt shut them all up. With cash, I assume."

"Did you find out how much he's paying for the land?"

Mary told Lizzie that her diligent research of city records hadn't yielded much, until she tried a different tactic. That day she pushed a basket of orchard-fresh Pink Lady apples across the counter at the county clerk's office, with a smile.

The clerk on duty, a short, balding man with thick-rimmed glasses, perked up when he saw the apples and listened to her question. He leaned in toward her to share that he "might have access to intel on this particular issue." Mary raised an eyebrow.

The clerk held up a finger, checked his surroundings, stepped away from the counter, and slipped into the back room. He returned with a manila envelope, which he placed on the counter and slid across to Mary.

She didn't open it there, but thanked the clerk and promised to bring more apples the next time she came. When she got in her car, she opened the envelope.

"Fourteen million dollars!" Mary said.

Lizzie dropped her wheelbarrow. "We have no chance, do we? Even if we tried to raise more money—that's a lot of recycling and bake sales. There's no way."

Mary set her wheelbarrow down on the slope. "It looks that way, but it's not set in stone. He's required to provide a plan for development. From what Ralph told me, he doesn't have a clue what he wants to do with this place. He's simply being vindictive at this point."

"Either way, we're totally screwed." Lizzie sighed. "I guess it's time to tell the membership it's over, huh? Move on to the next step."

The truth of Lizzie's words rattled inside Mary's head. Were they really out of options? Giving up? After thirty-plus years, what else could they do? She had run out of ideas, but had hoped Lizzie and the other young people in the garden would have been cleverer than she. Outside of lying down in front of a bulldozer, Lizzie said she couldn't imagine any way for the garden to stop the sale. Mary didn't have the heart to tell her she couldn't either.

"I need to talk to Ned." Mary rubbed the cuff of her sleeve back and forth across her forehead, an effort to smooth the worry creases that had formed over the past few months. "Don't tell anyone until we decide what to say to the general membership."

Lizzie agreed, but it was obvious to Mary that silence wouldn't prevent people from reading Lizzie's face.

"What will you do once all this is gone, Mary?"

Mary sighed. "Take up knitting, I suppose."

"Really?"

"God, no. But I'll be able to spend more time with my grandkids. They're almost old enough to hold a real conversation. Things should get more interesting from here on out."

"I didn't realize you had grandchildren," Lizzie said. "I should have known that." She paused. "I'm sorry I never asked."

"Everything is different, isn't it?" Mary looked out toward the ocean.

Lizzie nodded. "You're right. Ever since Charlie's memorial service, I've learned so much about the people I see all the time, but never knew. It's *The Wizard of Oz*, black and white suddenly turned color: your grandchildren, Bernice's work at the homeless shelter, Sharalyn being married—that was a shocker."

"You didn't know that?"

"See what I mean? It turns out, deeper friendships are more fulfilling than distance and safety. I'm afraid those connections will end once the garden disappears." Without waiting for an answer, Lizzie lifted the wheelbarrow up to continue down the hill, but then stopped in her tracks. She dropped the handles of the wheelbarrow and pulled off her gloves.

"Why are we doing this? Why bother to put the land back the way we found it if he's only going to tear it up?"

Mary looked at her sideways for a second. "You're right. I guess they could seize our funds. But why don't we throw one hell of a party to blow it all instead?"

Lizzie folded her arms and nodded once in agreement. "Fantastic idea."

The women stood still for a moment eyeing each other. As if they'd each read the other's mind, they both lifted a foot to the rim of their wheelbarrows and tipped them over. Mulch spilled out, tumbled down the slope.

"Let them deal with it," Lizzie said. "We're losing everything."

"Yeah, screw 'em," Mary added. They turned to hike back up the hill in search of Ned.

When Lizzie and Mary arrived at the crest of the hill, they looked for that signature straw hat wandering between plots. Mary always relied on the magical way he appeared whenever she invoked his name. This time, he didn't surface.

Mary spotted Bernice standing next to Ralph and shouted across the pathway to her, "Bernie, where's Ned?"

Bernice shouted back, but Mary couldn't decipher her words. She and Lizzie shuffled toward Bernice and Ralph through a group of gardeners who were laboring over bags of mulch.

"What?" Mary said. "I can't understand your accent from this far away."

Bernice gave Mary a sour look and rolled her eyes. "If you must know, Ned said he had an appointment with the city."

"What?" Mary said. "He didn't mention it. Well, I doubt it will do any good. I tried for weeks, but they sent me packing every time."

"Could it be because you're rude and overbearing?" Bernice said with a smile.

Mary smirked. "No, Bernie, that's you."

Bernice shook her head and waved Mary off. "Well, you asked, so I've told you. If you don't mind, we're off to comfort several weeping gardeners in my section." She took Ralph's arm, then turned in the direction of the meeting area.

Mary shrugged as Bernice and Ralph walked away from them. "She's doing much better," Mary said to Lizzie. "She almost has a sense of humor now."

CHAPTER 24
The Big Day

Late November

Winter came unseasonably early to the garden. A mild autumn suddenly turned cold and windy. Irrigating became a loathsome task when the once-tepid water that flowed from the hoses turned icy. Southern California rarely saw a frost, but this year it descended with startling force, much earlier than the December date the *Farmer's Almanac* predicted. It put an end to any remaining tomato plants and ruined the summer basil that had still clung to life. Lizzie hid her glee about the icy weather in front of other gardeners. She anticipated that her brassicas—especially kale—which improve with frost, would taste sweeter, and hoped her root crops—parsnips and carrots, in particular—

would take on the coveted sweetness otherwise unattainable in the warmer weather of Los Angeles. How ironic that this first frost would mark the end of the garden itself.

Finally, the day that Vista Mar gardeners had dreaded arrived. The sale of the seven-acre property where the garden had stood for more than thirty years would be final at the end of business that day. The end of four hundred plots, seven hundred and sixty members, and countless living plants. Though they had until the end of the year to clear the property, all growing, meeting, and composting was to cease.

Lizzie and Sharalyn walked together through their section, trying to imagine buildings or a parking lot in place of plots. Jared followed behind them.

Lizzie pointed to a plot with waist-high weeds that had cropped up since the last rain. "I was going to write him a citation this week."

"You still can, if it makes you feel better." Sharalyn let out a weak laugh.

"Want me to get your citation booklet?" Jared joked. Lizzie turned, reached back, and squeezed his hand.

They walked on in silence, looking toward the ocean, taking in the view they would no longer enjoy.

"It still doesn't seem possible," Sharalyn said. "This garden has stood as a landmark of the community for so long, it's impossible to imagine it wiped off the map without a second thought, much less a fight."

"That isn't true," Lizzie said. "We fought. And there's plenty of fight left in most of the gardeners here."

She glanced up the hill to the row of picket signs that bobbed back and forth across the fence line. Their numbers matched the group of protesters down on the street at the entrance. People honked in support as they drove by, but that was the sum total of any proverbial olive branch extended by the neighboring community. Lizzie guessed no one wanted to make too much noise, especially if they lived near Kurt.

News cameras came and went, with lip-glossed reporters stationed in the parking lot. They told the tale of tragedy and loss for the city to their viewers. Yet no one came to the garden's aid.

"Maybe the garden was too cut off from the neighborhood to be part of the community," Sharalyn said. "Maybe we're an elitist garden club to them."

"That might explain why no one stepped in to help," Jared said.

Still, the news vans buzzed with activity, this momentous day.

Sharalyn pointed to the road. A black Mercedes crept up the hill. "They're here."

Propelled by the arrival of the suits, Lizzie, Jared, and Sharalyn ran across the garden to find Mary. As a result of Mary's request at the last meeting—that every member of the garden show up for this moment—the parking lot was packed with cars, the garden full of people. Mary hadn't been able to save the garden, but she did convince the county clerk to insert a clause in the paperwork that a copy of all documents must be presented in person to Vista Mar's chair on-site.

Lizzie summoned the gardeners scattered across the hill. "It's time!" She waved her arms over her head to signal for everyone to assemble.

Gardeners flowed like ants out of their plots and into pathways, clogging Mary's passage as she tried to reach the gate. "Come on, people," Mary shouted, "make some room! Thank you! But stay close together. We want them to experience the magnitude of what they're about to destroy."

Mary pushed her way to the front of the group in time to meet the two men in black suits. This time, the gray-templed man wore a vindictive smile. The younger one was solemn, his eyes downcast.

"Good morning, ma'am." The smiling man's smirk stretched wider across his smug face.

"Might be good for you." Mary appeared stoic, on the outside. Inside, she wanted to strangle the rat bastard for that "ma'am" crap. "Let's get this over with."

The smiling man cocked his head to the right. "We've received the final paperwork this morning with regard to the sale of these seven acres. You'll find everything in order here." He waved a thick manila envelope. "Escrow closes on December 31, at which time your members shall vacate the property, and the land must be returned in its original condition, in accordance with the agreement on record."

The solemn man took the envelope and held it out to Mary.

She hesitated to touch it at first, but swallowed hard and accepted the package.

This is it. It's really over. What more could we have done?

The smiling man said, "Our client would appreciate if your members removed all foliage from his property by the end of today. He's planning a site visit tomorrow with several contractors and wants a clean slate."

Rumbling voices swelled from the crowd of gardeners.

"That's impossible!"

"That's illegal!"

Mary lifted her hand behind her to quiet the group. "We have until the end of next month, gentlemen, and my gardeners plan to utilize that time."

"I'm sure you'll find in the documents you now hold a clause that states, 'Compliance with regard to removal of all foliage on the date of delivery of said documents is required.'" The smiling man stood taller, while his partner shrank behind him.

Mary tore open the envelope, pulled out the thick stack of papers to find the clause in question.

"You'll find everything in order," the smiling man repeated. "Have a nice day."

As he turned and left, the solemn young man looked up from the ground and watched his partner walk away. He stepped forward to the gate and lowered his sunglasses. Mary read the sadness in his eyes.

He cleared his throat. "I'm sorry," he said, then turned and exited to meet his partner. The suits were accosted by news reporters as they walked to the car.

Mary looked down at the paperwork in her hands. She flipped through the pages, searched for something that referenced what they had said about clearing the plants today. Too many pages; she'd never find it.

Gardeners called out to Mary, "Is it true?"

"Hang on a minute!"

Lizzie and Sharalyn stepped up to look over her shoulder to help.

"This might take some time," Mary said. They passed over the surveyor's records, the sections about legal liability, and the copies of the original permit documents from thirty-one years earlier. They reached the end of the stack of papers without finding the clause. Mary fanned back to the beginning when Lizzie shot her finger out at a page as it flipped by.

"Wait a second!" Lizzie blurted out.

Mary folded back the page marked by Lizzie's finger. Lizzie leaned in and flipped a few pages back to find what had caught her eye. Mary focused on the spot where Lizzie pointed: a scribble on a black line, under which read "Buyer signature." The signature was indecipherable. But decipherable enough to know that it wasn't what she expected.

"Oh my God," Mary said. She leafed through to other pages and discovered the same signature. "What the . . . ?"

She returned to the first page and read the typed print. She looked up toward the parking lot, toward the cluster of reporters surrounding the suits.

"Gentlemen!" she bellowed.

The men stepped away from the cameras to address Mary through the fence.

"Is there a problem?" the smiling man said, though he'd stopped smiling.

"Did you look at these documents, gentlemen?" Mary said. "I believe you might want to look more closely at these documents."

Mary's heart pounded, and her exhilaration rose as the no-longer-smiling man flung open the gate and stepped into the garden path. She rotated the stack of papers to face him. He looked down to inspect the page where Mary pointed. Sudden shock colored his face. His partner walked over to join him.

The man ripped off his sunglasses, grabbed the documents from Mary, and flipped through them. He muttered under his breath, "How did this happen?" He turned to his partner and yelled, "How did this happen?"

"What?" His partner took the papers to look them over. A single burst of laughter escaped his lips. He looked up at Mary, Lizzie, and Sharalyn, then to his partner.

"I have no idea. I picked the package up from the office this morning. They said everything was in order. It was sealed, as you know."

The no-longer-smiling man reached for the paperwork, but Mary was faster. As she snatched the pages to her chest, the envelope that held all the documents fell to her feet. Lizzie bent down to sweep it up and reached in to remove a folded piece of paper. She unfolded it and turned to show Mary.

It was a photocopy of a cashier's check written in the amount of $850,000. The signature matched the one in the documents; it was not Kurt Arnold's.

Sharalyn stepped up to read the check and pointed to the memo line. "Five percent good faith deposit." Mary watched Sharalyn add it up. *850,000 dollars is 5 percent of . . .*

"Seventeen million dollars!" Sharalyn said. "I thought it was fourteen million. I'm confused."

Mary smiled for the first time in weeks. "Apparently so is Mr. Arnold. He lost a bidding war and his minions are clueless."

Oh, this is good, Mary thought. Nice to discover that someone wanted the property more than that spiteful curmudgeon. But who? And what did they plan to do with the land?

People from the crowd shouted out for Mary to explain. They sensed something was up but didn't know whether to expect good news or bad.

"Calm down, people," Mary spoke over the crowd with calm authority. "Give me a second until I figure this out, okay? I'll make an announcement once I have."

Just then, the rumble of an old Ford Falcon station wagon filled the air. The familiar squeaks grew louder as it teetered across the parking lot toward the exit. Mary, Lizzie, and Sharalyn looked up. They saw Ned's arm out the window, his finger drawing an imaginary line in the air. He rolled up to them, slowed his car to a crawl.

Over the squeal of rusty brakes, Mary called out, "Ned, you've got to see this!" She stepped toward his car.

Ned didn't stop. He kept rolling past them, but Mary noticed a grin on his face.

"I'll talk to you later, Mary. I've gotta go." With that, he drove off around the corner and disappeared.

"Ned!" Mary shouted after him. What a rotten time to leave. This was the most important day in the garden's history, and he had his mind on other things. It didn't make any sense.

The exhaust from Ned's station wagon drifted like a fog rolling in from the ocean. Mary watched it curl up in thin wisps, evaporating into invisibility. The familiar smell of Ned's clunker seeped into her brain, where something clicked.

"Oh, no, you didn't," she said to the air. As her awareness returned to her hands, she found she was still clutching the stack of documents to her chest. Her fingers were stuck to the pages. She loosened her grip on the paperwork and blinked a few times to achieve focus.

Where are my bifocals, damn it?

Mary looked at the first page of the document with fresh, albeit blurry, eyes. She held the stack at arm's length and squinted. She didn't recognize the name of the buyer listed, "The Chuck Trust," but when she looked through the pages at the indecipherable signature, it suddenly became clear. She had read that signature for years: on meeting notes, sign-in sheets, purchase orders. But today, it jumped off the document in her hands.

Kurt Arnold had lost the bidding war to their very own Ned Flossman.

CHAPTER 25
The Garden Master

The Next Morning

Ned hurried down to his plot as the sun sent long beams of light across early dewdrops, in hopes that no one would see him, especially Mary. A few hidden minutes alone in the garden before all hell broke loose—a good kind of hell, but hell nonetheless. He needed to get his story straight. They were bound to ask questions.

He was such a prominent fixture at Vista Mar Gardens that people often forgot he had lived a different life before he became garden master. They considered him as perennial as the magnolia tree in the center of the property, a steadfast landmark for members to orient themselves by. He pictured the day the garden first opened, when they had planted that tree. At the time, he was busy working as an engineer—he'd had no idea that decades later he would oversee the whole place.

It was like sweeping a dusty attic as his mind drifted back to those days; each brush forward kicked up memories that floated into the light of his mind's eye from all those years ago. As with many engineers, Ned's obsession with tinkering superseded his quest for order. As a young man, he'd spent his afternoons taking things apart and putting them back together—a trait that poor Charlie had inherited.

Ned laughed to himself. *Between the two of us, it's a miracle we didn't have crates of "extra" parts lying about.*

It was much further back, in his younger years, that Ned had first started gardening with his parents. He'd noticed his hand pruners were dull more often than not, and it bothered him how they never quite had enough spring in the grip. Without a second thought, Ned set out to invent a better set of shears. At the time, pruning shears sold in the United States had either a welded bolt or a rivet that held the two crosspieces together.

What a pain in the rear to clean and sharpen. Sometimes I had to resolder the bolt back into place.

Then—in '42, was it?—his father had read to him about Félix Flisch in Switzerland, who was developing a new type of pruning shear. Ned had his own ideas, and he wanted to share them. He wrote letters, sent drawings to Félix, with suggestions for how Flisch could improve upon the typical welded-bolt concept. Ned proposed a bolt that resembled a gear with tines, which he used as a locking mechanism to keep the shears closed when not in use. He also suggested selling the pruners with a special wrench that facilitated disassembly and cleaning.

Ned was overjoyed when that first reply had come in the mail. Félix Flisch was impressed with young Ned's ideas, and a friendship blossomed across continents. Over the next four years, Félix and Ned perfected what became known as the Felco pruner. Félix promised Ned that he would reward his ingenuity with a percentage of sales. It took a decade or so, but that promise had made Ned a very wealthy man.

The members of Vista Mar Gardens never suspected a thing. Every time someone had tried to convince him to send his rusty Falcon to the junkyard, he waved them off.

"It's a perfectly good, working car. I don't need another one."

Sure, he could buy any car he wanted, but he never said that aloud, and he didn't buy extravagant things. No one knew about his secret riches. He saved it all. It wasn't always that way though.

Good Lord, did I go to town.

When those first royalty checks arrived in the mail, he bought diamonds for his wife—his girlfriend at the time—and bought a big house in an up-and-coming community called Santa Monica. Paid for it outright. They took expensive vacations, and he entertained the idea of buying a hot air balloon. *That might've been fun*, he reminisced.

When Charlie arrived, everything changed.

Once Ned had formulated a plan to provide for his son's future, he diverted most of each royalty check into a trust for Charlie. He acted as though that money simply didn't exist and went back to engineering, assuming the life of a regular workingman. Easier than trying to make people comfortable around a rich guy. As it turned out, leisure didn't suit him well, and his wife had convinced him he ought to keep busy. *She was always right, wasn't she?*

When Charlie grew old enough to understand, Ned told him about the trust in his name. That only made him more ambitious. Charlie was determined to build his own empire, not to rely on his father's money for success. Like father, like son; both of them lived life as if the money didn't exist. Ned laughed out loud.

Ned was downright frugal when it came to spending money for garden supplies or tools. If a valve broke, he'd rather fix it than buy a new one. If someone asked him for a new shredder blade, Ned shopped for days before settling on the best price. Now, ironically, he'd spent it all on the garden.

Lizzie hunted for Ned as soon as she arrived through the gates. She didn't need to look far; she found him in the most obvious place: kneeling in his weedy plot. She stood in front of his mailbox, waited for him to acknowledge her. He didn't notice her standing there, so she grabbed her gloves out of her back pocket and dusted off the mailbox with a few good slaps.

He looked up. "Oh, hi, Lizzie."

"So, Ned"—she put her hands on her hips—"Mary is bursting with theories on how you pulled this off, not to mention where you got all that money."

Ned leaned back onto his heels and brushed his hands off on his pants. He smiled. "Aw, it's a long story. I'll tell you some other time."

"Are you kidding me? Come on, Ned. We never saw this coming. What did you do?"

He pursed his lips, looked to one side. "What did you tell the members?" he said.

"We didn't. Mary made something up on the spot. Generous donor, or some such thing. She wanted to hear it from you first. I'm sure she'll be here any minute."

"Yeah, she left about ten messages on my answering machine last night. I figured I'd let her stew a bit." He chuckled. For a moment it looked as though he wasn't going to tell Lizzie, but he leaned forward and pointed a finger at her.

"All right, but you have to promise to keep this top secret. Not one garden member, only the board, you hear?"

She couldn't imagine that it wouldn't leak out to the membership in a heartbeat, but she could speak for herself. "You have my word."

Ned unfurled the tale. In secret, he'd gone to the city offices to uncover the history of the garden, as Mary had. Once he discovered the right person to talk to in the Real Estate Division, he'd made an appointment, with help from Ralph, who hacked into the director's calendar and scheduled a one-on-one for Ned. Once in the meeting, Ned asked whether anyone other than Kurt had bid on the property. It was common knowledge among the board that the city had recently suffered from drastic budget cuts. The director told Ned how happy she was that someone had offered 50 percent over the asking price for the property, enough to obliterate the multitude of other offers, but she was still nervous that Kurt Arnold might back out. Especially with the mayor breathing down their necks to favor Kurt's bid.

"She said it was 'a tragedy that someone planned to destroy a garden'"—Ned mimicked the director's lilting voice—"'but times being what they are,' they had already spent the money in their minds. When I informed her that I might have a better offer, the director lit up like a Christmas tree. And I'll tell you, when she found out that I worked for the garden, you've never seen someone so grateful. She actually bowed to me across the desk."

Lizzie laughed. She pictured Ned on a throne, with the city official bowing in reverence before him, like Fred Astaire at the beginning of *Royal Wedding*.

Ned continued. "All of a sudden she was very helpful and introduced me to everyone in her office. She directed me to a good real-a-tor to get all the paperwork in order. I guessed a counteroffer had to be pretty big to steal it out from under that old curmudgeon and the rest, so Ralph did a little research into Kurt's financial affairs, and I made sure my counteroffer was out of his reach, at least enough for the city to consider it a final offer."

Ned grew quiet. He looked down at his hands, rubbed them together.

"What else was I going to do with it?" His voice cracked. "I saved everything for Charlie, and outside of him, this place is the only thing I've got. I contemplated giving my money to a charity when I drop dead, but this made a lot more sense. I may have lost Charlie"—the side of his mouth turned up—"but today I've left a legacy to seven hundred and sixty kids."

Lizzie stood speechless, stunned by his show of generosity. She'd never experienced anything like this before. Tears welled up in her eyes, though she tried to blink them back.

"Why are you crying?" Ned said.

Lizzie shook her head and wiped her eyes, tried to form words. "I'm . . . I'm honored to be one of your seven hundred sixty kids, Ned."

She lunged forward and threw her arms around his neck. He patted her on the back and squeezed her shoulders.

"Aw heck, it's my pleasure."

Kurt Arnold pushed past three people in line at the county clerk's office, demanding to speak to the moron who had screwed him out of a deal that was rightfully his. The clerk stared back at Kurt, until she recognized who he was. Fear washed over her at first; she edged herself away from the counter on her rolling office stool. She tried to ignore the flurry of insults Kurt flung across the counter and instead stared at his finger repeatedly tapping on her glass blotter. She wondered if it might crack from the pressure.

She wasn't sure what to say to this man, though she fought her natural inclination to give him a piece of her mind. Her position required her to be polite at the very least.

"I'm sorry your offer wasn't chosen by the department, Mr. Arnold," she said, as formal as possible. "We received several."

"Exactly! I should have been informed of any counteroffers. Why wasn't I?" His voice echoed off the dark wood walls, as did murmurs from those behind him in line.

She glanced over his shoulder and smiled at the waiting customers.

"I'm not sure how that was overlooked, sir, but I recall that there was an issue with your qualifications."

"Qualifications? That property was mine to buy. It is mine. The mayor—"

"I'm sorry, sir, but the mayor mentioned you're under investigation for accessory to arson. Does that ring a bell?" The clerk rolled on her stool to the bookshelf behind her. She leaned back, reached for a gift basket overflowing with fresh Pink Lady apples, persimmons, dried Champagne grapes, and pomegranates. She plucked an apple out of the basket and offered it to Kurt. "The department chose the best offer, sir. Care for an apple? They're locally grown and in season." She smiled.

The look on Kurt's face was priceless. She couldn't help giggling after he stormed out of the office, though it wasn't at all professional. He got what he deserved, and those nice people got to keep their garden.

She took a bite of the crisp apple.

"Next, please."

CHAPTER 26

Fertilizing

December

Lizzie kept her word and made Mary promise the same. They told only the board about Ned's dealings downtown. Board members, in turn, had sworn themselves to secrecy to keep Ned's generosity under wraps, to protect him from the rumor mill that spun unhindered through the garden. Ned didn't want anyone to view him differently.

"I got this far without anyone knowing I've got money, and I want to keep it that way." Ned stood next to Mary after the meeting.

"Your secret's going to burn a hole in my pocket, Ned, but I swear I'll never tell anyone," Mary said. "Well, maybe my hairdresser."

"I'll make Bernice president if you do." Ned laughed.

Mary reached for Ned's face with both hands and kissed him, just for shock value. She shook her head and left Ned chuckling as she strode off.

"Let's make her vice president," Mary yelled back over her shoulder. "We could use the help."

After months of tension, the garden members breathed a collective sigh of relief. Peace had returned once more.

The news they received was that a "friend of the garden" had bought the land and donated it back to Vista Mar in perpetuity. There was a sense of awe and wonder for the place, weeds and all. Gardeners looked upon their vegetables as precious gifts. They decided to throw a community harvest party to celebrate the holidays.

Even though December's chill blanketed the rest of the country, Los Angeles experienced a weeklong heat wave. The members took full advantage. They arrived laden with baskets of fresh-baked fruit cakes, armloads of newly harvested salads, and garden-grown casseroles prepared with love. The group acknowledged this was more than a holiday party; this was a celebration of a new beginning—independence. Before the property sale, there was an air of stinginess about the garden. Everyone had believed the eviction signified their last chance to grow their own food, so they hoarded their harvests for themselves. After the sale, generosity led the way.

Mary saw evidence of this renewed generosity as she walked along plot rows. Deep green leaves of lacinato kale passed from one soil-covered hand to another across plot borders. She found harvest baskets of all shapes and sizes stationed at the big magnolia tree, the garden's central location for free giveaways. Citrus from the orchard was piled high in cardboard boxes, up for grabs for all members. Mary smiled at the sight of it. The garden had shifted even more toward becoming a true community; she was proud to be part of it.

She had also discovered a different brand of abundance closer to home. When she walked by Bernice's plot, she noticed it looked less formal than it used to be. She couldn't quite put her finger on it, but it appeared more casual, more human. Then it dawned on her—Bernice had planted wildflowers. While it was true she had planted the flowers in neat rows along the edges of the plot where her roses once stood, they were wildflowers nonetheless. Mary heard laughter at the end of the pathway in the distance. She squinted in the low morning sun to identify who it was. There, dressed in holiday red and green, furry Santa hat included, stood Bernice, chatting with a group of her neighbors.

Something has definitely changed. She headed toward Bernice to get a better look.

Bernice reached into her tote bag and produced a stack of envelopes. She shuffled through them, pulled out a green envelope decorated with cellophane-wrapped candy canes, and handed it to Ralph, who stood next to her.

"A little something." She gave him an awkward smile. "Happy Christmas, Ralph. Oh, bloody hell, I keep doing that. Happy Chanukah, dear."

"It's okay, I celebrate both." Ralph grinned down at the candy canes. "Thanks, Bernice. These look homemade."

"That's because they are, dear." Bernice bubbled with excitement. "I'm taking a confectionery class, and these are my first batch. No, I take that back, my second. The first batch was a disaster. I mixed the colored stripes too quickly and the whole thing turned brown. It was quite depressing, actually. I dare say these look much improved."

The group erupted in laughter, and after a moment's hesitation, Bernice joined in. She looked alive for the first time in months. It was good to see. She glanced up at Mary and excused herself from the others. As she approached, she held out a card.

"Happy Chanukah, Mary." She placed the card in Mary's hands.

"Aw, thanks, Bernice. This is lovely," Mary said. "You look well."

"I'm trying." Bernice nodded. "Much better since Ned's shenanigans."

"Well, I'm glad. I noticed your wildflowers. That's a nice addition."

"Do you think so? I'm still adjusting to it, but I needed . . ." She paused.

Mary finished for her. "A change?"

Bernice met her eyes and smiled. "Undoubtedly."

"Good," Mary said. She took a beat before asking, "Have you seen Arthur lately?"

"Every once in a while, at the shelter. Still the same. But at least I see him."

The two stood together, looked out over the garden, and took in the festivities.

Mary's stomach growled. "Come on. Let's go get some of those gingerbread cookies before they're gone."

"I take it this isn't the time to question your priorities."

"Bet your ass, Bernie." Mary took Bernice's arm, pulling her toward the golden light of the buffet.

Before they reached the meeting area, Mary caught sight of something and turned to get a better look. A few rows over, she spied Ned in his plot. A cloud of gray dust billowed around him.

"What on earth?" She pulled Bernice down the hill.

Bernice trailed along, miffed by the sudden change in direction. "What is it . . . ? Oh!"

She, too, noticed the mysterious cloud of gray dust emanating from Ned's plot. He stood pensive in the cloud. When they got close enough to see, Bernice gasped.

Ned held the urn with Charlie's ashes. The lid was open.

"What are you doing, Ned!" Mary said.

Ned looked startled, but he put his hand out to stop them.

"I know this looks weird, Mary, but it's something I need to do. Stand back or you'll get it all over you."

Ned waited for the breeze to subside. At the right moment he tipped the urn with both hands to sprinkle the rest of Charlie's ashes over his soil like fertilizer. Mary and Bernice stood motionless. They watched Ned distribute his son's ashes around his plot, mostly in a small trench along the perimeter.

After a moment of silence, Ned spoke. "Now that I'm sure this garden will always be here, I want him here, you understand?" He paused. "This way, I'll always be with him and he'll help me grow. That's what kids do, don't they?"

Bernice and Mary nodded. Mary understood, even if it was unconventional, and probably illegal. They stood silent next to Ned while he swirled the soil and ashes together with his foot.

"Besides"—he looked up with a smile—"this soil could use some ash anyway. I overdid it with gypsum once, made it too acidic."

Despite Bernice's attempt to be solemn and respectful, she burst out laughing. Mary followed suit, then Ned. The women cringed at the idea, but they agreed that Ned had done the right thing. There were no words between them, but they shared the unspoken truth: Ned's garden would forever be connected to his love for Charlie.

CHAPTER 27
Sprouts

Late January

The holidays swept through Vista Mar, ushering in a new year and a renewed sense of dedication. Gardeners devoured seed catalogs over Christmas vacation, and eagerly anticipated the arrival of new seed varieties in bundles of crisp packets through the mail. Advanced gardeners began their ritual of seed-starting in professional growing trays and mini greenhouse covers. Some simply started seeds in collections of yogurt or cottage cheese cups under a homemade tent of sticks and plastic sheeting. The buzz of possibility was palpable.

Lizzie had her own set of seed adventures to try. As a New Year's resolution, she planned to experiment with a few unexplored varieties of heirloom lima beans and a rare salad green or two. She included the usual suspects, too: sweet peas, Swiss chard, tomatoes, peppers, and green onions, but left room to dedicate some space to edamame. Enough for snacks with Jared.

One day as they stood in Jared's plot, she offered to help him plan out his garden as well, but he said no thanks. He had a few tricks up his sleeve.

"I'm going to plant a lemon tree," he announced.

Lizzie sighed. "Jared, you know the rules. No trees in plots."

"Works every time." He winked and revealed a handful of tangled bare-root Alpine strawberry seedlings from behind his back. "Broke down and paid the extra shipping costs to get them right away."

Lizzie smacked him playfully on the shoulder, then kissed him. She had a ways to go before she'd learn to recognize a joke in Jared's eye, but she was learning. *Pretty soon, he won't get anything past me.*

She took a deep breath to broach a subject that had been on her mind for two weeks, which is how long it had taken to build up the courage to ask. "I know you want to plan your own garden, but if you're up for it, maybe we could . . . strategize a little? I mean, it's silly for us both to plant chard when we could consolidate it in one plot and use the other space for something that takes up more room." She paused to wait for Jared's reaction to the idea.

Jared looked at her wide-eyed, cautious. "You mean cross plot boundaries?"

Lizzie felt a lump form in her throat and realized her body was gearing up to hyperventilate. Maybe it was too soon. She had toyed with the idea in her mind, but it meant a new level of commitment they might not be ready for. Jared continued to stare at her. She didn't know whether to retract the offer or continue her pitch.

Jared broke the silence. "You mean like growing *our* greens in your plot, and growing *our* pumpkins, zucchini, and sweet potatoes in mine?"

Lizzie exhaled slowly, trying to stave off the anxiety stemming from this excruciating experiment in willful vulnerability. "Yes, but stop saying it like that or I'm going to throw up."

"You want to share plots?" A huge grin spread across his face as he reached for her shoulders. He kept her from doubling over and instead pulled her into a bear hug. "You're ready?"

"Shut up and say yes, okay?" She buried her face in his chest.

Jared let go of Lizzie to reach into his back pocket. He pulled out a folded piece of paper and handed it to her. "Open it."

Lizzie unfolded the paper to reveal a schematic of two plots, his and hers, annotated with crop locations and question marks. She glanced up at Jared. "How long have you had this?"

"Mmm, a couple weeks."

They were on the same page. Lizzie scanned the design for issues. Only one or two items would require negotiation; the rest was in alignment with what she had in mind. They sat down in the mulch pathway to review Jared's ideas together.

Lizzie's fears of losing herself and, of course, losing Jared, had muddied her thinking during their entire relationship thus far.

But with Jared in agreement, she felt she could breathe again. More than that. She realized that, as with the garden, the future held its secrets and she could neither divine nor control them. Lizzie knew she would thrive, even if the partnership fell flat on its face. Something had switched on, anchored her in a way that helped her relax in the face of uncertainty.

They decided to each keep a section of their gardens separate for themselves. Jared planted the Alpine strawberries in his; Lizzie planned to grow asparagus in hers. Together, they calculated enough space to grow everything they wanted—well, no gardener ever has enough for everything, but by the end of the discussion, they were content with their two intermingled plots.

LIZZIE, BOLSTERED BY a new confidence when challenged with the unknown, indulged her curiosity outside the garden. She felt more comfortable venturing from the beaten path on occasion. One day on her walk home, she dared herself to walk into that sketchy-looking shop, the Past's Future.

"It's time to find out what's going on in there," she murmured as she took a deep breath and swung open the door.

A musty odor reminiscent of Grandma's basement greeted her. Gold-gilded books, crystal chandeliers, and about a hundred vintage movie cameras were displayed in glass curio cabinets lining the walls.

The clerk popped out from behind an antique sewing machine. "Looking for anything special today?"

Lizzie stood amazed. *Wow, this is not the psychic-palm-reader drug front I expected.* Her eyes landed on an antique weather vane, with a gleaming sun and arrow above the four directions. She pictured it atop the metal trellis in her plot. A perfect fit.

Lizzie brought it to the register.

"First time here?" the clerk asked. Lizzie nodded. "Here's a coupon for ten percent off your next visit."

"Thanks. I'll have to bring my boyfriend."

That sense of calm, what was it? She was in love. Sanely in love. Though she had no idea where this relationship would go, it somehow didn't matter. She had already gained something from giving in to the experience—old wounds had healed. Her excitement about the journey overrode the fears that had prevented her from feeling safe in the past.

Ned and Ralph walked up from the compost area toward the main shed. Ned eyed Ralph, who appeared more animated than Ned had ever seen him. Ralph was midstory, telling Ned about his recent trip to Comic Con with Bernice.

"I dressed her up as Blind Al from *Deadpool*, and I, naturally, went as Weasel because"—he gestured to his current attire, zip-up hoodie and sweatpants—"that took no effort. People loved Bernice. She got asked for selfies on every aisle."

Ned grinned. "The attention probably did her good."

"She's actually pretty fun to hang out with, once you get her out of here."

Ned noticed that ever since Bernice gave Ralph the holiday card with homemade candy canes, the two spent a lot of time together outside the garden. Bernice had told Ned they went to museums, watched movies, and kept each other company on New Year's Eve.

"She's like the grandmother I never had," Ralph said.

Ned laughed. "Go figure."

Ralph went on about how Bernice had taught him how to make toffee, in exchange for teaching her to use internet voice-mail. They helped each other in the garden, as well, Bernice giving Ralph tips on growing roses and Ralph assisting with Bernice's new, conveniently located compost bin. If anyone asked, Bernice laughed and said that Ralph was her wild affair. But the truth was that Ralph filled the void Arthur had left behind years ago. She never looked happier in all her years at the garden, and Ralph thrived on being essential to someone else. It warmed Ned's heart to see Ralph connect with other people at Vista Mar. Charlie's legacy would carry on in these friendships.

CHAPTER 28

Growth

One Year Later—January

The following winter, Vista Mar bustled with gardeners old and young. While many parts of the country lay dormant, they harvested winter greens, brassicas, root veggies, and peas. Once again, Angelenos were hard at work plotting out warm-season crops and starting seeds indoors for tomatoes, peppers, eggplant, and squash. Spring was already here.

Down the slope in Lizzie's plot, she and Jared worked together to shovel compost into one of her raised beds. Their experimental "open-border" gardens had proved successful in the past year: higher yields with less work, and more time to relax together. Now, it was time to map the spring layout.

Lizzie sat down with her notebook and a pencil at the entrance to her plot. She browsed the list of specialty crops they had made the night before. Erba Stella 'Minutina,' a rare salad green, would go in her plot, while Jared wanted to try giant pumpkins in his.

"Are you sure?" she asked.

"I want to take it out into the ocean—you know, for one of those giant pumpkin boat races."

"Okay, Jack Sparrow." Lizzie just hoped the squirrels wouldn't eat it before it matured.

Jared pointed from where he knelt to her potting table off in the corner.

"Hey, can you grab my canteen over there?"

"Sure thing, sweetie."

She stepped over Jared's feet toward the potting table, upon which sat a small cluster of clay flowerpots bursting with hyacinth bulbs in full bloom. She loved the fragrance and leaned forward, closing her eyes to smell them. She opened her eyes to find another pot nestled behind these: tiny, without flowers, but filled with soil. Tucked into the rich earth in the terracotta pot—as if grown from the soil—sat a diamond ring. She gasped.

She put her hand to her mouth. "Oh my God."

She spun around to find Jared standing a few feet away with his arms out to his sides, grinning.

"What do you think?" he asked.

"Are you kidding me?" Lizzie dropped her notebook, rushed forward to kiss him. Jared stopped her gently, held her back.

"Wait, wait. I want to be official." He stepped back and took hold of her hands. He inhaled and settled his eyes on hers.

"Lizzie, I want nothing more than to grow old with you. Will you garden with me forever?"

"Of course!" Tears welled up in her eyes as she kissed him. She ran her fingers through his hair, held his face in her hands. She wanted to capture forever how he looked in this moment. He kissed her forehead. They looked up the hill toward a few gardeners working in their plots. Jared let out a hoot, and all eyes turned to the couple.

"She said yes!" he shouted.

Lizzie laughed. "It looks like we have more than just spring garden plans to make."

Over the past year, no one had received a complaint from Kurt Arnold. Ned wondered what had become of him after he lost the bid on the property, but the answer came one day when a large truck arrived in front of Kurt's house. Ned shouted out to anyone within earshot and pointed across the field as the roll door lifted on the truck. He had overheard at the post office that Mr. Arnold had bought a place in Beverly Hills. Looked like it was true. Kurt Arnold was moving out.

Gardeners clambered to the crest of the hill to see what Ned was hollering about. No one had noticed the For Sale sign in front of the house—Kurt Arnold was old news. The cluster of gardeners watched as overall-clad workers began to load furniture and boxes into the truck. Kurt had yet to make an appearance, but he didn't need to. The message was clear: he had lost, and the garden view from his front window served as a constant reminder.

Mary appeared next to Ned and startled him when she cheered like a fan at a baseball game. Together they gazed across the field.

Mary asked, "Is he going to prison?"

"Naw," Ned replied. "They never found enough evidence, but the investigation ruined his chances of buying this place. Good thinking, Mary, pressing charges for arson."

"Thanks, but we know who the real hero is here." She turned on her heels toward the shed. "Be right back, moneybags."

Mary returned moments later with an armful of plastic chairs from the meeting area. She glanced at Ned as she handed out the chairs. "We're going to need cups, Ned."

He pondered her words for a second, then with a knowing smile, set off for the office. On his way, he watched Mary go to her car, open the trunk, and unearth her insulated lunch box from beneath a mound of empty seed flats.

Ned returned from the office carrying a stack of paper cups and several cans of ginger ale tucked in his pockets. Mary and her fellow members had set up chairs in the field to watch Kurt's possessions travel from house to truck. Mary unzipped her lunch box and produced a small assortment of cheeses and crackers, which she distributed among her fellow gardeners along with fresh oranges from the orchard. Others found snacks to share from their own private supplies, and suddenly everyone had something to eat: granola bars, juice boxes, beef jerky, and even a suspicious flask to which Mary gave the stink eye.

Ned pulled the cans of ginger ale from his pockets as he caught his breath. "They're not cold, but they'll still taste good."

He poured a round. Gardeners sat to watch. It took a few hours, but everyone stayed for the end. Someone ordered pizza delivery to keep the party going. They smiled and raised a glass as the last box disappeared into the truck and the movers slid the door closed.

Mary held her glass aloft. "Goodbye, neighbor."

The other gardeners followed suit with cheers and salutations while they clinked their glasses in a farewell toast. Ned sat down next to Mary. Ralph and Bernice sipped their warm ginger ale side by side. They all waved to the truck as it pulled away from the empty house.

Ralph leaned forward in his chair toward Mary. "Do we know who's moving in?"

Mary shook her head. "I have no idea, but I hope they're aware of what they're getting into."

They all laughed, then Sharalyn cleared her throat.

"They are," she said.

"They are what?" Mary twisted in her chair to face Sharalyn. The look on her face made Mary ask, "Do you have something you want to share with the class, Ms. Sharalyn?"

Sharalyn took a sip of ginger ale. "I'm just sayin', I know who bought that house." She shrugged.

The group bubbled with questions. Ned flipped his chair around to face Sharalyn. They all settled their eyes on her in anticipation, eager for details of their new neighbor. Sharalyn was silent until Mary blurted out, "Spill the beans, Missy Thing. I'm dying here."

"Well . . ." Sharalyn stretched it out as long as she could. "With all this gardening going on, two plots aren't enough. I figured I better get off the water and put down some roots . . ."

Her words were drowned out by cheers from the group.

Mary jumped up out of her seat and tried to pick Sharalyn up out of her chair. When that failed, she hugged her and wished her well in her new home.

"Somebody's got to watch over this place," Sharalyn said. "It might as well be me and my husband."

"But what about your boat?" Ned's question halted the festivities.

Sharalyn waved her hand. "We'll get another one someday. You wouldn't believe the bidding war we had between two vintage houseboat enthusiasts. It was crazy, but we ended up with a nice down payment for the house. And my husband just got a promotion, so we took the plunge. One of Charlie's friends we met at the memorial negotiated the price down for us. Seems the seller was eager to move out of the neighborhood." She tipped her head back and hooted. Everyone around her joined in.

"My brothers were furious with me, but as soon as I mentioned my new guest room and invited them out here to visit sunny California, they got over it quick."

Bernice congratulated Sharalyn, then stepped aside to make room for Ralph, who offered a fist bump. The trio raised their glasses in a new toast—to their new neighbor and new home-owner.

"To new beginnings," Bernice said.

Their toast was interrupted by a voice from the driveway. "Excuse me." They looked over to see a young woman with teal green hair leaning out the window of her car. "I'm looking for Ananda? She's giving me a garden plot today."

Ned caught a glimpse of Ralph's face when he spotted the new member. He watched Bernice study Ralph's expression for a few seconds, then she leaned in. "Are the angels singing, dear?"

Ralph turned his head to Bernice. "You hear them, too?"

Bernice patted him on the arm and said, "Why don't you go help that young lady find her new section rep." She scooted him off in the direction of the driveway, smiling after him.

Ned chuckled and turned with Mary toward the sunset to take in the beauty of their second home. Patches of green glowed in the golden afternoon light. The two veteran garden-ers breathed in the ocean air and stood silent next to each other for a moment.

"Yup," Ned said.

"We're spoiled," Mary finished. She put her hand on his shoulder. "What's next, Garden Master?"

"I have no idea, but I'm sure we'll find out soon enough."

As spring arrived at Vista Mar, new life sprang forth from the soil. Plants and trees adorned themselves with fragrant blos-soms and the promise of fruit. The cycle of life came full circle, and as before, the gardeners at Vista Mar speculated about what Mother Nature held in store for them next.

AFTERTHOUGHTS

While Vista Mar Gardens is based on a real community garden in Los Angeles, California, it is important to state that all the characters and events that take place in *Garden Variety* are fictionalized. Many of the characters are composites of three or four people, some of whom have been members of the community garden over the past twenty-four years. There is a lot of fodder for story in a community garden, and there are glimpses of truth throughout this book to reflect that. But my characters took on their own lives and stories early on. On more than one occasion, something I wrote in the manuscript years before would suddenly come to pass in reality at the garden. I claim no powers of divination, merely coincidence. I also want to mention that during the decade-long process of writing this book in fits and starts, weather patterns changed dramatically from the first to the final draft. "Wildfire smoke" used to be "fireplace smoke," and the fall planting season shifted two months later. I attempted to be as accurate as possible with Southern California seasonality, but I expect that in the not-too-distant future, the gardening calendar year illustrated here will become yet another piece of history. Last but not least, while Felco pruners are a real thing, as is their inventor Félix Flisch, my fictitious character Ned Flossman had nothing to do with their invention.

ACKNOWLEDGMENTS

The journey from first draft to the book you hold in your hands was lengthy, and I couldn't have done it without the help of the following people: To my "writers' group" of gals, including Lynn Jordan, Colby Devitt, Paloma Cain, Tree Wright, and Nancy Perlman, who first mentioned that *Garden Variety* should be a novel, not a screenplay. They asked the right questions and helped hone early drafts. To Terrie Silverman and my Creative Rites classmates—despite the state of my first draft you were kind. To my husband, Andrew Cheeseman, for suggesting at the very beginning that he record an interview with me about the characters. In that conversation I realized Ned's critical story arc. To my classmates in UCLA's Novel III and IV classes, who scrutinized every word, and to Mark Sarvas, our instructor, who guided and, in a good way, intimidated us into being better writers. To my first set of readers: Kinga Toth, Mary Grace Castelo, Shifra Teitelbaum, Corrine Lightweaver, Hexie Cheeseman, Jane Rose Linesch, Julie Mann, and Dana Morgan. Their insights brought the manuscript to the next level. To my editors: Jennifer Silva Redmond, Ashley Patrick, Lucia Macro, and everyone at William Morrow, thank you for your keen eye and gentle address. And to my agent, Priya Doraswamy, who saw *Garden Variety* the way I did, was equally excited about it, and found it the perfect home, I cannot thank you enough.

About the author

About the book

Insights,
Interviews
& More . . .

Meet Christy Wilhelmi

Inga Ornelas

CHRISTY WILHELMI empowers people to grow their own food, to be more self-reliant, and to reduce pollution and waste, one garden at a time. She is the founder of Gardenerd, the ultimate online resource for garden nerds, where she publishes newsletters, her award-winning blog, informative videos, and a top-ranked podcast. Christy also specializes in small-space, organic-vegetable garden design and consulting. She holds regular organic gardening classes in California and has co-taught organic gardening at the Esalen Institute in Big Sur, California.

Christy was a board member of Ocean View Farms Community Garden in Mar Vista, California, for more than twenty years, and she gardens almost entirely with heirloom vegetables. Between 70 and 80 percent of her family's produce comes from her garden of less than three hundred square feet. Her writing has appeared in many publications, including *Edible Los Angeles* and *Edible Westside* magazines, *Heirloom Gardener* magazine, and the weekly column Mar Vista Farmers' Market Wrap Up for Patch.com. She is also the author of nonfiction gardening books such as *Gardening for Geeks*; *400+ Tips for Organic Gardening Success: A Decade of Tricks, Tools, Recipes, and Resources from Gardenerd.com*; and *Grow Your Own Mini Fruit Garden. Garden Variety* is her debut novel. ∿

10 Takeaway Gardening Lessons from *Garden Variety*

1. Create your ecosystem. Create habitats or living spaces for birds, butterflies, and other wildlife in your garden. Explore your yard and observe where you can install birdhouses, feeders, owl boxes, hawk perches, and toad houses, where applicable. Plant beneficial insectary plants (like members of the *Umbelliferae* or *Apiaceae* family) that attract good bugs. Good bugs help police the bad bugs for you, so you don't have to work as hard. Grow trap crops like nasturtiums, calendula, and marigolds to attract pests toward them and away from your tasty produce. Flowers of all kinds attract bees to increase the yields of many crops, from squashes to berries. Each of the plants listed above can be part of a healthy garden ecosystem. Vista Mar Gardens had many of these elements in play.

2. Plant cover crops. Not only do cover crops provide habitats for some beneficial insects, they also help condition garden soils in many ways. Leguminous crops like peas, beans,

and hairy vetch pull atmospheric nitrogen out of the sky and "fix" it in the roots of these plants. When you cut down the cover crop, leave the roots in place. Nitrogen nodules on the roots will break down and release the nitrogen for future crops to use. Cover crops also build soil structure, provide protection from sun and wind, and make a home for microbes to colonize around their roots. Lizzie grew cover crops each year over winter to help turn her sandy soil loamier.

3. Use compost. Compost is a key ingredient to keeping plants happy and thriving, both before and during the growing season. Compost contains some nutrients but is mostly an inoculum to fortify soils with beneficial microbes. Those microbes create networks of soil aggregates and improve your garden soil's ability to hold moisture, drain well, and synthesize nutrients for plants. Compost also makes clay soil more porous and holds sandy soil together like a sponge. It's the multipurpose fix-it ingredient for troublesome soil. Apply compost to garden beds before planting new crops each season. Mix compost ▶

with organic fertilizer or worm castings midseason and sprinkle it around your plants for a boost as they begin to flower and set fruit. Members of VMG knew that compost was the best ingredient for their soil. That's why they lined up early to get it.

4. Water with kelp. Kelp emulsions and extracts are great for a couple of reasons. Kelp offers a low level of broad-spectrum nutrients that help ease transplant shock when you first plant your seedlings. Water with diluted kelp to give plants these micronutrients and they will thank you for it. Kelp also has potassium, which encourages flowering and fruiting and overall plant vigor. Keep kelp emulsions and extracts in your arsenal of tricks. It was a secret Ralph employed to win the unofficial first-tomato contest every year.

5. Know your seeds. If you want to save seeds (and therefore money) from your garden produce, grow heirloom and open-pollinated varieties. Open pollinated (OP) means that any seed saved from an OP plant will grow out to look and taste just like its parent. Heirlooms

are also open-pollinated seeds, but they have history, sometimes dating back hundreds of years. Hybrid seeds, on the other hand, are grown in a controlled environment, and the seeds saved from these parent plants are wild cards; they won't breed true to type. You may end up like Ananda, with Early Girl tomato seeds that grow into something else entirely.

6. Pick one zucchini plant. Some of us feel that six-packs (aka pony packs) of zucchini seedlings shouldn't be legal to sell. One zucchini plant is more than enough for most families. Each zucchini plant will produce dozens of squashes in a season. And if you leave for a weekend, you'll have baseball bats when you return. One of those bats is enough to feed an army. You can always plant another squash as your one zucchini plant begins to wane—if you aren't sick of it by then. Sharalyn learned the hard way when she ran out of people on whom to off-load her surplus.

7. Grow bulb fennel, not wild fennel. This isn't a common mistake, but it can happen. Wild fennel is terribly ▶

invasive, and while it is a member of the *Umbelliferae* (or *Apiaceae*) family, this is one to avoid. It sends down deep roots that make it difficult to eradicate. It can take over a patch of soil in no time and never give it back. Be diligent when selecting fennel plants and seeds at the nursery and keep an eye out for wild types. Wild fennel is all over California and was pervasive at Vista Mar Gardens.

8. Cut back on water. When growing potatoes, you'll notice the leaves will start to turn yellow or brown toward the end of the growing season. Resist the urge to water your potato patch or else you'll end up like Sharalyn did (and the author), with rotten, putrid potatoes and anaerobic soil that smells like garbage. Instead, let the potato foliage continue to die back as the tubers dry down. This will firm the skins and make the potatoes more resilient to bruising and damage during harvesting.

9. Consider using ollas. If you live in a dry climate with either compacted or fast-draining soil, consider adding

ollas to your garden. These unglazed urns sit underground, with only their necks showing above the soil level. Fill the jugs with water and your plants will appreciate the slow percolation right where the roots need it most. Gardeners at Vista Mar Gardens utilized these Spanish ollas when they couldn't water midday during the drought.

10. Prune your roses in four steps. Follow Sharalyn's simple process for pruning roses in winter:

- Remove all the leaves before pruning. More experienced gardeners don't have to do this, but it makes the plant's structure more visible for beginners. It also helps to prevent diseases like rust and mildew, usually found on the leaves, from overwintering on the rosebush.

- Remove all horizontal canes, especially those growing toward the center of the bush. This opens the center and creates space for future growth. Cut them back to the main vertical canes.

- Prune back vertical canes to the desired height. Shrub roses can ▶

10 Takeaway Gardening Lessons from *Garden Variety* (continued)

> be cut down to twelve inches, but floribundas and tea roses can be taller.
>
> - Dab a dot of Elmer's glue on the tip of each freshly cut cane. This prevents cane borers from finding their way into your roses.

For more tips like these, check out Christy Wilhelmi's nonfiction books *Gardening for Geeks* and *Grow Your Own Mini Fruit Garden*. ∾

Small-Space Growing Tips for Home and Community Gardens

Not everyone is graced with acreage or a big backyard in which to grow fruit and vegetables. In fact, many people are limited to a balcony, patio, or postage-stamp-sized yard. Those who have even less space opt to apply for a plot at a community garden. We gardeners have the burning desire to grow as much food as possible in the space we have. So how do we bring our homesteading dreams to life? The answer is biointensive gardening methods.

The word *biointensive* is an umbrella term that means "grow a lot of stuff in a small space." Biointensive methods make efficient use of resources through tight plant-spacing techniques, while building a foundation of abundantly rich soil. Think about it this way, if you want to grow a bountiful garden, it begins with great soil.

How do we build great soil? Whether you are growing in containers, raised beds, or your existing soil, the best amendments include compost and worm castings. Compost is magical in that it can solve problems in both clay and sandy soils. In clay soils, compost adds space between particles, allowing for better drainage and air ▶

Small-Space Growing Tips for Home and Community Gardens *(continued)*

flow. In sandy soils, compost acts to hold soil particles together, making them more able to retain moisture and nutrients. Worm castings (a nice way of saying *worm poop*) are loaded with nutrients, humic acids, and enzymes that not only make plants grow but also help fight off insect pests. Mix this into your soil and you're off to a good start. Next, if needed, add organic vegetable fertilizer (especially if growing in containers) to provide the big three: nitrogen, phosphorus, and potassium. These three, along with other nutrients found in organic fertilizers, will help plants grow well in close quarters.

Once your soil is ready, we can move on to planting techniques. If you aren't yet familiar with *Square Foot Gardening* and *Grow Biointensive* methods, begin learning as much as you can about those. These growing systems will save you space, time, and resources once they're established. They can take some time to learn, but it's worth it when you see the abundance coming from your tiny garden.

Let's explore some additional techniques:

To utilize your growing space to the fullest, consider interplanting: plant small, quick crops in between larger crops that take longer to grow. For example, summer squashes, winter squashes, and watermelons take several weeks to get established before they take over a garden planter. Use that available space in between to grow a quick crop of arugula, radishes, or cilantro. The quick crops will be ready to harvest before the larger crops eclipse them. You'll get two harvests from the same space.

Explore planting crops of different heights or those that occupy different root zones in the same bed as well. For example, a Three Sisters garden grows corn, beans, and squash in the same planter. Corn grows tall, beans use the corn as a trellis, and squash plants function as a living mulch around the base of the corn. The beans' roots (which are nitrogen fixing) also provide extra nitrogen for the corn as it grows. As another example, try growing lettuces or spinach under the canopy of a taller crop like okra. Leafy greens prefer cooler temperatures, and if planted behind a trellis of pole beans, they will benefit from the shade those taller crops provide.

Vertical gardening is another way to grow food in small spaces. There are growing towers of all sorts available, some better than others. But trellising is one of the best ways to make the most of your growing space. Why allow cucumbers to sprawl all over the place when you can coax them up a trellis or ▶

Small-Space Growing Tips for Home and Community Gardens *(continued)*

wall? Herbs and strawberries grow well in hanging wall planters, and if the planter is deep enough, it can also support heavy-feeder crops like tomatoes.

These are just a few ways to maximize your growing space in a small garden. You'll find more ideas and in-depth strategies in Christy's nonfiction books *Gardening for Geeks* and *Grow Your Own Mini Fruit Garden*. ∽

Reading Group Guide

1. We all know someone like Kurt, someone who does not seem to have the power to be happy. Why do you think Kurt has turned so sour? He feels that the community garden ruined "everything" when it comes to his house. Do you ever feel sorry for him? Why or why not?

2. The *Rules and Regulations* booklet seems to dictate nearly everything that goes on in the garden. In what ways is it important to have stringent rules when dealing with such a disparate group of people? In what ways do the rules and regulations cause more problems than create solutions?

3. We're told that "Lizzie had a knack for choosing the right movie with the right life lesson at the perfect moment." Are there any movies you feel give you the right life lessons regarding conflict, love, friendship, or work?

4. Jared breaks the rules and lets his drunk friends into the garden, and Lizzie is furious. Is Lizzie's reaction justified? Do you think she acted too harshly? ▶

5. How is your growing season different from the one described in *Garden Variety*?

6. How do the seasonal changes, month by month, at Vista Mar Gardens manifest in its members' behavior?

7. What did you learn about gardening that you didn't already know?

8. Lizzie mentions how climate change has altered the Southern California growing season. How has climate change affected your own garden, town or city, and hardiness zone?

9. Were Mary and Ralph right to act as they did when they discovered what Kurt had in store for the garden? Why or why not?

10. In what ways might Bernice choose to act differently toward Arthur? Do you think she is doing the best she possibly can? Is "letting go" sometimes the only course of action? ᘯ